ALWAYS BEEN YOURS

DESTINY FALLS

ALEXA RIVERS

PROLOGUE – 16 YEARS AGO

*"Your first love isn't the first person you give your heart to—it's
the first one who breaks it."*
~ Lang Leav

GRACE

I STOOD on Nate Braddock's doorstep, a bag of lemon drops in one hand and my heart in the other. I knocked, my breathing shallow. I couldn't believe I was going to do this. Two years after my out-of-control crush on my best friend started, I would finally tell him how I felt.

When no one answered, I cracked the door open and peered through the gap. A light was on in the living room, and I could hear the TV. I pushed the door open further, took my shoes off, and padded in. Max, Liam, and Connor—three of Nate's brothers—were sprawled on the couch and armchairs, watching an action movie. Liam greeted me with a smile, Connor with a slight tip of his head, but Max, Nate's twin, seemed to pale.

"Hi," I said. "Is Nate around?"

"He's in his room." Connor sounded bored. "Or maybe the shower."

"Um." Max wet his lips. "You might want to wait for him to come out."

I frowned. "Why?"

Nate and I shared everything with each other. Max had never suggested I shouldn't just go in to see him before.

He hesitated, visibly lost for words. Before he could say anything, a little girl skipped into the room, nearly tripping over the ends of her flannel pajamas.

"Toby won't let me into the toilet," she whined. "Max, tell him to hurry up. I'm tired, and he's been in there for ages."

Max sighed, and I took advantage of his distraction to slip past them and down the hall. I'd come to ask Nate to be my date to the senior dance, and I wouldn't be distracted from my mission. It had taken me weeks to work up the courage, and once I had, I'd wanted it to be perfect, so I'd bought a bag of his favorite candy and waited for a night when I knew his parents would be out. If I didn't ask soon, I might explode.

I knocked briefly on Nate's bedroom door, then pushed it open.

I stopped short.

There, lying on his bed, wearing nothing but one of Nate's rugby T-shirts, was Maddy McLaren from school. My heart sank and my stomach rolled nauseatingly. Maddy raised an eyebrow at the sight of me and made a show of tidying her tousled blonde hair. I bit my lower lip, unsure of what to say. Maddy was everything I wasn't. Confident, outgoing, flirtatious. I'd had no idea Nate might be interested in her, but my eyes didn't deceive me. Whatever I'd walked in on wasn't innocent.

Maddy swung her legs off the edge of the bed and sashayed toward me with a sexiness I'd never be capable of. She reached out, and I thought for a moment she was trying to take my hand, but then she snatched the bag of lemon drops from me and smirked.

"Thanks." Her voice was husky and self-assured, as if she was found half-naked in guys' bedrooms every day. "It was so sweet of you to bring these over for us. I know how much Nate loves them." She winked. "I'll make sure he gets them."

I didn't move. I couldn't. I was so shocked.

Maddy McLaren was here in Nate's bedroom. In his shirt. On his bed. Had they…?

Oh god. I didn't want to think about it.

My heart felt like it was battering against the inside of my ribcage, and I struggled for air. I was too late. I'd missed my chance. Nate was with someone else.

Maddy seemed to take my hesitation as a refusal to leave, because she narrowed her eyes and leaned close. "Look," she hissed. "I know you and Nate have some weird BFF thing going on, but he's mine now. I've been with him in a way you haven't, and if I were you, I'd leave before he gets out of the shower. If you stay, you'll only embarrass yourself more."

My eyes burned. A choked sob rose up my throat, and I clapped my hand to my mouth and backed away. I wished I had something snarky to say back—a way to put her in her place—but I'd always been better with words on paper than in person. Besides, she was right. She had Nate and I didn't.

I turned away and noticed Max standing in the hall. I hung my head and refused to meet his eyes. As if this couldn't get any worse. He must have known what I was about to walk in on, and he'd tried to warn me, but I hadn't paid attention.

I backed out of the room and began to brush past him, but he wrapped an arm around my shoulders and guided me to the room next door. His bedroom. I entered, barely noting the organized desk and rows of academic awards on his shelves. It was all I could do to hold myself together.

Max pulled me into his arms, and I buried my face in the crook of his neck. All of the Braddock boys were tall, but I was unusually tall for a girl, so we fit well.

"I'm sorry," he murmured. "He's an idiot."

I sniffled, self-conscious about getting snot and tears on him. "I'm the idiot. I should have said something sooner, or just realized I didn't have a chance." I huffed. "If he was actually interested, he'd have already done something about it."

Max didn't deny my claim, which only made me feel worse. He hugged me close, and for a brief second, I wished with all my heart that *he* was the Braddock I wanted. Max was smart, kind, and he and Nate were supposedly identical —although with their different haircuts and clothing styles, it wasn't difficult to tell them apart.

Why couldn't it be him?

My heart gave a pathetic squeeze. Oh, yeah. Because Max wasn't my best friend. He wasn't the guy who'd threatened a bully when they'd been making fun of my height. He wasn't the boy who'd listened as I confessed that I sometimes hated my parents for leaving me here, even though they'd done so in order to help communities living in extreme poverty in Sudan. You weren't supposed to hate people who devoted their lives to others like that, but Nate understood my bitterness. He sympathized. I wasn't sure Max would do the same.

"I'm sorry," Max said again. He pulled back and swiped tears from my cheeks.

"What am I going to do now?" I asked hopelessly. "When Maddy tells him—"

"She won't," he interrupted. "Their thing is new. You're his best friend. She won't say anything in case she loses him."

I pressed my lips together. Even if Maddy stayed quiet, I wasn't sure I could go on being Nate's best friend while seeing him with her. It would hurt too much. But then, I couldn't give him up either.

"Look." He scanned my face, waiting to make sure I was listening. "It's up to you what you want to do next, but if you keep acting like things are normal, Maddy will stay quiet. At least, for now." He sucked in a breath, held it for a moment, then released it slowly. "If you come to the dance with me, she'll probably forget about it altogether."

"Go... with you?" I patted my pocket, where the two tickets I'd purchased sat ready for use. "Like, as a date?"

He shook his head. "Just so we both have someone to go with. We'll have fun together, won't we?"

I thought about it. He was offering to help me save face. Even if no one else had witnessed what happened tonight, I knew I'd be obvious if I turned up to the dance solo and sent longing gazes at Nate all night. If I was good at anything, it was making the best of a situation.

I straightened my spine and nodded. "Okay, let's do this."

1

GRACE

WHERE WAS my nude pink lipstick?

I studied the contents of my purse, but the tube didn't magically appear. With a groan of frustration, I rushed to the bathroom and searched the drawer where I kept my cosmetics.

I was going to be late. I didn't do late. I was always punctual. I prided myself on it. But if I couldn't find my favorite lipstick in the next few minutes, I wouldn't be.

I glanced at myself in the mirror and pulled a face. If I hadn't already started my makeup, I'd dispense with it entirely, but I couldn't leave it without a finishing touch. Sighing, I chose an alternative from the drawer and applied it. The color was a bit brighter than usual, but it still suited my outfit, so it would be fine. Especially just for dinner with Kennedy.

I didn't know why I was making such a big deal of this at all, except that the lipstick wasn't the only thing I'd lost recently. Just last week, I'd misplaced my favorite blouse and

I hadn't found it yet. Neither of these things was significant on their own, but I was an organized person. I wasn't accustomed to losing things. And after what had happened on my property earlier in the year, which had stirred up memories I'd tried to bury, the disappearances put me on edge. My subconscious kept whispering that someone had taken them.

Don't be crazy, I told it. *I'm just paranoid because of what happened to Kennedy. I'm being absentminded and forgetting where I put things, that's all.*

Unfortunately, my imagination knew no bounds when it came to 'what ifs'. A less than ideal side-effect of earning a living as a writer.

I blotted the lipstick, reapplied it, and spritzed myself with perfume. At least I hadn't lost the perfume too. Destiny Falls was in the middle of nowhere, so replacing items like lipstick and perfume could be more of a nuisance than if I lived in a city. I slipped the lipstick into my purse, grabbed a jacket from my closet, and headed out, locking the door behind me. I hadn't always bothered to lock up in Destiny Falls, but after having a violent stalker drug and kidnap Kennedy from my property, I'd become warier. More of that annoying paranoia.

The walk to Drunken Destiny, the local pub, didn't take long. I clutched my jacket around me, trying to stay warm in the cool winter air. Even though it was only six, night had already descended. The main street was mostly empty, the voices and laughter spilling out of Drunken Destiny the only source of noise.

As I entered the pub, I looked around, catching sight of Kennedy in a back corner. I wasn't surprised. She liked to stay out of the way as much as possible—although being a celebrity in a small town meant she never went completely unnoticed. I smiled at her, then greeted Eugene, Nate's Dad, who stood behind the counter. His wife, Heather, was seated at a bar stool on the other side. Meanwhile, Bailey, the bartender, was serving beer to a pair of young men who seemed more interested in her than in their drinks.

I made my way over to Kennedy and dropped into the seat opposite her. "Sorry I'm late."

She glanced at the clock on the wall. "I think three minutes late still counts as on time."

Usually, I would have laughed, but today I didn't have it in me.

"Hey, are you okay?" A line formed between Kennedy's dark brows.

I debated whether to be honest but figured that if anyone could understand how unsettled I was, it would be her. "It's probably nothing," I said slowly. "But I couldn't find my lipstick today, and last week I lost one of the blouses I wear all the time. I know I'm just being paranoid, but it's making me anxious."

Kennedy's expression clouded with concern. "Do you think someone might have stolen them? Do you have any guests at the bed and breakfast at the moment?"

I shook my head. "Both of the cottages are empty, although there are plenty of people coming and going from the house, so I suppose someone could have taken them, in theory. Honestly, though, I think I'm making too much of it. People lose things all the time."

"They do." Kennedy cocked her head. "But if it's playing on your mind, you could consider getting more security just so you feel safe."

I pulled a face. "Having a security system in place didn't stop Tyler from getting to you, so I don't think doing that would make me feel much safer." I tried to force it from my mind. "Don't worry, I'm sure it's nothing. Like I said, I'm oversensitive because of what happened." And because of the incident from my past. But no one in Destiny Falls knew about that. "I'm sure you're extra vigilant about everything too."

"I am," she admitted. "It's slowly getting better though."

Eugene appeared by our table. "Evening, ladies. What can I get you?"

We each rattled off our orders, and he noted them down and left.

"Maybe you should get a dog," Kennedy suggested when he was out of earshot. "Having Daisy around has been incredible for helping me relax. She hears every time someone comes and goes and lets me know so I don't have to worry about missing anything."

I hid a smile. I should have known the conversation would head in this direction. Ever since Kennedy and her husband Liam had adopted a Labrador cross from the local animal shelter, she'd been raving about how much she adored Daisy. I didn't think a dog would help me though. Or at least, not one like Daisy. She was too sweet. Too much of a goofball. Perhaps her alertness helped Kennedy, but I didn't think that was enough for me. If I were to get a dog, I'd want it to be one that would make intruders think twice.

A flicker of an idea played in the back of my mind. Daisy might never scare anyone or make me feel safer in my own home, but that didn't mean that no dog would. The right one could be a game-changer. I'd always liked the idea of a pet. I worked from home, and I was as settled as I'd likely ever be, so why not?

"You might be onto something," I told her. "I know someone who breeds and trains Rottweilers. Maybe I'll get in touch."

Kennedy laughed. "You're going to get a Rottweiler?"

"Why not?"

"No reason. I just pictured you with something classier, like an Afghan hound or a poodle."

I chuckled. "I doubt a poodle would get the job done the way I'm picturing."

"You never know." Amusement shone in her eyes. "Those things can be ferocious."

"If you say so."

Bailey bounced across the bar with so much energy, I was surprised the drinks on her tray didn't slosh over the rims of the glasses. She set them in front of us. "Sav blanc for Kennedy and a pink gin and tonic for Grace." She grinned and tucked a lock of silky black hair behind her ear, obviously pleased to have anticipated our orders. The perks of small-town life. "Can I get you anything else?"

"That's perfect, thank you," I replied. "Nothing else for now."

"I wonder what has her so smiley," Kennedy said. "She's always cheerful, but that was something else."

I shrugged, about to say I didn't know, but then I spotted a cluster of tall, handsome men making their way toward us, and it all clicked into place. "Braddock brothers," I murmured under my breath.

Kennedy's head shot up. She spotted Liam within the group and pushed back her chair to greet him. He kissed her thoroughly—a display more fit for the privacy of their own home than the local pub. The sight made my heart give a happy thump. I loved seeing them together. Especially after watching Liam—the oldest Braddock son after the twins—mope, broken-hearted, for far too many years. They deserved their happiness.

My gaze swept over the others in the group. Toby, the youngest—except for his twin, Summer—stood front and center, beaming his mischievous smile that always gave the impression he was about to do something naughty and that you'd like it. In the back were Max and Connor, the quietest of the brothers. Max smiled warmly at me, and Connor nodded. Which left only Nate. The man who'd been my best friend for nearly twenty years and with whom I'd been miserably in love for most of that time.

"Hey, Gracie." Nate leaned over and kissed the top of my head, the faintly woodsy scent of his cologne tickling my nostrils. His rugged face creased in a smile as he pulled back, and his familiar blue-green eyes crinkled at the corners. I wanted to fold myself into his arms the way Kennedy had done with Liam—to breathe him in and let him hold me—but that wasn't my place. I was the trusty friend. The comfortable old jeans that never let him down.

"Hi, Nate." I smiled back. It took no effort. Just looking at him made me want to smile.

"Tess is with her mum tonight," he said, as if I didn't already know it was his daughter's week with Maddy. "So we thought we'd get together for a few drinks. Mind if we join you?"

"Not at all." I kept my expression neutral and prepared myself for another evening of pretending I wasn't in love with my best friend.

———

By the time I got home, I was ready for a shower and bed, but first, I had to make a call. I removed my shoes, placed them in their usual spot on the rack, and stretched my feet out. I liked wearing heels, but it always felt good to take them off. I made my way through the mostly dark house, past the rooms used for guests, and into the private quarters. I switched a light on and sat on the couch, tucking my legs beneath me. I scrolled through my phone until I found a contact I hadn't spoken to in far too long.

Ryan Gentry.

I studied the phone number, nibbling on my lip. I liked Kennedy's suggestion about getting a dog. I often felt lonely in this massive house by myself. I could use the company. And I had an in with someone who could provide a well-trained dog that might actually make me feel less like jumping at shadows. But did I really want to make the call? Ryan was my friend, but there was a reason we'd barely spoken in months. It was easier to leave him in the past. But that wasn't really fair. It wasn't Ryan's fault I'd dug myself into a massive hole where he was concerned.

I hit the Call button. It rang and rang. For a few seconds, I considered hanging up and pretending the past two minutes had never happened, but then the line clicked, and a rasping masculine voice said my name.

"Hi," I whispered.

"It's been a while." I could hear the smile in his voice and knew he didn't take my absence from his life personally. We understood each other. Perhaps better than anyone. Ryan knew things about me that even Nate couldn't possibly imagine.

"You know how it is."

"Yeah." He cleared his throat. "So, what's up? I'm guessing you didn't call me after ten at night for no reason?"

I rolled my eyes. "I knew you'd be awake, Ry. You're never asleep before midnight."

"This is true. I'm sketching a design for one of tomorrow's clients." Ryan was a tattoo artist based out of a popular shop in Auckland.

"I bet it's gorgeous." All of his work was. That was why I'd trusted him with my one and only tattoo. "Um, does Felicia still breed and train Rottweilers?"

"She does." He sounded intrigued. "Why?"

"I think I'd like one, if she has any looking for a home."

"She probably does. Would you like me to check with her tomorrow and get back to you?"

"That would be great." I curled a few strands of hair around my finger. "Thanks."

"No worries. How's everything with you?"

I spent a few minutes catching him up on the latest news, then listened while he told me about the clients he'd been working with and how his family was. I felt a pang of guilt. Ryan wasn't the only person I'd neglected. I hadn't caught up with his parents or Felicia either.

"Hey, I have an idea," he tacked on the end of a story about a tattoo mishap he'd been fixing. "How about, if Fel does have a dog for you, I bring them down? I'd love to visit. I miss your face."

Nerves twisted in my gut. Having Ryan in Destiny Falls would be tempting fate. I didn't want the two parts of my life to collide. If anyone found out who he was to me, I'd never find my way out of that massive hole I'd dug, but I cared for him, and he was doing me a favor. How could I possibly say no?

With my insides tied in knots, I managed to summon a smile. "Sure."

2

———

NATE

IT HAD BEEN a hell of a shift. Dealing with snobby tourists who thought they were too good to be ticketed for speeding up a dangerously slippery mountainside, putting themselves and their fellow commuters at risk, didn't bother me too much most of the time, but one of the men I'd spoken to today had pissed me off. I needed to vent, which meant I was heading to Grace's place with beer and wine. On the weeks Maddy had our eight-year-old daughter, Tess, I often went to Grace's place instead of home after work.

When I pulled up, there was an unfamiliar Jeep in the drive. I frowned. Grace drove a sleek silver sedan that was as well-groomed as she was, whereas this battered Jeep was clearly past its prime. A bumper sticker on the rear advertised a tattoo parlor and was nearly illegible from years of fading. My frown deepened. Perhaps the jeep belonged to a guest. I got out and tried to look through the windows, but they were tinted. Scowling, I strode past and made my way up the steps. All I wanted was a beer, a heater, and Grace's excellent listening skills.

The door was ajar, so I let myself in. We didn't usually bother knocking at each other's houses. Her place was basically my second home. I passed the showier guest area and heard laughter as I approached the private kitchen. My eyebrows hitched up. Grace wasn't alone. Perhaps Kennedy had dropped by to see her. The two women were close—a fact that had bothered me when Kennedy first moved back to Destiny Falls, but we'd resolved our issues since then. As long as she made my brother happy, she was okay with me.

I entered the kitchen and stopped, unable to understand what I was seeing. Grace stood at the kitchen counter side by side with a dark-haired man—someone I'd never seen before—and a black-and-tan puppy sat near their feet. She and her companion were deep in conversation. As I watched, he said something too softly for me to hear, and she laughed and elbowed him in the ribs.

Something caught in my chest.

A man and a woman, preparing a meal. This looked like a date. But it couldn't be, could it? Grace didn't date. There was hardly anyone around here for her to date, and their body language said they were more comfortable with each other than a first date would allow. This was someone she knew.

The thought sprang to my mind that the whole scene was wrong. I didn't know where it had come from, but the sense of wrongness clawed at my gut. I set the beer on the ground, and the slight sound alerted the puppy to my presence. It leaped up, growling in a way that might have been menacing if it had been more than a couple of months old. Grace looked over her shoulder, and the color drained from her face.

My stomach rolled unpleasantly. Yeah, this was a date.

Why else would she look so horrified to have me walk into the kitchen as if I lived here?

The man turned, his vivid green eyes locking on mine. He grinned, wiped his hands on his jeans, and extended a heavily tattooed arm toward me.

"Hey." His tone was friendly. Welcoming. "You must be Nate. I feel like I already know you."

I shook his hand, noting that his grip was firm but not crushing. Whoever he was, he didn't think he had anything to prove. For some reason, that annoyed me.

"Who are you?" I demanded.

His forehead furrowed. "Oh, sorry. I'm Ryan. Grace's ex-husband."

I laughed. There was no other suitable response.

Ryan's frown deepened. "Why is that funny?"

He glanced at Grace as if asking for an explanation, and so did I. Her complexion was waxy, her eyes wide. One look at her shocked face and I realized Ryan wasn't kidding. She couldn't seem more horrified if she tried. My chest tightened.

Grace had been *married* and I hadn't known?

She'd had a wedding and shared her life with a man and I'd had no idea? How was that possible? I knew everything about Grace, didn't I? She was my reliable best friend. We didn't have secrets from each other, and there was no way I could have overlooked something as massive as that.

"But Grace has never been married," I protested, my voice too loud in the quiet room. The puppy barked, then glared at me.

"Nate..." she trailed off, looking lost.

"You can't have been," I said to her, placing the bottle of wine on the counter with more force than necessary. "We know everything about each other." Or at least, I'd thought we had. Her expression was beginning to make me wonder. Was there something I'd missed?

Ryan looked between us and cringed. "I'm sorry, man. I didn't know…."

My stomach heated with frustration at his interruption. At his presence, here in her home. Her *ex-husband*. I shook my head, refusing to believe it. Grace didn't keep things from me. She was steady and dependable. Always.

"Gracie, tell me what I'm missing." She'd clear this up. She was the clever one. Sometimes I needed things spelled out for me.

She touched my arm. The brush of her fingers singed me like an open flame. "It was years ago."

"What?" I stared at her. For the first time in my life, she looked like a stranger. I catalogued her features, each of them as familiar as my own, but I couldn't shake the feeling that I didn't really know her at all. Somehow, at some point, Grace had become a person who hid things—parts of herself—from me, and that wasn't okay. "So it's true? You married this guy?"

She sighed and visibly pulled herself together. "Yes. But we divorced five years ago."

"Five years ago." I spoke to myself as much as her. Back then, she'd just returned to Destiny Falls. How could I possibly not have noticed that she was in the midst of divorcing her husband? It should have been the talk of the town. Although, come to think of it, I'd been going through my own separation about that same time and juggling work with raising my tiny daughter. Still, I didn't understand how on earth the subject hadn't come up. Had I been so engrossed in my own problems that I'd been blind to hers?

"Why is he here?" I asked, focusing on the present. If Ryan had come in some kind of attempt at reconciliation, he could back the hell off. I didn't know what had caused their separation, but Grace was the kindest person I knew, so if she'd left him, there must have been a damn good reason for it.

"He brought Duke down for me. His sister, Felicia, breeds Rottweilers."

I glanced at the puppy, taken aback. Now that she mentioned it, I recognized the trademark characteristics of the breed. I'd been too distracted to pay attention to them earlier. The small creature stared back at me, less hostile than it had been, but it didn't move from its position near Grace.

"I didn't know you wanted a dog." That felt like another betrayal. I never held anything back when we spent time together. I told her all of my thoughts, and I'd believed she did the same with me, but it would seem I was wrong. Either that, or I'd simply not paid attention, and if I hadn't paid attention to this, what else might I have overlooked when it came to her?

Ryan grabbed a glass from one of the cabinets and held it out to me. "Sorry for dropping a bombshell on you." He shot Grace a look I probably wasn't supposed to see. "Why don't you pour yourself a drink, and we can sit down and talk this through?"

I backed toward the door, instinctively retreating. I couldn't sit down with this man and chat like we were buddies. My mind was rioting.

"Nah, I'm going to go. You two look like you've got a cozy evening planned." I turned toward Grace but didn't meet her eyes. "I'll catch you later."

"Stay," she whispered. "Please."

I left.

It was only as I pulled up my own drive that I realized I'd left my damn beer behind.

3

———————

GRACE

I RETURNED TO THE KITCHEN, having followed Nate out to his car in the hopes he'd at least pause and hear me out—although what I'd say given the chance, I didn't know. It didn't matter anyway because he'd driven off in a rush. I sighed, and Ryan handed me a glass of wine he must have poured while I'd been gone.

I sipped. "Thanks, I needed that."

He tilted his head in acknowledgment. "Want to talk about it?"

I scrunched my face. "Not really, but I suppose I owe you an explanation."

He caught my eyes, understanding reflected in his. "You never told him about us. I caught the gist of it."

"Yeah." I drank more wine. "I'm sorry. I know I should have. When we got married, it was fast and impulsive, and Nate had a lot going on in his life with a new wife and a baby on the way, so I didn't mention it." Part of me had longed to tell him and see if he got jealous—if there was any hint he might have feelings for me at all—but if I had confided in him and he hadn't cared, it might have broken me. On the other hand, if he had been upset, it could have torn his family apart. I'd decided I was better to stay silent and cling to a thread of hope without ruining anyone's life.

"After that, it became harder and harder to bring it up. How was I supposed to tell him I'd gotten married and hadn't mentioned it? When we divorced, I figured I could just pretend it never happened." My lips twisted. "I know that sounds awful, but I wasn't ashamed of you. I promise."

He poured a second glass of wine and leaned against the counter while he raised it to his lips. "I know." His smile was wry. "You forget that I know what it's like to love someone I can't have."

A beat of silence passed between us. It wasn't awkward. Nothing between Ryan and I ever was. Despite appearances, we had too much in common to ever feel awkward with each other. He knew my deepest secret, and I knew his. That bonded us in a way little else could.

"I should have told him." Guilt ate at me. "He deserved to know."

He nodded. "Yeah, probably. But I won't judge you for it. You'll do enough of that yourself."

I tossed back the rest of the wine, set the glass down, and bent to pat my new housemate, Duke. He pressed his head firmly into my palm and panted. Duke wasn't as full-on as Daisy, but he was sweet and well-trained. He'd also be big and intimidating once he was grown, which might ease the permanent case of jitters I seemed to have.

"We can talk it over more if you'd like," Ryan said.

My lips twitched. Ryan was such a talker. He liked to dissect everything. To take people apart and figure out what made them tick. Considering his career choice, that was a good thing. He never ran out of conversation with his clients.

He knelt beside me and gave Duke some love. "Talk to me, Gracie," he urged. "We might not have married in the most conventional way, and, sure, we're divorced now, but I'm always here to listen to you. You matter to me."

I kissed his cheek, feeling the rasp of stubble against my lips, and wondered for the millionth time why I couldn't have fallen in love with Ryan, or Max, or *anyone* other than Nate. I supposed it was the same reason Ryan had never been in love with me and could never have loved me in that way. My heart was otherwise engaged. It simply didn't have room for anyone else.

"Okay," I agreed. "But let's finish cooking dinner first. We can talk while we eat, and then I'd better head to Nate's place to explain."

I was not looking forward to that.

4

———

NATE

I RAMMED a gloved fist into the boxing bag hanging from my garage roof and grunted with the effort, pleased to feel the burn in my arm muscles. I swung again with my left hand, keeping my other fist up as if to shield my face from an invisible enemy. After what I'd just discovered, that seemed fitting. I'd been blindsided. Caught completely off guard. This morning, I'd been confident I knew all there was to know about Grace Smith. Now, I realized she had a whole other life separate from me.

Punch. Punch.

Why hadn't she told me she'd been married?

Punch.

Hell, why hadn't I been invited to the wedding?

Punch.

And, apparently, she wanted a dog. Why was this the first I was hearing of that?

Sweat rolled down my forehead and into my eyes. I blinked rapidly against the sting, my thoughts whirling.

When I'd gotten married, Grace had done a reading at the ceremony. I'd have had her in the bridal party if Maddy would have allowed it, but she'd been pregnant and emotional, and the only time I'd broached the subject, she'd gotten upset, so I'd backed off. It wasn't as if I didn't have enough brothers to be groomsmen. The point was, Grace had been there. She'd been involved. Why would she keep a wedding from me? Was she ashamed? Or had I been so wrapped up in my own drama that I'd made her think she couldn't come to me about it?

Whatever the case, I didn't like it. A soft voice in the back of my mind whispered that it didn't matter why she hadn't told me. I should have noticed. Even if it had happened while she'd been living in Auckland, studying toward her master's degree in creative writing, I should have been aware of something so enormous shifting in her life. But I hadn't. I'd failed her.

Fuck.

I gritted my teeth and threw another punch, the ripple of impact through my muscles grounding me in the present. But shit, whether my mind was in the past or present, I knew the truth. I'd been a crap friend to Grace. She hadn't felt like she could turn to me, and that wasn't good enough. I should always be there for Grace to lean on. If she'd been holding that back, what else might she have been keeping from me?

I backed away from the bag and wiped my face on my shirt. My stomach felt hollow. I hated the thought that there were things about Grace I didn't know. It showed how self-centered I'd been. Not that that should come as a surprise. I'd been a bad husband too. Maddy had told me so in excruciating detail when she'd asked for a divorce.

"Do better," I muttered to myself as I stripped off the gloves and hung them to air out. I yanked off my shirt as I strode out of the garage into the house and tossed it into the laundry. I then stripped off the rest of my clothes and took a hot shower. Winters in Destiny Falls could be harsh, and I let the water warm me all the way through.

I got out, and I'd only just started drying myself when I heard a knock at the door. Tentative. Probably Grace. I slung the towel around my hips and went to answer. I opened the door and waved her in quickly, wanting to keep the cool air out of the house.

"Am I a bad friend?" I asked as we appraised each other in the confined hallway.

"Of course not." She looked stunned that I'd ask.

I could tell from her expression she meant it. Something inside me relaxed. "Then why didn't you tell me?" I didn't specify what I meant, but she couldn't possibly misunderstand. "And what else is there you haven't mentioned? Do you secretly have a kid too?"

Her jaw dropped, and I immediately felt bad. This was on me as much as it was on her. "I'm sorry."

She shook her head. "Of course I don't have a child. Now, get dressed. I don't want you catching a cold on my watch."

I pressed my lips together to avoid smirking. She was such a caretaker. At least I knew that much about her for certain. I nodded and went to the bedroom, where I pulled on jeans, a T-shirt, and a light jacket. I found her perched on the sofa in the living room and sat beside her. She offered me a beer, and I took it gratefully.

"You left these," she said.

"Thanks." I cracked the tab open and drank. "So, are you going to tell me more?"

She drew in a shaky breath and squeezed her eyes shut. As she exhaled, they fluttered open and focused on me. I gazed into them. I'd always loved the hazel of her eyes.

Warm and comforting, like a hug after a stressful day. I offered her the beer, but she shook her head.

"I was in a bad place when I met Ryan," she said, turning those hazel eyes away from me. I wanted them back, damn it. I wanted to see her innermost thoughts. "He was having a rough time too. We got horrendously drunk together and came up with the brilliant idea that getting married would solve our problems."

I scowled. I didn't get it. "Did he need a green card or something?"

She laughed, but it sounded strained. "No. He's as Kiwi as they come. It was something else. The point is, we did it. We got married within about a week of meeting. We figured we'd give the relationship a shot. We liked each other." A smile softened her face as she spoke, and I felt it like a punch in the gut. "We had a lot in common."

I scoffed because from what I'd seen of him, he didn't look like someone she'd have much in common with. She silenced me with a look.

"We did," she said. "Still do. We dated for a while. Tried living together for a couple of years. But in the end, we decided we were better as friends than husband and wife, so we divorced."

I pondered her words, something she'd said earlier bothering me. "You were upset when you met him?"

Her mouth curled down at the corners. "Just man troubles."

My heart ached at the idea of her hurting and feeling like she'd had to turn to someone else about it. I should be the one she talked to when she needed support.

"You should have called." I touched her hand. "I'm sorry I wasn't there for you."

Her mouth didn't move, but I could see strain around her eyes. "You'd just gotten married," she said. "Maddy was due in a month. You had enough on your mind without me adding to it."

The ache worsened. I gave her a one-armed hug and kissed her temple. "Whatever is going on in my life, I'll always be here for you if you need me. All you have to do is ask. I'm a dumbass. Sometimes I need you to tell me what's going on."

Her lips tilted with amusement, and tension eased from my jaw in response. I hated seeing her worked up like this. I was pleased she was able to find some humor in the situation.

"You're not a dumbass."

It was a statement that didn't invite disagreement, but I disagreed anyway. "I feel like one."

She shrugged. "So do I. I married a man I didn't love who never loved me back."

I shook my head in disbelief. This Ryan guy had had Grace as his wife and been stupid enough not to fall in love with her? "He's an idiot."

5

———

GRACE

I STARED AT NATE, taken aback.

"How could he not love you?" he demanded. "He was fucking lucky to have you. You're the kindest person I know and beautiful too. So damned clever. What sort of moron could be married to you and not fall ass-over-heels in love?"

He shook his head as if even considering the possibility stumped him. Meanwhile, I struggled to hold myself together. Nate had no idea how bittersweet this moment was for me. He was saying things I'd longed to hear, but he didn't seem to realize the irony of the situation.

"He could never find a better woman," he added, sounding offended on my behalf.

I didn't know whether to cry or laugh. A strange sort of half sob emerged from my throat instead.

"Hey, now." He cuddled me closer. "Don't be upset just because your ex is stupid."

"He isn't," I protested, knowing he wouldn't pay attention. "Some people aren't meant for each other. He'll find his person, and so will I."

I hoped. Of course, there was always a chance I'd already found him but landed myself squarely in the friend zone through two years of inaction followed by more than a decade of hiding my feelings and digging myself into a deep hole of secrets and omissions.

"Any man would be lucky to have you." His tone was gruff. He wasn't one for talking about emotions, and this evening had been an emotional disaster.

I breathed slowly, trying to ease the tightness in my chest. Nate meant well, but Ryan wasn't the only man who'd seen me as a friend rather than a woman to treasure romantically. The thing was, even though I'd been married to Ryan, Nate's oversight hurt far worse. I'd always known where Ryan's heart lay. With Nate, I'd allowed myself to hope, only to watch his on-and-off relationship with Maddy finally escalate into marriage when she fell pregnant. The hope had never quite disappeared, but I'd forced myself not to act on it, afraid of how devastating it could be if I did. If he'd officially shot me down, I'd have been heartbroken, and if he hadn't, I'd have been a homewrecker.

"Thanks," I murmured, disentangling myself from him. I liked being held by him, but it made it difficult to remember reality. I needed to get my head on straight. "I'm sorry I never told you. We did it impulsively. You were busy with your own life, and I thought I'd wait until we settled down to mention it, but then I didn't know how to raise the subject. When we decided to divorce, I couldn't confide in you, since I'd never told you about the marriage in the first place. It felt like this pit of deceit I couldn't get out of." I sounded as miserable and sorry as I felt.

His lips pursed. He stayed silent for a long moment, then

released a whoosh of breath. "I can't say I get it, because I don't, but I appreciate the explanation."

Well, that was something at least.

"I should have done things differently." So many things. I'd wondered over the years if there was a single moment where I'd done or said one thing and should have done another, but I'd never been able to pinpoint the instant when I'd slid off the rails. What made it worse was that nobody seemed able to see me floundering. From the outside, I looked like I had my life together. My books made good money, and I got on well with almost everyone in town. There were no outward signs that everything was barely held together, intersected with cracks, like a vase that had been slammed down too hard but held together until one final touch shattered the pieces.

"It's okay." He glanced at me, a tenderness in his eyes that he let few others see. Despite his blustering exterior, Nate had a soft heart. "We're okay, Gracie. I promise." He quirked a brow. "Unless there are any other former husbands I should know about?"

I laughed, my relief palpable. "No. Just the one."

He grinned. "Thank fucking God."

6

———————

NATE

AT THE END of my shift the following day, I once again drove to Grace's house. She'd invited me over to play with the puppy, but I'd have come anyway because I wanted the opportunity to scope out her ex. When I arrived, I headed up the footpath past the garden and knocked on the door—to be courteous, since I'd barged in yesterday. When there was no response, I let myself in and wandered through, finding nobody. I followed voices to the small, private rear garden. It made sense they'd be out there with the puppy since it was the only fully enclosed part of the property.

I stepped onto the back porch and paused to watch the scene before me. Grace and Ryan were chasing the puppy around the lawn. The puppy, who she'd told me was named Duke, raced back and forth with a tennis ball in his mouth. Grace's laughter rang out, louder than I'd heard it in a long time. Her lips spread in a wide smile as she wrangled the ball from the dog and tossed it to Ryan. Her face shone with pleasure in the simple moment.

She stole my breath. Christ, she was beautiful.

I'd always known that in a general sense. With her long legs and feminine but understated style, it was impossible to miss. Not to mention the fact that a couple of my colleagues had asked for her number, and she'd gone on a date with one of them. But despite knowing that in my head, I'd never experienced her beauty so viscerally. She'd always just been Grace to me, but now it was as though my trusty best friend had been replaced by an intriguing stranger, and I didn't know what to make of it.

She glanced up, and her sparkling hazel eyes met mine. My stomach swooped and dipped. Ryan followed her gaze, also looking my way. The puppy whined, upset about his playtime being disturbed.

"Hi." I shoved my hands into my pockets. "It looks like you guys are having fun."

"We are." Grace strode over, gesturing for Ryan to follow. "Let me introduce you properly, the way I should have done yesterday. Nate, this is my ex-husband, Ryan. Ryan, my good friend, Nate."

I offered Ryan my hand, and he shook it. This time, we exchanged polite but wary smiles. I wasn't sure what to make of him, and it seemed he felt the same. The way he shifted closer to Grace and squared his shoulders should have pleased me. He clearly wanted to protect her and was worried I'd lose my temper again, but instead of being grateful she had his support, I was annoyed that I wasn't the one at her side. That was my role, and I didn't like it being usurped.

"Nice to meet you." I sounded sincere. Probably.

"You too." He assessed me, his green eyes searching my face for any flicker of aggression or disapproval. I tried to keep my features blank, but I'd never been good at hiding my feelings, so I didn't know what he saw.

"I'm sorry for being rude yesterday," I added. "I was surprised, and I reacted badly."

He tipped his head in acknowledgment. "It happens. If I'd found out one of my friends had been married and never told me, I'd have been upset too."

Why did he have to be so reasonable? Damn him.

"Are you visiting for long?" I asked, searching for small talk to make.

"Just until the end of the week." He tossed the tennis ball in the air and caught it, pretending not to notice the squirming puppy at his feet. "I had some leave owed, and I haven't seen Grace for ages, so when she called about getting a puppy, it seemed like a perfect opportunity."

My teeth ground together. I'd still like to know why she'd never mentioned to me that she wanted a dog.

"Ryan is keeping me company in the house." Grace patted his arm affectionately. "It gets quiet in such a big place all by myself."

A muscle in my jaw twitched, but I managed not to let on that I was surprised he was staying in the house rather than in one of the cottages. He was a friend, not a paying guest. I should have expected it.

"It's a lovely place." Ryan turned and lobbed the ball across the lawn. The puppy bounded after it, then snatched it in his mouth, tripping over his overly big paws and sliding snout-first across the grass. He got up, panting happily, and circled the lawn as if waiting for one of us to chase him.

"He doesn't understand the point of fetch yet," Grace said, nodding toward the dog. "He'll get the ball, but he won't bring it back."

I chuckled. "Why would he, when he went to all that effort to get it?"

"I guess you have a point." Ryan edged toward the dog, but Duke backed off, releasing a snarl from around the ball.

"Come on." She gestured toward Ryan and Duke. "Let's give him a bit more of a run around."

"Okay."

I pulled off my socks and followed her onto the lawn. We threw the ball for Duke—when we could get it off him—for another half hour, and then Ryan ducked into the house and returned with two beer bottles and a pink gin and tonic. For a few seconds, it surprised me that he knew Grace's preferred drink without having to ask, and I had to remind myself that they'd been married. Presumably, he knew more about Grace than just her drink preferences. Things even I didn't know. Like whether her sleek thighs felt as silky as they looked, and how her skin tasted. I shivered, startled by my own musings. I'd never wondered how Grace's skin would taste before, so why was the question popping into my mind now? Was it just because I'd realized that there was more to her than I'd imagined?

As we drank, each of us sitting on an outdoor chair positioned on her porch, my eyes kept flicking between them, almost without my permission. I cataloged their every caught gaze and shared smile, wondering if there were still feelings between them. Regardless of whether they'd been in love, they obviously cared for each other. Was attraction simmering quietly between them? I needed to know.

Grace called Duke over and scooped the puppy onto her lap.

"He'll be too big for you to do that before long," Ryan warned.

She smiled. "All the more reason to do it now." She checked her watch. "Time to get started on dinner. Nate, would you like to stay?"

I hesitated. Usually staying would be a no-brainer for me on an evening when I didn't have Tess, but I recalled how I'd felt when I'd walked in on them the other day. I didn't want to watch their banter and inside jokes and feel like an outsider.

"No, thanks." I softened the reply with a smile. "But I appreciate the offer."

To my surprise, Ryan looked disappointed. "Are you sure you can't stay?"

"Yeah, I have a few things to do before my daughter, Tess, arrives tomorrow."

"Ah." He nodded in understanding. "She's with her mum?"

"Yeah. We do alternate weeks."

"That must be hard."

My chest squeezed. "It is, but it's better than what a lot of fathers get. I'm lucky in that Maddy has always wanted me to be involved in Tess's life as much as she is."

"Of course she does." Grace took my hand and squeezed, then let it go. "You're a great dad, and she knows it."

Cheeks hot, I forced a shrug. "Anyway, I better hit the road. Bye, Gracie. See you around, Ryan."

As I left, even though I knew it made me an asshole, I couldn't help hoping that I would not, in fact, see Ryan around.

7

———————

GRACE

Ryan and I cooked together as smoothly as we used to. Both of us enjoyed being in the kitchen, and we had complementary strengths. I was better at baking, and he was the master of meats. Together, we created a delicious ravioli meal and then shared a bottle of wine while we ate. When we'd finished, we gorged on a dark chocolate tart and sprawled on the soft rug in front of the fire. My house had a great central heating system, but I still liked to light the fire for cozy nights in. Electronically generated heat simply couldn't compare to the warmth of a log fire.

"I'm sorry if I caused any issues between you and Nate," Ryan said as we nursed glasses of wine. "That wasn't my intention."

"I know." I gazed at him, noting the concern in his gemstone-green eyes. "You didn't. Any issues are because of me holding back when I shouldn't have, not because of you. I should have told him the truth years ago, but I didn't know

36

how, and then when I got the chance, I took the easy way out.”

“I don’t blame you.” He patted the floor and Duke trotted over and snuggled next to him. “Nate is full-on. I can see why you needed to get away from him for a while.”

I winced. “It wasn’t that.”

He rolled his eyes. “I know, Grace. Of all the people in the world, you know I understand how it feels to watch the person you love marry someone else.”

“I wish I could take away the pain for you.” I patted the puppy, focusing my attention on his furry head instead of on Ryan, who I knew would be trying to school his expression.

“I know you do, honey.” His voice was gruff, and he stretched over to kiss my cheek. “For what it’s worth, I’m not certain your feelings are as one-sided as you think.”

I laughed. “Sure.”

“No, really.” He sounded sincere, and when I glanced at him, I saw nothing but truth on his face.

I shook my head. “Don’t you think that if Nate felt anything for me other than friendship, I’d have figured it out by now? I’ve spent years analyzing everything he says and does for the slightest hint he might want me back. All he sees me as is his best friend. Trust me.” That being said, I’d never given him the ultimate test and told him about Ryan while we were actually together. I squirmed at the thought.

“Hey.” He paused in cuddling Duke, his eyebrows knitting together. “Listen. I know you’ve been telling yourself that for years, but he was very territorial about you for someone who’s just a friend, and he spent a lot of time watching us together. I think he was trying to figure out if there’s still something between us and whether he needs to feel threatened.”

The tiniest prick of hope spiked in my chest. I tried to

shut it down as quickly as it arose because hoping against the odds would accomplish nothing but getting me hurt. "You're being ridiculous."

"I'm not," he insisted. "You're too close to this. You can't see what I do. That man was worried I'd take you away from him."

"No." My voice shook. "He's just protective. That's all."

Seeming to notice my distress, Ryan nodded and didn't say anything for a while. He sipped his wine, then set it down far enough away that Duke wouldn't knock it over with his tail, and rolled the puppy onto his back. He rubbed Duke's belly, winking at me when he snuffled happily. After a while, Ryan eased away, and before much longer, Duke dozed off, the light from the fire playing over his fur.

"Nisha is pregnant," Ryan said out of nowhere.

I swallowed, my throat suddenly dry. Sympathy for him throbbed in my chest. Nisha was his best friend's wife. The woman he'd loved for nearly as long as I'd loved Nate. I closed my eyes, understanding how much he must be hurting. I'd been through something similar when I'd discovered Maddy was pregnant and that Nate planned to marry her. It hadn't been intentional—on his part, at least. It had crossed my mind that Maddy might have "forgotten" to take her contraceptive pill in order to lock him down. There was just something about the way she'd looked at me so smugly when they'd announced they were expecting.

I'd met Ryan a week after the wedding ceremony. I'd been drowning my sorrows in an Auckland bar, and he'd been half pissed and telling the bartender all about his doomed love for the woman his best friend had proposed to. I'd listened, fascinated by his story and for once feeling as though I wasn't alone. Before I knew it, we were drinking together, sharing our woes, and a few days later, we were married ourselves. But getting married hadn't solved the problem. It had been like putting a Band-Aid on a knife wound.

"I'm sorry," I whispered, reaching over to take his hand and squeezing it so he knew he had my support. No wonder he'd felt the need to visit me. To escape from his life. I couldn't even tell him it would get better, because I wasn't sure that was true. One day the pain might fade to a dull ache, but it might not ever leave entirely. "You're welcome to stay here for as long as you need."

It was all I could offer. A place to gather himself and figure out what to do next. Logically, he knew Nisha was unavailable to him whether she was pregnant or not—she was married to his best friend, after all—but this must feel like another nail in his emotional coffin.

He let out a sharp breath. "Thanks, but I'll just stay for the week. Any longer and I might not want to go back."

"That would be okay too. I have room here for you, and there isn't a local tattoo artist. If you set up shop, I bet you'd get plenty of customers from the tourists passing through."

His lips pursed. "Don't tempt me. My life is back in Auckland. But I might visit again if that's okay?"

I tangled my fingers with his. "Any time. You've always got a place here."

8

GRACE

I SHIFTED papers on my office desk, searching for the lilac-colored notebook I used to scribble my ideas for stories and random thoughts I had late at night. It didn't appear to be there, so I checked the desk drawers. Finding them empty, I strolled through the house, scanning the cupboards and tables, wondering where I might have left it. I often carried the notebook around with me, which meant it could be anywhere—although I could have sworn it had been next to my laptop when I turned it off yesterday. Hopefully, Ryan hadn't taken it to his room to snoop, or I'd have to wake him up to retrieve it.

"Alice!" I called, hearing footsteps in the hall. "Is that you?"

"Yeah." Alice rounded the corner, a coffee in a reusable takeout cup in each hand. "Here you go." She passed me the one with text printed on the front that read "Keep calm, it's only a first draft" and kept the other labeled "World's Best Assistant" for herself. She'd clearly just returned from her morning jaunt to the local cafe, Taste of Destiny.

"Mm." I breathed in the scent of fresh coffee. "Thank you. I need this."

She grinned. "Me, too. I stayed up way too late reading last night. I kept telling myself, 'One more chapter,' and before I knew it, I'd finished the whole book and started on the second in the series."

I laughed. "It's never just one more chapter."

"I know." She rolled her eyes, which were dark beneath carefully shaped and colored brows. Alice had only lived in Destiny Falls for a few months—although she'd become absolutely indispensable to me in that time—and unlike many newcomers, she hadn't eased up on makeup or fashion choices at all since arriving. She was always stylishly dressed and beautifully made-up. "Anyway, what did you want?"

I led her back along the hall, glancing through each doorway as I passed, double-checking whether I'd missed anything obvious. "You didn't happen to see my notebook before you left for coffee, did you?"

"As a matter of fact, I did."

My heart lightened with relief. "Thank god. I was worried I'd lost it."

"Check the kitchen. I'm pretty sure it was on the counter."

"Huh." I frowned. I didn't recall having used the note-book in the kitchen recently. "Okay. I'll do that."

I looked, and sure enough, the notebook sat on the kitchen counter near the containers I used to store breakfast foods for the guests. Strange. I shrugged it off and returned to the office, where Alice had already set up at the second desk. My author inbox was open on her screen, displaying over fifty new emails. I took a moment of silent appreciation for the fact that, because of Alice, I'd only have to read a few of them. She dealt with the majority of my correspondence and just gave me the highlight reel, pointing out anything that required my personal attention. The woman was an absolute godsend.

"Who's the hottie staying down the hall?" she asked, spinning to face me, her cup clasped between her palms. Her bright pink lips were tilted in a perpetual smile and the little flicks of eyeliner at the corners of her eyes gave her a pixie-like appearance. If I didn't know she was the same age as I am, I might have guessed her to be in her early twenties. Sometimes, I envied her youthful appearance, although at times, it could be a detriment. I knew she had a hard time getting some people to take her seriously.

"When did you see him?" I asked.

"As I was leaving for coffee. He clearly didn't expect me, because he was only wearing boxers." She waggled her eyebrows mischievously.

"It's not like that," I protested, smiling anyway. "He's my ex."

"Oh." She sounded disappointed. "Not a current love interest, then? No rekindling of the old flame? You know people love a good second-chance romance."

I laughed. "No old flames rekindling here. We're friends. He brought Duke down for me."

"Duke?" She cocked her head, her neat bob bouncing around her ears.

"Oh my gosh, you haven't met Duke!" I stood, everything else forgotten. "Come on, he's the cutest thing ever."

I steered her into the backyard, where Duke had just finished chowing through the breakfast I'd fed him earlier. As we approached, he glanced up, flecks of meat framing his mouth, and he seemed to smile.

"He's so sweet," Alice gasped, sinking to her knees in

front of him. He let her pat him once, then returned his attention to his meal. She giggled. "Well, he knows his priorities."

"Oh yes. He's got a lot of growing to do. He'll need that fuel."

"He's a Rottweiler?" she asked.

"Yes. Ryan—that's my ex—his sister breeds them."

She shook her head in disbelief. "I never pictured you with a Rottweiler."

"You're not the first person to say that." I recalled how surprised Nate had been and felt a twinge of guilt. To say I hadn't handled things well where he was concerned would be an understatement.

"Nate?" she asked knowingly.

"Exactly."

We made our way back inside, and I left the door open so Duke could come in when he'd finished. I'd gone a bit over-the-top and set up beds for him in the living room, the office, and my bedroom, so he had the run of the place. No doubt he'd harass us to play with him as soon as his breakfast settled. For the first time in a long time, my heart felt like smiling. There really was nothing that could compare with the affection and goodness of dogs.

"How did your BFF react to you having your ex to stay?" Alice cut straight to the heart of the matter, as usual.

"He wasn't thrilled, but he seems to have calmed down."

"I'll bet."

There was something in her tone I didn't understand, but I let it go.

"So, what's the priority today?" she asked, shifting gears as we reentered the office.

I grabbed the notebook from the desk and waved it. "I had some new ideas for Jewel and Rocky's story over the weekend. I'm going to make a start on those. I'm sure you've got plenty for the upcoming release to get on with."

She nodded. "Sure do."

One of my medieval romance novels was releasing soon. I wrote historical romance books over a range of eras, but medieval was my most popular. However, the story I was currently writing was a passion project set at the time Destiny Falls was established as a mining town, featuring Jewel and Rocky, who were loosely based on a real-life couple who had inspired the town's romantic mythology. I'd been doing as much research on the real couple—Pearl and Charles—as I could, but information about them was scarce, so I'd had to improvise a lot.

I sat and flipped through my notebook to the most recently used page. I skim-read my notes from the weekend and mulled over how to incorporate them into what I'd written so far. As I was thinking it through there was a knock at the office door. I glanced around. A sheepish-looking Ryan poked his head around the corner, holding up a pair of mangled high-heeled boots.

I groaned. "Isn't Felicity supposed to train them not to do that?"

He shrugged. "He's a puppy. Puppies do puppy things."

A whining sound came from near the floor. Duke sat there, somehow looking both proud and contrite.

A laugh burst from me before I could contain it. "At least he's good entertainment value."

9

NATE

"CAN we have fried potatoes for breakfast?"

I woke up with Tess hovering over me and blinked, trying to clear my blurry vision. Slowly, my daughter's beautiful face crystallized, surrounded by a halo of dark blonde hair. She batted her eyelashes, but I knew she wasn't trying to manipulate me with them. Tess honestly had no idea how adorable she was.

"Daddy?" she prompted. "There are leftover potatoes in the fridge."

"Yes, sweetheart, we can make fried potatoes." My voice sounded rusty. As it should, considering I'd been sleeping for hours.

I sat up, and she shuffled backward to sit on the edge of the bed. With her bottomless blue eyes that landed somewhere between the greenish blue of mine and the sky blue of her mother's, she watched me stretch a kink out of my back,.

"Have you washed your hands?" I asked.

She nodded.

"Good. How about you go and get out the frying pan and the butter? I'll be there in a minute."

She left quietly—the same way she did everything. It was strange that Maddy and I had managed to produce a shy child. Tess hadn't inherited either my directness or Maddy's social nature. The only two things she was willing to speak up about were food and books. She read more than any other kid her age, and when she hadn't eaten in a while, she gave hangry a new meaning.

I got up and dressed quickly, worried she'd turn on the stove if I took too long to get there. The fact that she'd woken me meant she was probably already on the verge of a hunger-induced meltdown. She didn't like to disturb either her mother or me if she could avoid it, no matter how many times we told her we were happy for her to do so. I hurried into the kitchen. She was waiting, a slice of butter already in the pan. I switched the element on and started the kettle to make coffee.

"Would you like a hot chocolate?" I asked, thinking it might take the edge off.

She gave me one of those shy little smiles that punched me in the heart every time it made an appearance. "Yes, please."

"Great. Grab the marshmallows and the chocolate powder. I'll get started on the milk."

She did as I said, her face furrowed with concentration, and my heart squeezed again. It was crazy to me that despite being a grumpy, hot-tempered bastard most of the time, I'd somehow helped raise a big-hearted, well-adjusted little girl.

Together, we made hot chocolate, and while she drank, I sliced potatoes and added them to the melted butter in the pan. I found a couple of leftover sausages and added them as well. I wasn't much of a cook, but Tess never seemed to mind.

"Can we visit Grace's new puppy?" she asked as I served her breakfast.

I dished my own potatoes and sausage and grabbed a fork, passing another to Tess. "Gracie has a visitor at the moment. It might not suit for us to visit."

Tess gave me a strange look. "But she always likes to see us."

"I know, sweetheart, but it's not polite to just invite ourselves over."

Her confusion wasn't surprising, considering how many times we'd done just that.

"What if her visitor doesn't want to see us?" I said, hoping that would make her think twice.

Tess's forehead creased in thought for a moment but then cleared. "Her visitors are always nice." She cocked her head. "What's the matter? Don't you like them?"

My expression grew pinched. "I like him just fine."

"It doesn't sound like it."

I squeezed the bridge of my nose in frustration. Tess was too perceptive. I didn't know where she got that from either, but it sure as hell wasn't me.

"Are you and Grace having a fight?" Tess's voice had dropped to a whisper. "Is her visitor going to be her new best friend? Is that why you don't like him?"

"No," I growled. I'd had enough of that line of questioning. "Grace is my best friend, and I'm hers. That isn't changing, okay? I promise. You've got nothing to worry about."

Nor did I. No matter the fact that—as Tess had so helpfully pointed out—I was behaving like a jealous child. Shame weighed heavy in my gut. I really hadn't done my best to reassure Grace that her lies of omission wouldn't damage our friendship or to try to connect with Ryan. I'd taken a couple of steps in the right direction, but I hadn't been all in. If I wanted her to confide in me more, I needed to do something so that she'd feel comfortable doing so.

"Okay." Tess's voice was small.

I sighed. "I'm sorry, sweetheart. Daddy woke up on the wrong side of the bed. Why don't I call Grace when we've finished breakfast to see if she minds us coming over so you can meet Duke?"

A smile crept across her face. "I'd like that."

Then that's what I'd do. Nothing was more important to me than my daughter. Sometimes, I just needed to get my head out of my ass to remember that.

When we'd cleaned up the dishes and I'd sent Tess to the shower, I called Grace, who was more than happy for us to come over. Tess was thrilled. We headed over, and while she and Grace were playing with Duke, I made an effort to get to learn more about Ryan. Whatever else could be said about the guy—and despite the fact that his tattooed, rugged exterior was definitely not what I'd imagined for Grace—he cared about her. That was undeniable.

But I was still relieved when he said he was leaving the next day.

Sue me.

10

GRACE

On Sunday morning, I bid farewell to Ryan and returned inside to get ready for a walk with Nate and Tess. During their visit yesterday, they'd invited me to bring Duke and join them for a stroll around the golf course on the edge of town. Local golfers rarely ventured out during winter because the ground was often hard with frost or covered by a light dusting of snow. Still, it was a beautiful spot, and I was sure Duke would enjoy getting off the property.

I wrangled the puppy into a coat and buttoned it shut beneath his chin. He stared at me balefully.

"You look very handsome," I told him. "You'll appreciate it once we get outside."

He didn't seem to agree, but his bad mood only lasted for as long as it took me to get the leash and attach it to his collar, then he pulled me toward the door. I opened it. Thanks to his training, he didn't bounce or try to snatch the leash from my hands, but excitement glittered in his eyes, and I could tell it was taking all of his self-control to behave.

"You're doing so well," I said. "You're going to be the best little doggy in Destiny Falls."

"Don't let Kennedy hear you say that."

I jolted in surprise and glanced up to see Nate and Tess standing on the path leading from the road to the house. They were both bundled up with scarves around their necks and knitted beanies covering their ears. My heart gave a little jump. They were so precious together.

"Sorry, didn't mean to scare you," Nate said.

"You're fine." I placed my hand over my chest and took a breath while my pulse slowed, then I locked the door, pulled a pair of thin gloves out of my jacket pocket, and slipped my forearm through the leash while I put them on.

"Hi, Duke." Tess moved slowly toward the puppy, wary of the slippery path. She extended her hand, and Duke snuffled it happily, then yanked me toward her. I stumbled and righted myself. Tess giggled in delight as she stroked him while his tail waggled wildly.

"Good morning," Nate said.

I met his eyes, and my stomach flipped over at the sight of something unexpected in his gaze. An odd light that heated my insides more effectively than my jacket or gloves ever could. "Morning. Are you ready for this walk?"

"The sooner we get moving again, the better. My nose is already frozen just from getting over here."

As I drew nearer to him, I saw that the tip of his nose was endearingly pink.

"Don't say anything," he muttered.

My lips twitched, but I didn't say a word.

"Can I walk Duke?" Tess asked as we started ambling along the path and joined the sidewalk.

I exchanged a glance with Nate, who gave a slight nod. "Of course you can. Just make sure you keep a strong grip on the leash, and if he starts to pull too much, pass it to your dad or me."

"Okay."

I handed her the leash and showed her how to wrap it around her forearm so that Duke couldn't take off suddenly and pull it from her hands. She paid close attention, checking to make sure she'd done it right twice before she was comfortable to continue walking. I crossed my fingers that Duke wouldn't do anything crazy.

"She'll be fine," Nate murmured, apparently noticing my concern. "She's had practice with Daisy."

I side-eyed him. "Daisy isn't a Rottweiler."

"Maybe not," he conceded. "But she's a full-grown dog. Duke is only a puppy."

"True."

Still, I kept a close eye on them, and it didn't take long to see that Duke was being the perfect gentleman. In fact, he was more obedient with Tess than he'd been with me. Something loosened in my chest. It was nice to know I wouldn't need to worry about him around children.

It only took a few minutes to get to the golf course. By the time we'd circled half of it, Tess handed the leash back to me so she could warm her hands in her pockets. She stuck close to us even when Nate said she could stretch her legs if she wanted to. She was just that kind of kid.

I adored her.

I'd feared when she was born that I might hate her for tying Nate to another woman, but I needn't have worried. The first time I'd held her, I'd fallen for her with my whole heart. Not only because she was a piece of Nate, but because she was willing to love everything and everyone around her unconditionally. As she'd gotten older, I'd become her favorite person to talk to about books. Neither of her parents was a reader, so we'd bonded over our shared passion.

"Have you read anything interesting lately?" I asked, pausing while Duke sniffed the base of a tree.

Tess was quiet while she thought. "I read a really cool book about a group of friends with ponies who solved a mystery."

"That sounds great," I exclaimed. "Why don't you tell me about it?"

She went into detail recounting the story while we completed our circuit of the golf course and emerged back onto the sidewalk. I listened, enjoying not so much her words as her obvious love for reading. It made me happy.

We stopped when we reached the corner where we usually parted. From here, it was only a few blocks to each of our homes.

"Tess and I thought we'd visit her Nana and Grandpa," Nate said, nodding toward a different street that led to the Braddock's childhood home. "Want to come with us? We can warm up in their outdoor hot tub."

"Ooh, yes!" Tess squealed. "I love the hot tub! Please come. It'll be better with you there."

My innards turned to marshmallow. I was nothing but fluff when it came to this gorgeous man and his wonderful daughter. "I'd love to, but what about Duke?"

Nate shrugged. "Mum and Dad will be happy to mind him. Hell, maybe he'll want to join us in the tub."

"Ew!" Tess protested. "No, Dad. Duke is not coming in the tub with us."

"He's not," I agreed. "Are you sure your parents won't mind?"

"They'll love it."

I told myself I only capitulated because I knew Eugene and Heather probably would love to meet Duke. It had nothing to do with the glorious pleasure-pain that came with the prospect of seeing Nate's broad, bare chest across the tub from me.

Okay, maybe it was that. Just a little. I was only human.

We headed to the Braddock family home together. When we arrived, Heather greeted us with a massive smile and a plate of freshly baked brownies. She insisted we help ourselves to them before getting changed. They were delicious, as usual, although I caught Tess trying to sneak some to Duke and had to explain that chocolate wasn't good for dogs—a fact she seemed horrified by. It was only once Tess and Nate had gone to change into their swimsuits that I realized I had nothing to wear.

"You can borrow something of Summer's," Heather said, waving me toward Summer's childhood room.

"But she's half a foot shorter than I am," I protested.

She rolled her eyes. "Height doesn't matter much when it comes to bikinis."

I pulled a face. I didn't have a comeback for that except that I preferred one-piece swimsuits. I went to Summer's room and sorted through the drawers. In the back of the top drawer, I found a selection of barely there bikini tops and briefs that would cover almost nothing. I grimaced and pulled everything out. Surely there must be something less revealing. But no, five minutes later, I hadn't found any other options. With a sigh, I chose the least startling swimsuit of the bunch and prepared myself to sprint for the hot tub as quickly as possible.

11

———

NATE

Tᴇss and I had nearly defrosted by the time the French doors opened. I glanced over, wondering what had taken Grace so long, and my mouth fell open. My best friend's svelte body was almost entirely exposed, goosebumps erupting over her skin as she emerged into the cold winter air. I'd seen Grace in swimsuits before, but she usually wore one pieces or more modest two pieces that concealed her lean torso, graceful curves, and legs that seemed to go on forever.

Now, it was as if learning her secret had made me see her in a new light—as a stranger in some ways—and I couldn't take my eyes off her. Her cheeks were flushed pink, and she was nibbling her lip, clearly uncomfortable with the outfit. It was only because of that that I was able to tear my gaze from her—but not before I'd noticed a flash of something dark on her right hip.

She hurried over and climbed into the water, easily clearing the edge of the tub. A vision of her wrapping those elegant legs around my waist flashed into my mind, and my dick started to thicken in my trunks. I shifted uncomfortably and reminded myself my daughter was present. Yep, that was enough to solve the problem.

"What's that on your hip?" Tess asked. Thank god for curious kids.

Grace glanced down as if she didn't know what Tess was talking about. "Oh, that's a tattoo."

My cock came back to life. Grace had a tattoo? How had I never known that?

"Is it new?" I asked.

"No." She angled her hip so we could both see her ink. It was of a sun and moon bound together with intricate mandala designs that was somehow a perfect complement to her classy beauty. The whole thing was only the size of my palm, and considering how low it sat on her hip, with the bikini knotted just beneath it, I understood how I'd never had cause to see it before.

"I got it years ago," she explained, tracing the outline with a fond smile. "Ryan drew the design. You know how awful my drawing skills are."

My stomach clenched. It was ridiculous, but I didn't like the thought that someone else had etched a part of themself permanently onto her body and I hadn't. For some reason, I wanted to know and have more of her than anyone else.

Don't be a dickhead, I mentally scolded myself. *You're her friend, that's all. Of course her ex knows her more intimately than you do.*

But I had to admit, it was getting more difficult to lie to myself. After years of viewing Grace strictly as a friend, I couldn't unsee the things I was noticing about her now.

"It's so pretty," Tess breathed, looking as closely at the fine lines of ink as I'd like to. I forced myself to hold back. My daughter could stare, and it was innocent. If I gave

Grace's sexy tattoo the same attention, there would be nothing innocent about it.

"Thank you." Grace smiled at Tess, then dropped her hip back beneath the water. Her eyes flicked toward me, then darted away quickly, as though trying to gauge my reaction.

Considering how I'd blown up at discovering her secrets recently, I couldn't blame her for being cautious. I looked away from her, staring at a smudge on the wall until my body had calmed down.

What the hell was wrong with me?

It wasn't as if I didn't know Grace was a woman. I'd seen her dressed to kill on more than one occasion, and I'd always been able to acknowledge how attractive she was without my insides getting tangled in knots over her.

This was different.

It reminded me of the months during high school when I'd wondered whether she'd say yes if I asked her out. We'd been great friends even then, and I'd passed a lot of nights dreaming about how she might feel in my arms, but she'd been so different from the girls I usually dated that I didn't know how to read her. I'd eventually decided not to make a move in case she shot me down and I ruined our friendship. The way I felt now reminded me of how mixed up I'd been over her then. But I was a thirty-four-year-old man. Not a teenager. There was no excuse for my reaction.

Still, as Tess splashed around and Grace rested her legs across mine, I couldn't help wondering how things might be different if I hadn't been too scared to take a chance. Of course, no matter how enticing the idea, I'd never go back, even if I had the choice. Being with Maddy had given me Tess, and that meant everything. My daughter was the single most precious thing in my life.

I made myself smile and concentrate on their conversation. They were discussing what kind of characters they liked best in books. There wasn't much I could contribute to that, since the reading I did was limited to police briefings and reports.

We stayed in the tub until Tess's fingers started shriveling up and then raced to the house so we could get dry before we froze. I did everything I could not to stare at the jiggling globes of Grace's ass, but when a throat cleared and I looked up to see Mum's raised eyebrow, I knew I'd been caught. My cheeks burned and I refused to meet her eyes again until after I'd returned from the bathroom, dry and clothed. Both Tess and Grace were still getting dressed, so I sat with Mum and Dad at the table. Duke lay nearby on an old couch cushion they must have given him to use as a bed.

"You three should stay for lunch," Dad said. "We've got plenty to go around."

"Oh yeah?" I had to admit, it would be nice not to have to go home and figure out what to cook for Tess. When I was alone, I tended to rely on sandwiches and protein bars more than I should.

"Unless Grace needs to be back to spend time with Ryan," Mum added slyly.

I narrowed my eyes at her. "How do you know about him?"

She winked. "You think anything happens in this town that I don't know about? I knew she had a male guest the morning after he arrived. It took a little longer to get his name, but give me some credit."

I grunted and studied the wooden grain of the table rather than giving her the satisfaction of seeing my surprise.

"Is he handsome?" she asked.

I shot her a glare.

"Eden from the cafe heard from Alice that he's gorgeous, and you know Alice has an eye for the handsome ones."

"Did you, uh, know they were married?"

"What?" She sounded shocked. "Of course not. I had no idea Grace was married. When? Where?"

Her astonishment somehow made me feel better. At least I wasn't the only one who'd been in the dark. I gave them a quick rundown of everything Grace had told me about their relationship.

"Wow," Mum said when I finished. "She sure kept that quiet." She paused, then added, "Do you think he wants to win her back?"

"Enough gossip, woman," Dad groaned. "It doesn't matter how gorgeous he is or how friendly he and Grace apparently are. They divorced for a reason, so don't meddle."

"He's gone anyway," I added.

"Oh." She had the audacity to look disappointed. "What a shame. Grace deserves a good man in her life."

I fought the urge to mutter that she didn't need anyone else because she had me. That wasn't what Mum had meant, and I knew it.

Voices in the hall caught our attention, and Grace and Tess entered the living area, wearing matching smiles. My heart gave a pang. Being here with them both felt familiar and new all at once. Their presence gave me a sense of being whole. As if we were a family. Except that we weren't, and the big-hearted brunette with her arm around my daughter was more of an enigma than I'd ever imagined. I couldn't let that stand. If Grace had more secrets, I was going to find out what they were.

12

———

NATE

AT THE END of my shift, I stripped off my work gear and changed into a T-shirt and a pair of track pants, then I stuffed everything into a duffel bag and slung it over my shoulder. I drove the short distance to Grace's place and jogged up the path to her front door, leaving the bag in the car. We needed to talk, and now that Ryan was gone and Tess would be picked up from school by her mother, there was nothing to get in the way of that.

I tried the handle, and when it opened, I let myself in. I headed through the house on autopilot until I stood outside the office door. It was shut, so I raised my hand to knock, but then a delicate palm with surprisingly strong fingers clamped around my forearm, stopping me.

"Don't you dare," Alice muttered. "She's finally got into the zone after trying and failing to hammer out words for hours. If you break her focus, there'll be hell to pay. Not just from me and her, but from her readers too." She scowled.

"No one understands how difficult it can be to really get into a good flow state."

"Okay." I backed off, holding my hands up to show her I meant no harm. "I'll leave her alone." I glanced at my watch. "If I go to the gym and come back in an hour, will that be all right?"

She tilted her head to the side, considering. The gesture emphasized the sharpness of her chin, which was at times matched by the sharpness of her tongue. "Come back and we can see. If she's still going at it, then you might just need to come back tomorrow."

I sighed. "Fine."

I wanted to see Grace as soon as I could, but I appreciated Alice looking out for her. Grace effectively ran two businesses: the cottage bed and breakfast and her writing career. She needed someone to help protect her valuable time, and Alice may look like the Disney princess version of that woman from *The Queen's Gambit,* but she could be fierce when the need arose.

I strode back to the car and headed to the gym, which was housed in an old industrial building near the fire station. Since Destiny Falls was a small town, the gym was simple and operated on a key-based system. I let myself in and connected my phone to the music system via Bluetooth. I scanned the space, which was fairly stark with only a couple of treadmills, a selection of free weights, a stationary cycle, and a set of bars for bodyweight exercises.

I warmed up on the treadmill and was arranging weights on the bench press when the door swung open and Bailey strolled in, beaming when she spotted me. She sauntered over, her hips swaying, her lips curved into a flirtatious smile that I knew didn't mean a damn thing. Bailey was Summer's best friend, and she'd practically grown up with us. She could flirt her little heart out without ramifications because none of us would ever go there. Honestly, with the nonstop attention she got from tourists at the bar, she probably liked knowing she was safe with us.

"Hey, Bailey," I called in greeting.

"Looking good, Nate." She conducted a thorough visual sweep of my body and winked. "All that police training is working for you."

I rolled my eyes. Perhaps her words would be better for my ego if I didn't know she'd say them even if I'd succumbed to the dad pouch that had been trying to develop since Tess had been born. Bailey was sweet. Not in the wouldn't-hurt-a-fly way that Grace was, but sweet all the same.

"What would you know about police workouts, Little Miss Peace and Love?" I teased.

She gave me a look haughty enough to befit royalty and strutted over to the bars. She bent her knees and launched into the air, pulling herself over one of the bars in a fluid motion. She paused for long enough to meet my eyes, then dove over the bar and seemed to glide in an arc before returning to her original position. She released her grip with one hand until she was holding herself in the air with only one arm attached to the bar. She was barely sweating.

I laughed. "Point made. I forgot you were a former gymnast."

"Nothing former about it," she said, lowering herself to the ground. "A gymnast is a gymnast regardless of whether they compete or not."

"True," I agreed. "And I hear you're a hell of a coach."

In addition to working at the bar at Drunken Destiny, Bailey also coached the Destiny Falls gymnastics team and maintained a health and beauty blog. I'd never fully understood it, but Summer had assured me she was successful enough not to need the extra bartending income. She only kept her job at the pub because she loved my parents. Everyone in Destiny Falls did. The Braddock family was an institution. Dad owned the local bar, Mum managed the information center, and between the six of us kids with our various careers, we formed a massive part of the local community.

Bailey grinned and headed for a yoga mat in the corner. Obviously unimpressed by my choice of music, she drew her earbuds from her pocket and put them in, then she began some kind of yoga flow. I hefted the bar off the rack and grunted through another set of bench presses.

My mind wandered. Thinking about Grace. Bailey. Women in Destiny Falls.

Unfortunately, the downside of living in a small community where everyone knew everyone else was that there were few women I'd be interested in dating if I ever wanted to put myself out there. Not that it mattered anyway. I'd decided soon after Maddy asked for a divorce that I should focus on Tess until she was grown. When she'd slapped divorce papers against my chest, Maddy had made sure to tell me of the many ways in which I'd let her down. I hadn't been there when she needed me. I worked too much. I didn't give her enough attention. I never wanted to spend time with her. She felt unappreciated. And the real zinger: I seemed to love Tess more than her.

The thing is, I did love Tess more than her.

But Tess was my daughter. How could anyone—even her mother—expect me to love them over her?

Nope. I'd failed at romantic relationships just like I had recently discovered I'd failed at friendship. I never wanted to make anyone else feel the way Maddy had—especially not someone I cared about, so it was best if I didn't try again. Maybe one day. But for now, I'd just focus my energy on being the best dad I could be and hope I didn't screw it up.

13

———————

GRACE

I CLOSED the door behind Alice and locked it. Ever since the incident with Kennedy, I'd been more careful when I was home alone—to the point of worrying I might be growing paranoid. Surely the odds of something happening in the same place twice, and to the same person twice, were negligible.

I knelt and fussed over Duke, who'd followed me to the exit. "Hey, buddy. It's just you and me. How about we stretch and then get a snack?"

He made a sound that could be interpreted as agreement, and when I stood, he followed me to the living room. I lay on the floor and stretched, feeling a tightness between my shoulder blades and in my upper back, then I turned onto my side for a spinal twist. I repeated the stretch on the other side, then got to my knees and threaded one arm beneath my body, leaning my weight on the shoulder to stretch out the shoulder blade.

I groaned. Damn, that felt good.

Outside, a vehicle rumbled up the drive. Duke barked, and I shushed him, recognizing the sound of Nate's car. I didn't move, knowing he'd let himself in. When some of the stiffness had gone from my shoulder, I swapped sides, sighing in relief. My muscles felt wrung out, and it was just what I needed. Sitting at a computer all day could be hell on my body. It was great when I had guests because I had to run through daily maintenance routines, but with the cottages empty and Alice taking care of most of my admin work, there wasn't any excuse for me to get up from my desk.

I listened as the front door opened, and Duke raced down the hall, barking frantically.

"It's okay, boy," I called, but I couldn't bring myself to move.

"Hey, Gracie." Nate's voice carried down the hall. "Where are you?"

"Private living room," I yelled as loudly as I could from my current position.

"How did the—whoa." His footsteps stopped abruptly. "What's up with you?"

"Sore back."

He tutted. "You have to take better care of yourself."

I wriggled around, sticking my ass higher into the air, trying to get a deeper stretch. I heard him mutter something under his breath, but I couldn't tell what.

"Get up. Let me help," he said.

Carefully, I maneuvered myself out of the pose and flopped onto the floor bum first, then turned to face him. He lowered himself onto the sofa and spread his knees. "Come on. I'll give you a back rub."

A full-body shiver rippled through me, and I couldn't help thinking what else I might like him to rub. But I was a good girl and behaved myself, sitting cross-legged between his thighs. When he dug his thumbs into my knotted muscles, I couldn't hold back another groan.

"Shit, your back is a mess." He didn't ease up, and my head fell forward in bliss. "You need to take breaks," he continued as he worked one knotted muscle and then another. "So you can limber up and move around. Hell, even getting one of those spiky massage balls would help."

My lips curved. "Why would I want one of them when I have you?"

There was absolutely no incentive. A massage ball couldn't possibly compare to having Nate's hands on me and listening to his gruff voice as he lectured me. His post-exercise scent—clean male sweat—surrounded me, and if not for the discomfort in my upper back, I'd have been in heaven.

"I can't always be here," he reminded me.

"I know, but you do such a good job when you are." When he handled me like this—tenderly, gently—it was easy to imagine he might love me the way I did him. Hazardous to my heart, perhaps, but addictive all the same.

He cleared his throat. "It's come to my attention that I might not have been the type of friend I want to be."

My stomach sank, and suddenly his touch was of little comfort. I shuffled away from his intoxicating scent and rose to my feet. "You're closer to me than any of my other friends."

I didn't meet his eyes as I breezed out of the room, knowing he'd be close behind me. Duke let out a woof of protest, apparently not ready to move. I didn't wait to see if he'd come with us.

In the kitchen, I considered pouring myself a glass of wine but started the kettle boiling instead. I'd had enough wine recently.

"I want to know whatever else I don't know about you,"

Nate said, leaning against the counter and crossing his feet at the ankles. "It's true that you didn't tell me about getting married, but I should have damn well noticed something was going on with you—both then and when you divorced. I'm sure there are other things I've been oblivious about and missed over the years, and I'd like to know what so I can do better at getting my head out of my ass in the future."

My hands shook as I prepared a mug of herbal tea. I didn't make one for him, knowing he'd rather help himself to a glass of water or beer from the fridge if he felt like having something to drink.

"You didn't do anything wrong." I faced away from him while the tea brewed. "You don't need to fix anything because there's nothing to fix."

"Grace." His tone said not to bullshit him.

"There's not," I protested. "Besides, I'm sure there are plenty of things you don't know about me, and vice versa. If you have a particular question, ask and I'll answer."

When a couple of minutes dragged by and he didn't say anything, I thought I'd gotten off scot-free, but as soon as I removed the tea bag from my mug and turned back to him, he started on the questions.

"I didn't realize you had an ex-husband. Are there any other significant exes waiting to pop up from the woodwork?" He sounded as if he was trying for humor, but his delivery fell flat.

I mirrored his position, the mug resting on the counter near my elbow while the tea cooled. "Like I told you, there are no other ex-husbands. I dated a couple of guys while I was in Christchurch during my undergraduate study, but nothing serious. I went out with Cal once, but there was no spark. I've had a few dates from apps, but nobody who warranted a second date. That's pretty much it."

Hopefully he wouldn't push for more. I could hardly

explain that I'd decided it wasn't fair for me to date others and lead them on when I was hung up on him. I'd thought Cal, the local veterinarian and Summer's business partner, might be a good match for me because of our similar temperaments. The handsome blond wasn't a hardship to look at, and we got along well, but we were too similar. He fit much better with his current girlfriend, who was awkward, endearing, and had a massive heart.

"Why?" He looked bewildered. "I know there aren't many single guys our age around here, but you're a catch. Surely someone would be willing to move towns if they fell for you."

"Maybe I didn't look that hard," I admitted. "Online dating isn't really my thing. I'm better in person."

Duke padded into the room and stopped at my feet. I bent to pat him, and he shoved his nose into my palm, looking for treats. "I've got nothing for you," I told him. "Later."

The dog gazed hopefully at Nate, who shook his head.

"He's going to eat you out of house and home," he said.

"But he'll be cute doing it."

I grabbed the handle of my mug and blew across the surface of the tea. I was starting to get hungry, and a glance at the clock told me it was after six. I'd need to begin cooking soon if I didn't want to eat late.

"What about Max?" Nate said, startling me.

I frowned. "What about him?"

He shifted from one foot to the other, obviously uncomfortable. "Did anything ever happen between the two of you?"

I snort-laughed and clapped my hand to my mouth.

"What?" he demanded. "He's a good guy, and you two are close."

"So are you and I," I pointed out. *Yet we're tragically not together.*

He grumbled. "I'm just saying."

I sipped my tea and, finding it too hot, put it down, then opened the fridge to see what I might be able to make for dinner. "Nothing has ever happened between Max and me. He's too much like my brother."

Unlike his twin. Unfortunately.

"Have you ever been in love?" he asked.

I scowled and dropped a kumara onto the counter harder than necessary. "What's with the third degree about my love life?"

He shrugged. "I feel like I let you down in that department while I was busy with my own shit. All this stuff that's coming up made me realize there's a lot I don't know about you, and I hate that."

"You know more about me than almost anyone."

"I don't want it to be 'almost.'"

I nibbled my lower lip as I rinsed the kumara and then searched for a vegetable peeler. It was hard to dismiss his question when his intentions were good. But if I told him I had been in love, he'd ask who with, and that would open a can of worms I wasn't prepared to deal with. I needed to distract him, but based on how persistent he was being, that would take something big. My mind sifted frantically through ideas, then my mouth seemed to open of its own volition.

"My books are spicy," I blurted, then felt heat rush to my cheeks. I squeezed my eyes shut and inwardly cursed myself.

What the hell, Grace?

14

———

NATE

"Um, spicy?" I asked, baffled. "I didn't know books could be spicy."

Her face was the color of cooked tomato. Whatever she meant, it was obvious she didn't want to explain, but she heaved a sigh and started talking.

"It means there's rather, uh, graphic sex in them," she said, raising her chin as though daring me to make a stupid comment. "A couple of my books have some light kink."

"Kink?" I repeated, like an idiot. "Like, whips and chains? I thought you wrote historical novels."

She pressed her lips together and scrunched her nose like she'd rather be having literally any other conversation. "I do write historical novels, but they're romances. Love stories set in different time periods. As for whips and chains, not so much. More like blindfolds and ropes." She moistened her lips. "Some dominance and submission, but nothing heavy."

I stared at her, half-convinced we'd slipped into an

69

episode of *The Twilight Zone.* My sweet, bookworm best friend was apparently a secret vault of information about sex stuff I'd never even considered.

Mind. Blown.

"You," I started, but couldn't think of what to say. "I... um.... Ropes, did you say?"

She laughed and rolled her eyes, her expression lightening for the first time. "Yes, Nate. Ropes. Bondage. Some people do that. Sometimes, it isn't even sexual."

I shook my head in disbelief. "When you told me you wrote historical novels, I was thinking World War II type stuff. But you're telling me it's more like *Downton Abbey* with kinky sex?"

"Close enough, but some of my books are sweeter than others."

Here I'd always thought of her as remarkably wholesome. Who was this woman with the tattooed ex she'd married on impulse and her secretly kinky stories?

"Can I read one?" The question was out before I could think it through, but if she thought it was strange, she didn't let on.

"Um, yeah. I guess so." She sounded awkward as hell. She hurried out of the room, but before I could regain enough sense to follow, she reappeared with a book in her hand and offered it to me. I took it from her, studying the cover. A woman stood with her back to the photographer, an elegant gown around her waist and nothing marring the alabaster skin of her back but a string of pearls looped around her neck. My eyes bulged. I'd seen some of Grace's books, but never one that looked like this. I'd definitely have noticed. After all, the main reason I hadn't delved into any of her novels was that reading wasn't really my thing, and it would take something more interesting than what I thought of as dry historical stories to tempt me.

I'd read that situation all wrong.

"Here," she said. "That's my most recent one."

"Thanks." I tucked it under my arm without opening it. I wasn't sure what I expected to see inside, but I didn't want to react in a way that might bother her, so I'd look later, when I was alone.

"Tess tells me she's been doing some writing," she said, turning back to the kitchen counter. "Have you read any of it?"

"Not yet." I latched onto the change of topic with relief. "She's very private about it."

She looked over her shoulder and smiled reassuringly. "Don't worry. She will share when she's ready."

I ran my hand over the buzzed ends of my hair. "Please tell me she hasn't read anything of yours. At least, not anything like this." I waved the book from under my arm.

Grace snorted with laughter and tossed a tea towel at me. "Of course not. Come on, grab a peeler. If you're here, you might as well help."

As soon as I got home after dinner, I settled on the sofa and opened Grace's book. I scanned the first few pages. They were innocuous enough. I could tell it would be a love story, but if not for the cover, I wouldn't have guessed it to be anything raunchier than *Pride and Prejudice*. I flicked through a few more pages until I glimpsed a word that brought me up short.

Cock.

I looked closer. I'd never heard the word "cock" come out of Grace's mouth before. Seeing it here in black-and-white, as a product of her imagination, felt dirty.

I couldn't look away if I tried.

I read a paragraph, then two. At first, I was a bit lost because I didn't have enough context, but it didn't take long for me to work out that the heroine was a widowed gentlewoman who'd stumbled upon a sex club, and the hero was a notorious womanizer who'd taken it upon himself to seduce her. The scene was incredibly erotic. I was glued to the pages as the man blindfolded the gentlewoman and stripped her of everything except her pearl necklace, which he used to tease her until she was a writhing mess. He was securing her hands above her head when I came to my senses and slammed the book shut. My heart beat wildly, and filthy images assailed my mind one after another. I closed my eyes, but there was no stopping them.

Grace, naked except for a pearl necklace and a blindfold.

Grace, gasping with desire as I trailed the pearls around her breasts, over the silky smoothness of her stomach, dipping between her legs.

My dick throbbed, fully invested in the fantasy.

Her cheeks would be flushed with passion—a delightful shade of pink nobody else ever got to see. Her slender legs would shift restlessly, seeking the release only I could give her.

Fuck.

I shot to my feet and bolted to the bathroom. With shaking hands, I turned on the cold tap and splashed my face. The bite of the icy water brought me part of the way back to reality. My dick deflated.

"You can't think about your friend that way," I told my reflection. "Not cool."

But damn if that horny bastard cared.

15

———————

GRACE

I WAS GLARING at the computer screen, trying to dig up more information about what had happened to Pearl and Charles after they married at Destiny Falls. Unfortunately, I was having little success. The front doorbell rang, and I flinched in surprise. Duke barked and raced out of the room.

"I'll get it," Alice said before I could seize on the distraction as an excuse to give up my research.

I clicked through the records Kennedy's private investigator had sent her after she'd hired him to look into the couple, but nothing new jumped out at me. Twisting my lips, I scanned the words I'd already read several dozen times. Giving up, I returned to Google. What I really needed was to find one of the couple's descendants—if only I knew how to track them down.

"Grace."

I glanced up at the voice, surprised. Usually, Alice did everything in her power to prevent people from interrupting my work. "What is it?"

"There's a guy at the door who's insisting he talk to you personally."

Adrenaline shot through me. I couldn't think of anyone who'd need to speak to me in person about anything important, and Alice would have recognized someone who was part of my life. I didn't like surprise visits with people who insisted on seeing me. They reminded me of what had happened with Darrel Weich in Auckland, earlier on in my career. The man had been a fan of my writing, and he'd somehow tracked me down to the home I shared with Ryan —although he'd watched me for weeks before he made himself known. But when he had.... Well, he definitely hadn't been subtle.

"Did he say what he wants?" I asked, twisting my fingers anxiously.

"I think he'd like to rent one of the cottages," Alice said. "That was the impression he gave." She lowered her voice. "But he's a bit strange. Do you want me to come with you?"

I considered her offer. "I'm sure he's harmless, but perhaps you could stay close, just in case?"

"Whatever you need." She gave me a small smile and touched my shoulder.

I soaked in her quiet support. "Thanks."

Duke bounced at our heels, and Alice scooped him into her arms, giggling when he tried to lick her face.

"Impressive," I remarked. "He's heavy."

She booped him on the nose. "I'm stronger than I look."

I rose slowly to my feet and walked out of the office. Alice hung back, walking a few steps behind me. Present, but not intrusive. As we neared the front door, I summoned my courage and pushed it open, half expecting to see Darrel Weich on the other side, but it was a stranger. He looked up, his dark eyes sweeping me from head to toe, but not in a creepy way. More like he was taking stock of me and working something out in his head.

"Grace?" he asked.

"Yes. You wanted to see me?"

He nodded, then took a step backward and dragged his fingers through shaggy chocolate-brown hair. He made a sound of frustration in the back of his throat and squared his jaw, which was covered with scruffy facial hair.

"I'm Ezra." He squinted as though that was supposed to mean something to me. I studied him. He was decent looking, perhaps a couple of years older than I, but I was certain I hadn't seen him before. "Ezra Mendel."

I smiled politely. "It's nice to meet you, Ezra."

"You're Grace Smith?" he clarified.

"Yes." I wondered if he might be a bit slow. I thought we'd already covered that part. "Can I help you?"

"Oh." His eyes widened, and he glanced around as if noticing his surroundings for the first time. "*Oh*. Ah. Yes. I'd like to rent a room."

I put my hand on my hip. "A cottage, you mean? I don't have any rooms available inside the house." I'd decided to stop renting those out once I'd moved back from Auckland.

"That's right." He nodded decisively. "A cottage."

Behind me, Duke barked, and Alice shushed him.

"For how long?" I asked.

"Uh...." He looked like he was thinking quickly. "I'm not sure. A couple of weeks, at least. Can I confirm with you later?"

I sighed, already knowing this guy was going to be more hassle than he was worth. Although it would be nice to have someone in the cottages. The place felt too silent when they were empty. "Okay, but if I get any other booking requests, I'm going to need you to firm up your plans."

"I can do that." A muscle jumped in the side of his face,

and a thread of anxiety wove through me. Whatever his deal was, Ezra was strange. Perhaps I'd be better off telling him to leave. But he didn't seem dangerous. Just unusual. And I wasn't one to rush into judgment about someone.

"What brings you to town?" During winter, we usually only had guests who were interested in skiing or snowboarding.

He shrugged. "I needed to get away from my life for a while, and this seemed as good a place as any."

Warning bells chimed in my head at the vague response. I'd have to keep a close eye on Ezra. He might seem harmless, but I didn't trust him. Perhaps I'd ask Nate to look into him. But then I winced, remembering how protective Nate could get when he thought I was taking an unwarranted risk. Maybe I wouldn't mention it after all.

"I'll show you to the cottage, and then Alice will get you checked in," I told him. I unhooked a jacket from a hanger behind the door and put it on, then I gestured for Ezra to precede me into the yard. "Along there." I motioned for him to walk the path beside the garden. He stopped in front of the first cottage—the one Kennedy had been abducted from. I stepped past him and waved at the other one. "You can stay here."

Desdemona had supposedly cleared the negative energy out of Kennedy's cottage, but I still preferred to put guests in the other one whenever possible. It wasn't that I was particularly superstitious, but it seemed polite to invite paying guests to enjoy the cottage that didn't have a history that included kidnapping unless there was no alternative. I took a key from my pocket and unlocked the door. The interior smelled faintly of lemon from the cleaner I'd used after the last tenant left.

"This is the living area," I said, waiting while he looked

around. "There are two bedrooms through the doors over there and a bathroom and a laundry off the hall."

He pushed his hands into his pockets, gazing around as though he wasn't quite sure how he'd ended up here. "It's nice."

"Thank you. There is tea and coffee in the pantry, and I can get you some milk for the fridge. We serve breakfast in the house in the morning if you'd like to join us. Otherwise, there's a fully equipped kitchen you can use."

"Breakfast would be great." He pivoted to face me and beamed. "Will it just be the two of us?"

"Unless my assistant or aunt are here. Sometimes they come for breakfast."

His eyes widened. "Your aunt?"

"Yes, she runs a shop in town."

"You'll have to tell me which, and I'll check it out."

"Sure..." Again, that sense of wrongness prickled at the back of my scalp. I felt a tickle of premonition. He was a little too eager. Something was going on here beyond him simply visiting Destiny Falls for a break. Was he another obsessed fan who'd gotten it into his head that I was the love of his life? He didn't look crazy, but then the most dangerous men rarely did.

"Will I see you often?" he asked. "Perhaps you could show me around town."

"I work from home," I said, choosing my words carefully. "My assistant and I share an office in the house, so you'll probably see us most days," I added, subtly letting him know I wouldn't be alone. "I'm pretty busy at the moment, so I probably won't have time to show you around, but if you need anything else, knock at the main door, and one of us will make sure you're taken care of."

"Got it." He offered a smile that was too tender considering we'd just met. "Thanks. I'm looking forward to staying here."

"I hope you'll enjoy it." I edged out without turning my back on him. Perhaps he was nothing more than he claimed to be, but I had a bad feeling about his presence here. This time, I'd listen to my intuition and tread with caution.

16

NATE

I MET Max at Drunken Destiny after work on Friday. I needed his advice, so I'd asked him to come earlier than the others. I asked Bailey for two pints of beer and took them to the table in the rear corner of the bar, as far from the other patrons as possible. I didn't want to risk anyone overhearing our conversation.

"What's up?" Max asked as I sat opposite him.

I wrapped my hands around one of the glasses and gazed into the foam rather than meeting his eyes, knowing he'd see too much. Despite the fact that we shared identical DNA, Max had always been the smart one. He'd been at the top of our year in school and gone on to become a doctor. He was perceptive and quick-witted, whereas I was hot-tempered and about as subtle as a battering ram, no matter how hard I tried to tone it down.

"I've been having some thoughts," I said.

His lips twitched ever so slightly. "I'm glad to hear it."

I rolled my eyes. "Shut up. What I meant is that I've been

having some thoughts about Grace." I swallowed, knowing I was about to cross a line I couldn't uncross. If I gave voice to my fantasies, they wouldn't be a secret anymore. They'd be out there in the world even if I trusted Max not to share them. "Romantic thoughts," I added, in case I'd been unclear.

Max's eyebrows flew up, and he leaned forward, resting his weight on his elbows. "Do you have feelings for her?"

I huffed. "It's not that simple." I fought to find the words, frustrated with my inability to express everything that was going on inside my head. "I've never thought of her... that way... before, but ever since her ex turned up in town and I realized I didn't know her as well as I thought, it's like I can't get her out of my mind." I gave him a meaningful look. "It's never been like that with her. *Never*. I don't know what to do about it."

Max sat back, watching me thoughtfully. He raised his beer and drank. When he set it down, he finally spoke. "It's not surprising you'd find Grace attractive."

I glanced around to make sure nobody had heard him, but they all seemed to be minding their own business.

"She's a stunning woman," he continued.

Hot jealousy flared in my gut and I battled to ignore it. Talk about inappropriate reactions. I had no cause to be jealous. Of course Max knew that Grace was gorgeous. He had eyes.

"Inside and out," he added. "In fact, she might be one of the most attractive women I've ever met."

A glass shattered nearby, and the bar fell silent. I flinched, unprepared for the sudden crash back to the present. Two tables over from ours, Bailey was on her hands and knees, collecting the shards of a broken wine glass while wine pooled around her legs. I grabbed a wad of napkins from our table and dropped to the floor to help mop up the spilled drink. Max offered Bailey his hand and helped her up. He carefully transferred the glass from her shaking hands to an empty plate that one of the patrons had passed to him. Bailey stared at the floor. She seemed uncharacteristically lost for words, and as soon as she got the chance, she escaped out the back to the kitchen.

We returned to our seats. The interruption had clearly amped up the tension between us. Max wiped his palms and fingers on a napkin and turned his blue gaze back on me.

"I'm not the only man who thinks Grace is attractive," he said quietly. "A lot of guys around here do, so it's understandable that you're seeing her that way."

"But I never have before," I protested. "In eighteen years of friendship."

He opened his mouth, then seemed to think better of whatever he was about to say and closed it. For a moment, I couldn't help wondering if he wanted Grace himself. It would explain why he'd been single for so long. But then, Grace had already told me it wasn't like that between them. Was she misreading the situation...or was I? Theoretically, it wouldn't be the worst thing if there was something romantic between them. Max was a truly good person. I should want someone like him for Grace. But I didn't. I couldn't.

I wanted her for myself.

Perhaps I was seeing the truth years too late, but I wasn't the top-scholar twin and I'd never claimed to be. I'd finally figured it out, and even though I knew I should keep my distance from Grace—I'd been a horrible husband and not the best friend—I didn't know if I could.

"So what?" Max asked. "Just, whatever you do, be careful with her. Make sure you know what you want before you go for it, or you'll end up hurting her."

I bristled. I didn't need advice on how to take care of

Grace. She was my best friend. I knew what she needed better than Max did. Or at least, I used to think I did. After all the secrets I was unearthing, who knew?

"I won't hurt her," I ground out.

He studied me long and hard, then finally nodded. "I believe you."

The pub door swung inward, and two more of our brothers staggered in along with Liam's best friend, Asher. The wind blew hard behind them, throwing the door open even further.

Toby scanned the bar and spotted us in the back. He waved excitedly and crossed the distance between us in a few strides. "Hey, Twin One and Twin Two!"

"Hi, Tobes," Max said.

"Can't you call us something more original?" I bitched.

Toby's eyes ping-ponged between Max and me. "How about Good Twin and Evil Twin?"

I groaned, knowing which role I'd been cast in. "No."

"Leave him alone," Liam said to Toby, amusement gleaming in his eyes that were nearly the same shade as Max's. He aimed a pointed look at me. "He's only trying to get a reaction."

"And he knows you'll be the one to give it to him," Asher added.

Liam laughed and clapped his friend on the shoulder. "Other than you, Ash."

Asher's nostrils flared, but he didn't argue because, like me, he knew his temper could get the best of him.

"Is Connor coming?" Max asked, noticing we were one brother short.

Toby sank onto a chair and helped himself to my beer, swatting my hand away as I tried to snatch it from him. He took a long swig, then passed it back. "You know Connor wouldn't come into town at all if he could get away with it. If the grocery store delivered, and Mum didn't guilt him into the occasional family meal, he'd be as feral as the wildlife he protects." He cocked his head, then added, "I'd be tempted to join him, but I met a really nice girl at the resort today."

We all groaned, and Toby looked affronted. "Hey, Brita is different. I think she might really be the one for me."

I sighed and met Max's knowing gaze. Toby always thought his next fling would be different. In all fairness, he genuinely seemed to want to find love, but if he thought he'd find it with some European vacationer who'd leave at the end of her trip and never look back, he was doomed to be disappointed over and over again.

"Why don't you tell us about her," Max suggested, extending an olive branch.

Toby brightened. "Okay, so here's what you need to know...."

17

———

GRACE

I WAS HALFWAY to the Braddock's place with Duke, who was sniffing the grass eagerly around us, when I realized I'd forgotten the homemade granola that was my usual contribution to brunch. The Braddock family brunch happened every few weeks, and we all knew our roles. If I turned up without the granola, I'd have at least two pouting Braddock siblings to deal with.

Sighing, I doubled back to my place.

"Come on, pup," I muttered, tugging the leash. "You've sniffed the power pole enough for one day."

I walked as quickly as I could, and it only took a few minutes to reach my driveway. I slipped Duke's leash over a post near the gate and hurried up the path. As I reached the door, I noticed a sound around the side of the house. I froze, my instincts blaring at me that something was wrong.

I dithered, unsure whether to investigate or back away. In the end, I reached into my pocket for my phone and edged toward the source of the noise as quietly as possible. I found Nate's number in my contacts and was just about to hit Call as Ezra came into view. He was standing beside the office window, and his expression looked guilty. I frowned. What reason would he have for being there? It was at least a couple of dozen yards from the path that led from the road to the cottages.

"Grace?"

I plastered a phony smile on and slowly backed away. "E-Ezra," I stuttered, glancing from him to the office window. "What are you doing?"

He smiled, but it didn't reach his eyes. "I was looking for you. The door was locked, so I thought I'd see if you were in your office." His forehead creased with concern. "Are you okay? You're a bit pale."

"I'm fine," I snapped, cringing as I jerked backward. "I'm going to brunch, but I forgot something, so I had to come back. You hadn't come over for breakfast yet, so I thought you must not want it." We'd shared one breakfast together, but it had been tense and awkward. He'd asked too many questions and yet, hardly told me anything about himself. I'd been relieved when he failed to show up today.

Somewhere behind me, Duke whined, seeming to sense my distress. Why hadn't I brought him with me instead of leaving him at the gate?

"I was running late." He moved closer, but when I backed away again, he stopped and held his hands palms out in a gesture of peace. "I really was just looking for you. Where are you going for brunch?"

I wondered if he was angling for an invitation. "To a friend's."

He nodded. "All right. Um, hey, you mentioned your aunt owns a shop. Which one is it? I'd like to have a look."

I hesitated, reluctant to tell him because of his odd behavior, but if he wanted to, he'd be able to find out just by walking into the café and asking. Any local there would know.

You're being paranoid again, I told myself. *He's a little overeager, that's all.*

"Destiny Fibers," I said. "It's on Centennial Street."

"Great." He smiled. "I'll go and check it out."

"Okay, you do that. I'm going to leave now." I jerked a thumb toward the road.

He frowned. "Didn't you say you needed something from the house?"

"I got it already." I grimaced, knowing the lie would probably be obvious. But I needed to escape—the sooner the better.

"Right." He looked at me like I was crazy. "I guess I'll see you for breakfast tomorrow."

I nodded briskly and left. Duke lunged toward me as I approached, as if sensing I needed him, but then he settled for the rest of our walk, perhaps noticing how withdrawn I'd become. Unfortunately, no matter how much I told myself I was overreacting, my paranoid brain wouldn't accept it.

I forced myself to smile as I strode up the Braddock's drive and paused outside the house to unclip Duke's leash. He ran a few steps away from me, then seemed to notice I wasn't following and came back. I scratched the top of his head and told him he was a good boy.

As I let myself into the house, Heather greeted me with a welcoming smile. "Hello, Grace. I'm so glad you came."

Her words warmed me. Sometimes I wished Heather had been my mother, but if she was, then that would make my feelings for Nate even more awkward.

She glanced at my empty hands. "No granola?"

Kennedy entered the kitchen, coming from the direction of the living area. Her face fell. "There's no granola? But I bought yogurt and fruit I thought would go with it perfectly."

"They'll still be delicious on their own," I assured her. "I forgot the granola this morning, and I had a little trouble when I went back, so I decided to leave it behind."

Heather's eyebrows knitted in an expression of maternal concern. "What kind of trouble?"

I told the two women about my run-in with Ezra and how shaken I'd been. "I might be making something out of nothing," I concluded. "But he makes me nervous."

"Oh, Grace." Kennedy pulled me into a hug. "I'm sorry this is happening. Especially so soon after Tyler kidnapped me there. It must be stressful for you."

"I'm on edge all the time," I confessed. "Even though I keep telling myself there's nothing to worry about."

"Listen to your gut," Kennedy urged. "I knew I was being stalked for ages before Tyler actually did anything, but I told myself I was being crazy, and look where it got me. Trust me, if you think something is off about him, then it probably is."

"Kennedy is right," Heather said. "Better safe than sorry. Maybe you need to take extra precautions around this Ezra guy."

A throat cleared in the doorway. "You should make him pack his bags and leave."

The flip of my heart told me who had spoken before I even turned.

18

NATE

MY STOMACH HAD HARDENED the moment I'd first overheard what Grace was saying to Mum and Kennedy, and now it sat like a rock in my gut. The idea of Grace being around someone who made her uncomfortable wasn't right. I couldn't handle her being in a potentially unsafe situation, especially after Kennedy had been kidnapped from Grace's property only a few months ago. It hit too close to home.

"Surely that would be overreacting," Grace replied, only the anxious light in her eyes showing her true fear. "He hasn't said or done anything to threaten me. He's just... a little intrusive."

I pinched the bridge of my nose and groaned. Grace and her big heart. She thought the best of everyone, and I worried that it would get her into trouble one day.

"Look, I haven't met the guy, but if he's making you nervous in your own home, he has to go."

Grace glanced at Kennedy, as if seeking her opinion.

Kennedy shrugged. "My radar system for detecting

dangerous men is broken," she said. "I saw threats where there weren't any and didn't see the danger where it actually existed. If I could go back, I'd be more cautious though. You never know what people are capable of."

Grace nodded slowly. "I'm not going to kick Ezra out just because I'm feeling jumpy. I've been on edge for ages because of what happened at the start of the year, so it's probably nothing to do with him."

I scowled, not happy with her decision. "At least promise me you won't have breakfast alone with him. Tell him the oven is broken or something. I need to know you're safe."

She tilted her head in thought. "I can do that. I'll make an excuse and offer to comp his breakfast at Taste of Destiny."

"Good." It was something, at least. I'd still prefer it if the guy was gone. "I wish you'd consider giving him the boot."

"I know you do." She sighed. "I promise I won't be alone with him again, and I've got Duke if I need him."

"Duke is still a puppy," I pointed out.

"But he's growing fast." She pursed her lips as if wondering whether to say what was on her mind. I silently urged her to do it. "Nate, I'd really appreciate it if you could run a background check on Ezra and let me know if there's anything worrying in his past, just for my peace of mind."

"Absolutely, but if he's lying about his identity, he's out."

"Agreed."

"Would you like us to come over more often to make sure you have plenty of company?" Mum asked Grace.

Grace smiled in response. "I'll never say no to seeing more of you."

Mum laughed. "So you think now. Just wait."

The women struck up a conversation and returned to preparing brunch. I hovered nearby, my mind buzzing. If I hadn't walked in when I did, would Grace even have told me about her encounter with Ezra, or would she have kept it to herself?

I was her best friend, damn it. Not to mention the most senior-ranked police officer in town. I needed to know these things so I could protect her.

I kept an eye on her, noticing Kennedy draw her aside for a few minutes before brunch, and wondered what they were talking about. They returned as Mum finished serving food, and we all filled our plates. During warmer months, we'd be eating outside, but today we all piled into the living room. Everyone was here. Even Connor turned up as we were starting to eat, a beard hiding most of his face as he greeted us and poured himself a coffee.

When I heard Grace laugh, sweet and slightly husky, my gaze was drawn back to her. Her chin was propped on her palm, and she was smiling at Summer across the table. Green flecks danced in her eyes, and I wished I was closer so I could lean toward her and breathe her in. I bet she smelled incredible.

"Stop staring."

I jolted at the words spoken only a few inches from my ear.

"I don't know what you mean," I muttered to Max.

He smiled knowingly. "Yes, you do." His lips barely moved as he spoke, and I appreciated that he was trying to be discreet. "Unless you've decided to go for it, you need to be less obvious, or other people will start to see what I do."

I shoveled scrambled egg into my mouth to buy myself time to think. When I swallowed, I knew I couldn't delay any longer. "Maybe I have."

The twitch of Max's eyebrow was all that showed his surprise. "Have you?"

"I'm not sure," I admitted.

I wanted her, there was no denying that. I'd even go as

far as to say I'd never been this taken by a woman before. But it wasn't that easy. She was my best friend. She fit perfectly into my family—which was a gift, but also something to be wary of. If we got together and it didn't work out, she might feel too awkward to attend family events, or my parents and siblings might make it unbearable for me, since I could be reasonably sure I'd be the one to screw it up.

I gazed at her, following the curve of her neck and shoulder with my eyes and tracing down her slender torso to the curves I ached to map with my hands. I tore my eyes off her and glanced at Kennedy seated beside her, only to see far too much interest in my sister-in-law's expression. She cocked her head questioningly, but I turned away, wondering how it was that I'd been oblivious to Grace as more than a friend for years, but as soon as that began to change, everyone seemed to know it. Had they all been waiting for this moment? Had they known it was coming? And if so, how had I been so blind?

19

———

GRACE

THAT EVENING, I locked all of the doors and checked that the windows were latched, wondering if perhaps I should have taken Kennedy up on her offer to stay over. She could tell how shaken I was and had offered to sleep in the spare room so I'd feel less vulnerable, but I hated to take her away from Liam just because I was overly sensitive, so I'd turned her down. I wondered whether the invitation still stood.

No. She can't stay here every single time you feel anxious. It wouldn't be fair.

I sighed. Perhaps she'd been onto something when she'd mentioned getting additional security devices a few weeks ago. Even though I knew they wouldn't necessarily stop a determined predator, they might give me peace of mind because I'd be able to check them from my phone wherever I was so I could be sure I was safe if I ever felt like I wasn't alone in the house. There was a lot to be said in favor of anything that might stop me from jumping at every shadow and freezing each time the floorboards creaked or groaned. I knew my reactions were likely over-the-top because of Kennedy's kidnapping, but I couldn't just turn them off.

I'd made a salad for dinner—not needing anything else since I'd eaten so much at brunch. I'd eaten my fill and packed the rest away for tomorrow. Now, I was lying on the sofa in the dark with Duke pressed to my side, trying to work up the courage to call the cottage's landline and tell Ezra there wouldn't be any breakfast tomorrow.

Just do it.

I'd considered going out to speak to him earlier, but I'd promised Nate not to be alone with him, so, ridiculous though it may be, I'd do it via phone. I'd switched the lights off before I sat down because I didn't want him knocking on the door to talk to me in person. If it was dark, he might think I wasn't home.

It's not a big deal. You're being hysterical.

I grabbed my mobile phone, found the cottage's number, and dialed before I had time to think too much about it.

"Hello?" Ezra sounded confused.

"Hi, Ezra. This is Grace."

"Grace, hi." I heard rummaging and then he was back. "Sorry, I was in the middle of making dinner. What's up?"

My heart thumped violently, and I drew in a slow, deep breath, reminding myself that Ezra had never been anything but nice to me.

"I'm afraid there was an incident in the kitchen today and it's out of commission until I can get some repairs done. I won't be able to make breakfast, so I'll call Taste of Destiny, the café on the main street, and ask them to comp a meal for you. It might be a while before everything is working again."

"Oh no! What happened?"

"A bunch of things went wrong at once." I hadn't been able to think of a single issue that would render the kitchen useless without also needing me to evacuate the house. "I'm really sorry for the inconvenience, but Taste of Destiny does delicious food."

"I know," he agreed. "I visited it earlier today." He hesitated, then said, "I have enough dinner for both of us if you'd like to join me. Not having a working kitchen must make things difficult for you, and I'd love to get to know you better."

Damn. I cursed myself for not having considered that.

"I ate with a friend earlier."

"Oh." His tone was laced with disappointment. "Well, perhaps we could both go to Taste of Destiny for breakfast together."

I frowned. Why was he so keen to spend time with me? If he was really here to get away from life, surely he'd prefer to spend time on his own.

"Alice, my assistant, will pick up breakfast for me."

"Are you sure I can't tempt you?"

"I'm afraid not. I'll keep you updated on the kitchen situation."

"Okay, but let me know if you decide to go out for lunch or dinner. I'll go with you."

"I will," I lied. "Goodnight." I hung up before he could issue any more invitations.

There was a knock at the door, and I flinched. Shit, he must have come looking for me. But then I heard a key in the lock and relaxed. Ezra didn't have a key to the house. It must be Nate. I shouldn't be surprised he'd turn up. I knew he'd want to talk to me more about Ezra, and he'd likely gone to the police station as soon as he'd left brunch so he could check their databases.

"Come on, boy," I said as I stood. Duke stretched, then bounced off the sofa and padded diligently along beside me as I switched the light on and went to the door. I checked through the peephole and smiled at the sight of Nate's scowling face before opening the door. "Hi."

For a second, something flared in his eyes, but it disappeared as fast as it came. He held up a few printed sheets of paper. "I have the background check."

"Thanks." I stepped aside to let him in. He headed straight for the living room, flopped onto the sofa, and propped his feet on the coffee table. I hid a smirk. He was so predictable sometimes. I sat beside him and waited for him to continue.

"Why was it dark in here?" he asked.

I pulled a face. "Because I just called Ezra to tell him not to come over for breakfast, and I didn't want him to know I was home."

His nostrils flared. "If he makes you that nervous, you shouldn't be keeping him around, regardless of the fact that his record is pretty clean."

"It is?" Relief filled me. I had been overreacting. I'd suspected it, but it was good to know for sure.

"Yeah. Ezra Mendel has no significant prior convictions." He sounded displeased. As if he'd actually hoped I might have a known violent criminal residing on site. "He's been ticketed a couple of times for speeding, but he paid the fines by the due dates. No other problems with the law. He's thirty-six and has been working as a physiotherapist for the national women's hockey team for seven years." He hesitated, then added, "His father recently passed away."

I felt a pang of sympathy. I knew how it felt to lose a parent, even if mine weren't technically dead.

"No reported break-ins or stalking behavior?" I asked.

"Nothing that made it onto his record, although I've reached out to my colleagues stationed nearest his house to find out whether there's anything that hasn't made it into his file. No reply yet though. I still think you should be wary of him," he said, reaching for the dish of lemon drops I kept on the coffee table and fishing one out. He popped it into his mouth. "Your instincts are warning you about him for a reason."

I rolled my eyes. "Yeah, because they see monsters in every shadow after what happened to Blair and Kennedy." And what had happened to me, even if that had been years ago. The impact of that kind of thing never really left a person.

"Don't dismiss them so easily."

He handed me the printed sheets of paper, and I flicked through them. There was a photocopy of Ezra's driver's license, a short list of the speeds he'd been recorded at and the fines he'd paid, and a typed statement that he'd attended university in Dunedin and attained his degree in physiotherapy before specializing in sports recovery.

"Thanks for checking him out." I kissed Nate's cheek, surprised when his body became stiff against mine. I'd kissed his cheek plenty of times over the years, and he'd always accepted it the way he would a kiss from his mother or sister. Why the sudden tension?

I backed away. Did he have an inkling of my feelings for him? That would explain why I'd caught him looking at me strangely over the past few days.

Please let it be something else.

I didn't want to lose Nate. Our friendship meant the world to me. If he cottoned on to the fact that I was in love with him, it could spell the end of everything, including my honorary acceptance into the Braddock clan.

"Let's watch *House of the Dragon*," he suggested. "I'm falling behind."

I relaxed. Perhaps I was reading too much into things. "What episode are you up to?"

"The fourth, I think."

I turned on Netflix and found the show. I started it playing and called Duke onto the sofa between us. Without him as a buffer, I feared I'd do something stupid, like snuggle against Nate's side and indulge in a fantasy that our love wasn't as one-sided as I thought and any moment he'd lean over and kiss me.

A light flickered outside.

"What was that?" Nate asked, suddenly alert.

"Probably Ezra turning on a light in the cottage," I said more calmly than I felt.

We moved to the window and peered into the dark. Ezra's cottage was indeed lit from within, but he wasn't inside. Instead, his silhouette was perfectly framed in front of the window beside the door.

"He's probably smoking," I said.

"There's no cigarette." Nate echoed a thought I hadn't wanted to acknowledge. "I'm going out there to talk to him."

"Don't." I grabbed his arm. He tried to pull away. "I'm a big girl. I can deal with my own problems."

He jerked his head toward the window. "He needs to realize he's scaring you."

I huffed. "All he's doing is standing outside a cottage he's renting. He has every right to be there. I'm just too jumpy."

Nate's lips pressed together mutinously, but he stopped trying to tug free. "Fine, but the minute he puts so much as a toe out of line, he's going to hear about it."

I smoothed my hand up his back, pleased he'd conceded even if I secretly liked his protectiveness. I didn't want any scenes tonight. I just wanted to watch TV and go to bed. "Come on." I took his hand and pulled him back to the sofa. Duke hadn't budged, which comforted me. The dog was quick to bark when he thought something was wrong. I was being overly sensitive, that was all.

I started the show again and settled back. A few minutes later, my phone buzzed.

"Who's messaging you at this time of night?" Nate asked.

I checked the screen. "It's Desdemona."

As I read what my aunt had written, a chill descended over me.

Desdemona: *I sense forces shifting in the cosmos. Prepare for change.*

I wanted to laugh it off. Perhaps at another time, I would have. But right now? I couldn't. Because I had a feeling she was right, and that scared me.

20

GRACE

DUKE and I wandered along the pavement. I kept my steps short and slow so I wouldn't slip, and he stayed firmly on the concrete, not daring to step off onto the frosty grass. It had been dark when we ventured out, but now the sky was dark gray, and daylight was beginning to creep up on us. At the front door, I kicked off my shoes and removed my gloves before finagling the key into the lock with partially numb fingers. As the warmth from the central heating system greeted us, I let out a sigh of relief.

"It's a cold one, hey, Dukie?"

He galloped inside, for once not wanting to delay returning from his walk. I disconnected his leash, and he took off, probably heading for one of his beds. I hadn't lit the fire, since I wouldn't be able to relax and enjoy it until after a day of work.

I tracked Duke down in the living room and took the little booties off his feet. He sniffed them curiously, as if he had no idea where they'd come from, and I couldn't help smiling. He was such a cutie.

I left him where he was and turned on the shower. Steam billowed around me as the water heated up, and my skin prickled with pins and needles as I got under the stream. I lingered in the water until feeling had returned to my fingers and toes and I felt warm all the way through, then toweled dry quickly before I had time to get chilly again. I wrapped myself in a fluffy robe and started coffee brewing before going to my bedroom to find clothes.

As I opened my underwear drawer, I noticed that my panties weren't arranged the way they usually were. My heart rattled uncomfortably. I rubbed my chest and glanced around, my skin crawling as though someone was watching from the window, but there was no sign that anybody had been in here. I looked back at the drawer. It was definitely wrong. Usually, I kept the panties I wore most often near the top so I could grab them easily in the mornings. Today, a selection of my sexier lingerie was arranged above the others. The sight of the silky thongs and barely-there lace panties turned my stomach.

Someone had been in my room.

They'd touched my underwear. Sorted through them.

Or had I rearranged them?

No. I shook my head. I wouldn't have done that. Not without good reason. I'd only have brought out my fancy panties for a date or if I needed a pick-me-up.

When had this happened?

I wracked my mind, trying to recall when I'd last opened this drawer. Yesterday morning, perhaps. I hadn't done any laundry since then. That meant that sometime between yesterday morning and now, somebody had been in my bedroom and put their intrusive fingers all over my personal belongings.

I shuddered. Who would do that?

If it had happened a few years ago, I could have imagined Darrel Weich going through my underwear, but he'd left me alone ever since I'd taken out a restraining order against him and paid for him to get the therapy he desperately needed. Darrel had moved on. Right? Or had he simply gotten sneakier?

I shoved the drawer shut, flinching with shock at the loud slam in the silent house. I backed away from the drawer, my hand at my mouth, wondering what to do. Someone had been in here, but I had no evidence. What would I tell the police in my official report? That my panties had been reorganized? I'd sound crazy. Nate would believe me, but how much would he actually be able to do?

I drew in a shaky breath and got dressed on autopilot, skipping the underwear. They were all going through the laundry before they touched my skin again. I backtracked to the kitchen, gnawing on my nails. If someone had been in the house, why hadn't I noticed? Or Duke? Had they come while I'd been gone? Had Ezra somehow gotten inside? Was he messing with me? If so, why? I'd never done anything to him.

In the kitchen, I inhaled the scent of coffee and looked around for my mug. It wasn't on the counter. I frowned. I could have sworn I'd left it there. I opened the drawer where I stored mugs and found it inside. My fingers trembled as I lifted it out. Maybe I was going crazy. I glanced from the mug to the coffee machine, uncertain what I expected to see, but everything looked normal. Perhaps I'd only thought I'd gotten the mug out earlier.

I finished making the coffee and was about to take a sip when footfalls sounded behind me. I jumped in fright. Coffee spilled down the front of my blouse, the scalding liquid burning my skin.

"Shit!" I cursed, dumping the mug on the counter only seconds before I would have dropped it to the floor.

"Oh my god!" Alice slung her handbag onto the counter, grabbed a tea towel, and ran cold water onto it.

I peeled off my blouse and she pressed the cold compress onto my skin.

"Hold this," she said. "I'll get ice out of the freezer. If we don't cool it down quickly, it might burn you."

"You scared me." My voice sounded shrill to my own ears. "I didn't hear you arrive."

"I walked today." She opened the freezer and withdrew a bag of ice cubes. "I knocked at the door, but when you didn't answer, I let myself in."

"Duke didn't bark."

She shrugged. "Duke likes me. I sneak him treats when the boss isn't looking."

I couldn't bring myself to laugh.

Alice looked at me more closely as she offered me the ice. "Are you okay, Grace? You're very pale."

"I don't know." I took the ice and pressed it to the red splotch where the most coffee had landed.

"You look like you've seen a ghost." Concern showed on her face. She put her hand on my upper arm and guided me out of the kitchen. "Why don't you sit down, and I'll find you a clean shirt?"

"Thank you." As I settled onto an armchair, my mind wouldn't rest. It kept zinging from the underwear drawer to the coffee mug, the missing lipstick and blouse. Seeing that silhouette outside the cottage. A flashback to Darrel Weich circling my home, refusing to leave until my supposed captors set me free to be with him, the way he was certain I wanted to be.

What on earth was going on? Because I was no longer so

sure I was imagining anything. Perhaps I'd call Kennedy later and ask what she thought.

When Alice returned, she'd brought one of my favorite loose-fitting shirts, which would cover my scalded skin without hurting too much. My eyes welled with unshed tears. However crazy the day, I was so glad I had Alice. She always knew exactly what I needed.

"You're amazing," I told her.

"Don't get sentimental on me." She winked. "I'm just doing my job."

"Speaking of." I bit my lip, hesitating for a moment.

She straightened, hands on hips. "Yeah?"

"Would you be able to call a security company and have them install some more cameras around the house?"

"Absolutely. I'll do that right now." She took my wet shirt and balled it up. "Is everything okay, Grace?"

"I hope so." But honestly, at this point, I had no idea.

21

———

NATE

With Tess in the back seat of my car and Grace in the front seat, driving up to Destiny Peak to spend the day skiing felt like a family road trip. It was so familiar—we made a point to go skiing at least a few times each season—and so comfortable that I had to remind myself we weren't actually a family. Not properly. Tess might look up to Grace, but there was no official relationship between them. Grace wasn't her stepmother, no matter how well she'd fit the role, and, in fact, Maddy might pitch a fit if she were. She'd said before that she worried Tess might see Grace as a substitute mother figure because of how much time they spent together and the fact that they shared a hobby. She didn't want anyone taking her place. Not that they could, in Tess's eyes, but Maddy had always been a bit insecure about Grace.

Grace craned her neck to check on Tess, who had her nose buried in a book, then turned to me and spoke quietly.

"I had security cameras installed in the house," she said. "Particularly in the guest areas, but also one in my bedroom and the living area."

My grip on the steering wheel tightened, my knuckles going white. I would have helped with the cameras if she'd asked. "You should have mentioned. I would have been there to help."

"I hired professionals to do it."

"Even so." Didn't she know how much I needed to protect her? "Did something else happen to change your mind about them?" Last I'd heard, she hadn't thought they'd be worthwhile.

She shrugged one shoulder. "I got the feeling someone had been in my bedroom and messed with my things, but nothing was taken."

My jaw clenched. "That's bad, Gracie. You should have called. I could have had a look around and then helped make sure the cameras were in the best places."

She gave me a strange look. "I'd feel weird knowing you had access to a camera feed into my bedroom." Her cheeks colored. "Not that I think you'd spy, but it was easier just to get them to do it when they delivered the system."

The back of my neck heated at the thought of what I might see if I had a live video link to her room.

Stop it, I mentally scolded myself. *She doesn't need you fantasizing about her when she's vulnerable.*

"Fair enough." I managed to sound calm, and I could sense her look at me in surprise, but I kept my eyes on the road. "But please tell me if anything else happens. It's my job to keep you safe, and I could never live with myself if I let you down."

She was silent for a moment, but then she laid her hand on my thigh and gave it a brief squeeze. I willed myself not to respond. "Okay, I will. But I've been keeping an eye on the camera feeds and, so far, nothing seems unusual or out of place."

"Thank you." I relaxed my shoulders, which had climbed up around my ears. "Your safety is vital to me, Gracie."

I glanced over in time to see her expression melt into sweetness. "Yours is to me too."

We drove in silence after that, and I took a moment to scan the road ahead of us. There were dozens of cars on the way to the ski fields, which wasn't a surprise considering how perfect the weather was. Sunny with clear skies but low temperatures. In the back, Tess closed her book and put it on the seat beside her.

"Can you tell me about the story you're writing?" Tess asked Grace. "The one about the man and woman who started the tradition of couples swearing their love at Destiny Falls."

"Sure thing." Grace smiled at her, putting our more serious conversation aside. "What do you want to know?"

"What were their names?"

"Pearl and Charles," Grace answered. "But they went by Jewel and Rocky."

"Why?" Tess's tone was curious, but not demanding.

"I don't know. Perhaps their nicknames felt like a better match for who they were than their real names did. Rocky was a miner. A lot of them used nicknames rather than their legal names. For Pearl, it might have been to keep her secret life with Charles separate from her family, who were rich and wanted her to marry someone else."

"So it's true that they weren't supposed to end up together? Like Romeo and Juliet?"

Grace laughed. "Pearl and Charles had a happier ending

than Romeo and Juliet. As far as I know, no one died from anything other than old age. They married at the falls and ran away together, then lived a long and happy life."

"Huh." Tess picked up her book and thumbed absently through the pages. "But if they had to go somewhere else to be together, why does everyone say that Destiny Falls is such a romantic town?"

I glanced at Grace, curious how she'd respond to the question. Many locals were defensive of the town's status as a romantic symbol.

"That's a good question." Grace didn't sound bothered. "Perhaps because it was at the waterfall where they married and promised to love each other. A lot of people find star-crossed lovers to be romantic, and in this case, it isn't tainted by an unhappy ending."

"I guess." Tess didn't sound satisfied. I thought that might be the end of the matter, but then she spoke again. "Do you believe in real-life love stories?"

"I do."

Grace's quick reply surprised me. I'd always thought of her as a pragmatist, and surely, it wasn't pragmatic to dream of fairytale princes and happily ever afters.

"They just don't always look like they do in books or movies," she added. "I think real love is more about the small moments. It isn't about grand gestures—it's about being there for the other person every day and caring for them. Real love doesn't have to be showy or dramatic. It's steady and reliable. That's what matters. Having someone who you know will be your soft landing place when you need one."

"Like Mum and Dad are for me?" Tess asked, and my heart swelled so big, I had to blink back a few tears. Damn, I loved my daughter.

"Kind of like that," Grace said. "But different too. It's hard to explain unless you've felt it."

Have you felt it, Gracie?

I longed to ask her. Had she loved her ex, Ryan? Had she loved someone else?

Could she ever love me?

22

GRACE

At the ski field, we hired equipment and got ready on a bench near the beginner slope. After so many winter days on the mountain, I was competent enough to ski the intermediate runs, and even a couple of the more advanced ones, but Tess wasn't confident when it came to sports. She could ski well for her age, but she liked to be on familiar ground, and I didn't mind staying there with her. Honestly, I preferred spending time with Tess and Nate to challenging myself on a black run. Their company made it feel like everything was right with the world.

I skied down the slope, slowing at the bottom, near where they waited. "Like this," I said to Tess. "Remember?"

"Uh-huh." She mimicked the pizza-style stopping motion I'd shown her.

"Why don't you and your dad have a try?" I suggested. "I'll wait here."

She bit her lip, adorably nervous. Hopefully it wouldn't

be long before the basics came back to her and she regained some of her confidence. "Okay."

I waited while they made their way to the top of the slope. When they got there, Nate helped Tess get ready to go and then paused until she'd made a start before following. Tess skied smoothly down the slope, her only glitch coming when she tried to stop too quickly, but she righted herself. Nate, on the other hand, was a disaster. He veered from side to side, barely slowing as he drew near us. I stepped in front of him and caught him before he could collide with anyone or anything else. Laughing, I backed off but held onto his shoulders until I knew he was stable.

"I had that," he protested, but his grin showed in his eyes.

"Sure you did, Dad." Tess sounded doubtful.

"I would have figured it out, Miss Sassy-Pants."

Tess giggled. "But you're even worse at skiing than I am."

He straightened. "Sometimes it's hard to be this awesome."

Tess and I met each other's eyes and snickered.

He narrowed his eyes at each of us and heaved an overly dramatic sigh. "Neither of you could possibly understand."

"Da-ad." Tess swatted his arm. "Don't be silly."

He yanked Tess into a hug and wrestled her into a head-lock while she giggled and flailed. "I don't know what you're talking about. I'm not silly, am I, Grace?"

"I plead the Fifth."

He chuckled. "You know New Zealand isn't subject to the U.S. Constitution, right?" He released Tess and tousled the ponytail poking out from beneath her beanie. "Okay, you're both better than me. Is that what you want to hear?"

"We can teach you," Tess said.

Nate and I exchanged a smile. Her confidence was on the rise. Mission accomplished.

"I don't think there's any saving your dad," I stage-whispered to Tess. "He has two left feet."

"No, we can help," Tess insisted. "Let's do it again—all of us."

"Okay, sweetheart." Nate looked at her with so much love in his eyes that it almost hurt to witness. He was such a wonderful father, and I knew he could be a wonderful partner too. Just not for me.

We went up and down the slope a few times until Tess felt comfortable enough to try somewhere different. Nate's skills didn't improve much, but I was certain he was secretly proud of his inability to ski. Nobody who'd lived in Destiny Falls their whole lives could truly be as appalling as he was unless it was intentional.

At the bottom of another beginner slope, I looked up from helping Tess to find Nate watching me with an expression I couldn't interpret. Anxiety churned in my stomach, but I told myself I was imagining the strange look. Then I saw it again as he took my hand to guide me onto a ski lift and again as I supported Tess while she removed her skis when she'd finally had enough.

What was going on? Was this about the security cameras I'd mentioned during the drive, or was something else on his mind?

A flicker of nerves made me clumsy, and my fingers tripped over each other as I fumbled with Tess's skis. Had he seen my love for him in my eyes earlier? It was always harder to suppress when I watched him with Tess. He was so good with her, teasing her and encouraging her to come out of her shell while giving her enough space that she didn't feel pressured.

"Can we get hot chocolate?" Tess asked as we returned the rented equipment.

Nate glanced at me. "What do you think? I could do with a hot drink to warm me up."

"Sure."

We headed past the shop and to the main lodge, where a sign directed us down one of the corridors to the restaurant. The owner, Tabitha, had hired an incredible chef a few years ago, and people came from miles away to eat here. We were lucky there was a separate cafe section that couldn't be booked, or we'd never have found a seat. A waiter came and took our orders. Nate got a cappuccino, Tess got her hot chocolate, and I asked for a trim latte.

While we enjoyed our drinks, I studiously avoided meeting Nate's gaze. I felt exposed. As though I'd let myself—once again—start thinking of us as a family, and he'd somehow seen it in my face. In my heart, Tess was partly mine. Not in a way that lessened her connection to Maddy or Nate, but in a way that added to it. She had them, but she also had me. I might not be her mother—by name or anything else—but I loved her all the same.

Sometimes, I let myself dream.

I knew better, but I couldn't seem to stop.

I was relieved when we finally made the journey home and Nate parked outside Kennedy and Liam's house where we'd met up, since Kennedy had volunteered to babysit Duke.

"Are you sure you can't come over for a while?" Tess asked.

"I'm sure." I ignored my own disappointment. "I have some work to catch up on, and Duke needs a walk."

I caught Nate side-eyeing me, and I wondered what was going on inside his head. It must be obvious to him that I was looking for excuses, but he didn't call me on it, and for that, I was grateful. I needed to remember my role and what it wasn't. Fast.

23

NATE

THE CALL CAME LATE in the afternoon on Sunday. A nineteen-year-old girl was missing from the ski resort, and her friends had grown worried enough to report her disappearance. The resort had called Connor, who headed up the local search-and-rescue team, and Connor reached out to the other team members, including me.

"She was last seen on one of the black runs around ten this morning." Connor's voice was gruff, his summary to the point. "Her friends lost sight of her, but apparently she wasn't as skilled on the slopes as most of them, so they assumed she'd had enough and returned to their room. When they finished and realized she wasn't there, they asked reception and were told nobody on staff had seen her since she left with them in the morning."

"Why did they wait so long to report it?" I asked, frustrated. If she'd veered off course on the side of the mountain, every minute counted. She could have hypothermia by now. Especially with the snowstorm that had descended around lunchtime.

"They thought she might have gone into town and gotten stuck." Connor sounded as annoyed as me. "Unfortunately, that means it's going to be hard to find her with a fresh layer of snowfall."

"Have we checked that she's not somewhere in town like her friends thought?" I asked.

"None of the shop owners have seen her," Connor replied. "She could be in someone's home, but surely she'd have called her friends to let them know if that was the case."

"Probably," I acknowledged.

"I've got the GPS coordinates for the last run she was seen on, so we'll start there," Connor said. "We're lucky the storm has settled."

I glanced out the window, noticing that snow was now gently drifting down—a stark contrast to the situation a few hours ago.

"Can you meet us at the resort? We'll have a briefing in the parking lot and go from there."

I nodded. "You got it."

"Thanks."

He hung up.

I glanced at Tess, who was curled on the couch, her feet tucked beneath her, reading a book with swirling purple mist on the cover.

"Tess?"

She looked over, visibly struggling to pull her attention from the page of her book. "Yeah?"

"A girl has gone missing on the mountain. Search and rescue have been called. I have to go out. I'm going to see if you can stay with Grace while I'm gone." I preferred to have Grace or my family babysit Tess when I was on duty rather than bothering Maddy. We were on speaking terms, but I didn't want to give her any reason to think I couldn't handle having fifty-percent custody of our daughter.

"Okay." She resumed reading. If I hadn't said anything, she might not have even noticed if I'd just left.

I made a quick call to Grace, who assured me it was fine for Tess to visit with her until we found the missing girl or canceled the search for the night. I bundled Tess into the car and grabbed the duffel bag I kept on hand for search-and-rescue situations. I tossed it in the trunk and drove us to Grace's place as quickly as possible in the snowy weather. She was standing out front, a single sentinel waiting for us. Gratitude rushed through me.

"I don't know what I'd do without you," I called through the window as Tess got out. "Thank you."

"No problem." Grace wrapped an arm around Tess. "We're going to have a great time. Stay safe out there. Good luck."

As I pulled away, I wished I could be heading to Grace's warm living room to join them in front of the fire rather than venturing into the snow.

I met with the search-and-rescue team and listened while Connor explained who'd be searching where. I was partnered with Toby. I wasn't surprised he'd turned up. As a ski instructor, he knew the mountain better than any of us. He and I were assigned to the area immediately beneath the black run the girl had been on. When there was no sign of her, we continued into another search quadrant even as the sky rapidly darkened and we were forced to turn on our headlights.

"We're going to have to call it a night." Connor's voice crackled over the radio strapped to my waist. "It's too dangerous to stay out here."

"Fuck," I muttered. I wanted to search until we found her, but I knew Connor had made a sensible call.

"Wait." Toby grabbed my arm. "What's that?"

He pointed into the distance. I squinted, unsure what he was pointing at, but gradually, my vision adjusted, and I could make out a spindly thread of smoke against the dark horizon.

"That's where the old musterer's cabin is," Toby said. "The one where—"

"I know the one you mean," I cut him off. "Nobody should be renting it this time of year. That would be crazy. Perhaps she saw it and went there for shelter. Is it far?"

"Not too far, but I think Liam and Asher are closer to it than we are."

"Connor," I said into the radio. "There's smoke at the old musterer's hut. Perhaps Liam and Asher should check it out before heading in."

"Good catch," Connor replied. "I'll get them onto it."

———

AN HOUR LATER, the teenager had been collected from the old musterer's hut and transported to Destiny Falls Medical Center where Max was looking her over. Asher had done a preliminary check and declared her to be hungry, dehydrated, and cold, but not in any serious danger. Max was determined to do a full workup before discharging her.

He and Asher agreed that she seemed to be in shock. She sat on one of the clinic's chairs, her shoulders slumped and a blanket wrapped around her. She'd changed into an outfit Summer had supplied, so she was dry, and I'd made her a mug of hot chocolate loaded with sugar in the hopes it would perk her up. During the drive over, she'd admitted that she'd gotten lost and had taken shelter at the hut when it started to snow, but otherwise, she had hardly spoken.

"Can I call one of your friends for you?" I asked. It was too late for anyone to safely drive down the mountain, but perhaps it would comfort her to hear a familiar voice.

"Please don't." Her voice trembled.

I settled onto one of the other chairs, ignoring Max as he listened to her breathing.

"They were very worried about you," Connor rasped from his position in the doorway. Everyone else had made themselves scarce so as not to overwhelm her.

"Yeah. Well."

I tried again. "Is there anyone you would like us to call?"

"No. I'll be fine. I was stupid, but no one else needs to get dragged into it."

Max caught my eyes and nodded toward the door. Connor backed out, and I followed. Max was close behind.

"We need to know what happened that led to her getting lost," I said quietly, hoping she wouldn't overhear. "Especially if her friends were somehow involved."

Connor grimaced. "I doubt they were. The ones I talked to were on the verge of panic. They definitely care about her."

"That doesn't mean they didn't upset her," Max murmured. "If she was emotionally compromised, it's more likely she'd have gotten distracted from the trail." He pursed his lips. "Maybe she needs a woman to talk to. I could ask Summer to come over."

"Don't do that." When they both stared at me, I added, "If we're trying not to overwhelm her, then Summer isn't the best option. She'll be too forceful. I'll call Grace. She's great at listening, so perhaps she'll get further than us." She'd messaged earlier to say that Desdemona had joined them for dinner, so Tess wouldn't be alone if Grace left.

Connor nodded. "Good thinking."

"Do it," Max agreed.

I called Grace, telling myself that the little spark in my chest at the sound of her voice was simply an aftereffect of adrenaline. I explained the situation to her and asked if she'd come.

"I'll be there soon," she replied. "And she's welcome to stay at my place if she has nowhere else to go. I have a spare bed made up."

I relayed her offer to Max, who shook his head.

"I want to monitor her overnight," he said.

I passed the message back to Grace, and I could tell from the muffled noises coming down the line that she was already preparing to leave. "Drive carefully."

I ended the call and found my brothers both watching me curiously. "What?" I demanded.

Connor just shook his head, but Max's amused smirk spoke volumes. They knew I was in knots over Grace. It seemed everyone fucking knew—except Grace.

Damn it.

24

GRACE

I'D BEEN SHARING dinner with Desdemona and Tess when Nate called. After we hung up, I cast a longing look at the hearty quiche remaining on my plate and sighed.

"I'm needed at the Medical Center," I told them. "They've found the girl, but there's something they've asked for my help with."

Tess pushed her chair back. "Can I come?"

I pursed my lips. Nate hadn't explicitly said anything, but I imagined he'd want Tess to remain here. The back end of search and rescue could be messy and time consuming. "No, sorry, sweetheart. Your dad has to be able to focus on work, and if you're there, he's going to want to give you all his attention."

Tess pouted but didn't argue. She wasn't the type to make a fuss, although she was obviously disappointed.

"How about I teach you to do a three-card tarot reading after we've finished dinner?" Desdemona asked Tess, meeting my gaze and winking.

"Thank you," I mouthed, gratitude for my eccentric aunt swelling within me. She'd been the one constant in my life since my parents had left me in Destiny Falls and taken off for one of the most dangerous parts of Africa. She might not be a traditionally maternal figure, with her iron-gray hair and a pair of colored dreadlocks framing her face—not to mention her penchant for fluffy knitted clothes in outrageous colors and the occasional joint she liked to smoke, but she'd given me more unconditional love and support than anyone else ever had.

"You could teach me that?" Tess asked, effectively distracted.

"Easy as pie," Desdemona said. "Just finish your quiche and let me find my cards. I know I left a set around here somewhere."

I smirked. I knew exactly where Desdemona's cards were. She'd stashed them in my nightstand in the hopes I'd eventually take to using them the way she did. The thing was, I'd always been happy not knowing what the future held because if it wasn't what I wanted, I'd rather be blissfully ignorant.

"I'll see you two later," I promised. I carried my plate to the kitchen and stored the leftovers in the fridge, then rinsed the plate and stacked it in the dishwasher. I grabbed a jacket, gloves, and one of the knitted beanies Desdemona had gifted me and went to the door. Duke tried to follow, but I blocked his exit. "Sorry, bud. You're better off staying here."

I drove to the Medical Center and entered through the back door, which had been left unlocked. I found Connor and Nate lingering in the hallway outside the overnight observation room.

Nate kissed my cheek in greeting. "Thanks for coming. Max and the girl—her name is Cissy—are in there." He jerked a thumb at the door. "We didn't want to leave her alone, but she isn't talking. Hopefully she'll open up to you."

I nodded, nerves swooping in my gut. I wasn't sure I'd live up to their expectations—I was hardly an expert with teenage girls—but I was willing to try. I opened the door slowly and eased inside. Max was perched at a small desk in the corner, typing on his laptop, while a short, compact girl with damp hair sat on the bed, her knees pulled up to her chest and her back against the wall. She was wrapped in blankets but didn't look warm. Her dark eyes flicked over to me, then returned to focus on a point just beyond her knees.

Max got up, closed his laptop, and tucked it beneath his arm. "I'll be in my office if you need me," he told the girl. "This is Grace. She's going to sit with you for a while."

Cissy gave a slight nod, her gaze darting to me and away again. As Max left, I sat on his chair and pulled it closer to the bed.

"Hi," I said.

"Hi." She looked uncomfortable. "So are you a counselor or something?"

I laughed. "No, I'm a romance author, actually, but I'm good at listening, and Max thought you might need to talk."

"A romance author." Cissy gave a bitter laugh. "That's just perfect."

I frowned, unsure whether she'd intended to insult me. "Why?"

For a moment, I thought she might not answer, but then she sighed and hugged her knees closer. "Because the whole reason I'm here is that I fell in love with the wrong guy."

Oof. I felt that in my heart.

"What do you mean?" I asked, careful to keep my tone soft and undemanding.

She rolled her eyes. "I'm totally in love with one of the boys in our group. I'd hoped this trip might give me a chance to get closer to him, but instead, I caught him making out with my friend."

I rubbed my chest, able to feel her pain like a tangible thing. "When was that?"

"When I got to the bottom of one of the slopes this morning." She rested her head on her knees. "I pretended I didn't care because none of them know how I feel about him, but I couldn't get it out of my head, and when we started down the next run, I slid out of control and tumbled off course. I shouted, but none of them could hear me. It wasn't too cold then, so I figured I'd just stay there a while until I had my emotions back under control, but then the storm started, and I couldn't see where I was going."

Her voice caught. "I was so scared. It felt like a miracle when I found that hut." Her lower lip wobbled. "I'm not sure if I'd be here if I hadn't." She squeezed her eyes shut. "I'm so stupid. If I hadn't thrown myself a pity party, none of this would have happened, and everyone could have all been at home instead of out looking for me in the freezing cold." She buried her face between her knees. "Now I'll have to apologize to everyone."

"Hey." I eased closer and reached out slowly, hesitant to touch her even though she seemed to need reassurance. She didn't flinch when my hand landed on her back, so I stroked gently up and down, hoping to soothe her. "It's okay. The search-and-rescue team doesn't care about being in the cold. They're just happy you're safe. I'm sure your friends will be too."

She raised her head, and her eyes were filled with misery. "But I'll have to explain why I got lost."

"You don't have to tell them anything you don't want to," I said, keeping up the soft, rhythmic movement. "You can say you lost control and couldn't get back to them. They don't need to know what was going on in your head at the time."

Cissy chewed on her lip, then growled and swiped at her watery eyes. "Ugh, I'm so pathetic."

My heart squeezed with sympathy. I glanced at the door, wondering whether it was soundproof. I didn't think the Braddocks would be in the hall anyway. They'd probably retreated to give us some privacy. Connor may have even left. Getting home to his cabin would be a challenge after the weather we'd had. I sucked in a shallow breath. I wanted to do what I could to help Cissy feel better, but baring my heart was difficult after keeping everything to myself for so long.

"You're not pathetic," I whispered, glancing toward the door again. "Want to know what is pathetic?"

Her eyebrows drew together. "What?"

"I've been in love with one of those guys out there—Nate —since I was younger than you."

Cissy's eyes widened. "Does he know?"

"I don't think so." At least I hoped not. "But we've been friends since we were young, and I had to watch him marry and have a baby with someone else. It was awful, so I understand some of what you're going through."

To my surprise, Cissy took my hand. "Does it get any easier?"

I wished I could tell her that the feelings lessened. Perhaps for her they would. But mine had never wavered.

"You either move on or learn to live with it," I said. "Personally, I've learned to live with it, although he's divorced now, which makes it easier." If I had to see him and Maddy together—or him with anyone else—it would ruin me. Selfish, perhaps, but I couldn't help it.

Cissy leaned closer. "So you have a chance with him."

I barked a single laugh. "After being friends for so long? It seems unlikely."

"Don't give up," she urged, squeezing my hand. "Tell me about him. Maybe it will distract me."

I sighed, reluctant to give her what she asked for while knowing it might help both of us. "Okay."

We chatted for an hour or so until Max returned to check on her and she started to look tired. I slipped her my number before I left in case she wanted to talk more.

Nate guided me out with his hand at my elbow. "What did you say to her?" he asked. "She's like a different kid from the one we brought in."

I shrugged. "We found common ground."

He arched a brow. "Oh?"

"Mm." I wasn't going to share the details. No way.

He cocked his head, and the look in his eyes—fondness and something deeper, unfamiliar—made my tummy flutter. "Well, okay, then. Keep your secrets this time, Gracie. But just so you know, you're incredible."

I turned to face him, realizing too late how close together we were standing. All it would take was a slight shift from one of us, a sway toward the other, and we'd be kissing. I held my breath as his head dipped closer, wondering if it was finally going to happen. If Cissy had been right, and after all this time, there was still hope. But then he straightened and cleared his throat.

"I'll finish up here and come over soon to pick up Tess." His voice was hoarser than usual—or was I imagining that?

Don't be ridiculous, I told myself. *You've had a lifetime to get used to the fact that he only sees you as a friend.*

I forced myself to smile. "I'll take her to your place so she can go to bed. It must be about that time of night."

"Thanks. You're a lifesaver."

25

NATE

By the time I parked in my driveway, exhaustion weighed on my shoulders like a cloak. A light glowed from the living area, and my heart overflowed with gratitude as I let myself in. I detoured up the hall to check on Tess. My daughter was asleep in her bed, her eyelashes dark against cheeks that were pale in the light cast by my phone screen. Something eased inside of me at the sight. No matter what happened, my little angel was home, safe and peaceful. Nothing could be more important than that.

Grace was in the living room, her legs stretched along the sofa as she stared intently at the screen of her e-reader. Emotion caught in my chest. She looked perfect there. As right as Tess had looked curled in her bed. Grace belonged here with me. She was part of our family, official or not.

She raised her eyes and smiled, but I could see her weariness. She started to move so I could sit beside her, but I gestured for her not to bother. I lifted her legs and rested them across the top of my thighs, relaxing back onto the cushions.

"Thank you." The words gusted from my mouth on a heavy exhale. "I don't know how, but you always seem to know exactly what I need."

A smile started to curl her lips, and I could already see her gearing up for a gentle rebuttal. She honestly didn't realize how much I relied on her and how much it meant to me to be able to do that.

"Let me finish." I raised my hand. "I don't know what I'd do without you. You make my life better."

Emotion shone in her eyes. I couldn't tell if it was what I'd hoped to see there or not, but whatever it was, she felt it intensely. My throat tightened. How had I been blind to Grace as a woman for so long? She was beautiful from the inside out, and I'd never doubted that. For some reason, I'd just never let myself go there since those first curious wonderings in high school. She'd become my trusty best friend, and I hadn't looked beyond that.

Could I do it now? Would I be worthy of her? Or would I let her down the way I had Maddy? I gritted my teeth. If I hurt Grace like that, I'd never forgive myself. Was it worth the risk?

"You're my friend," Grace replied. "You've always been there for me. That's just what we do. I'm glad I was able to help."

I felt a pang of guilt. I hadn't always been there for Grace. I'd failed her before. She hadn't even felt able to tell me she'd gotten married.

"Besides," she continued. "I love Tess and so does Desdemona. Spending time with her is no hardship."

"I know you do." Seeing that love made me want to gather her in my arms. "Gracie...."

She glanced down at my hands, and I realized I'd begun rubbing her calves.

I stopped and mentally fortified myself. "Have you ever wondered if things could be different between us?"

Her expression froze, and I caught a flicker of something in her face that reminded me of a cornered dog. Wide-eyed and panicky. She masked it quickly. "How do you mean?"

Her tone was all careful politeness. It made me wary. I tugged my lower lip between my teeth, realizing I was going to have to spell it out for her.

"Have you ever thought maybe we could be more than friends?" I did my best not to sound as edgy as I felt.

Grace stared at me, that cornered dog expression on full display. "I, uh, um." She jolted upright, swinging her legs off my lap, and backed away several paces. "I just remembered that I left the pantry door open. I need to make sure Duke hasn't got into it."

She turned on her heel and bolted.

I sagged against the couch, that little flame of hope fizzling out.

I guess I had my answer. It just wasn't the one I wanted.

26

GRACE

MY HEART BEAT like crazy as I rushed out of Nate's place and fumbled with the keys for my car. It took me three attempts to push the button that would unlock it, and when I did, I didn't allow myself a moment to stop and process what had happened. Instead, I slammed the car into reverse and shot backward, the tires slipping as they gained and lost grip on the icy road.

I sucked in a breath and let it shudder out, then gathered as much composure as I could and drove toward home. My thoughts were a jumble, and although I fought to keep my breathing steady, my head spun and my vision seemed to blur and sharpen with each beat of my panicky heart.

How had Nate known? Had he somehow overheard my whispered confession to Cissy?

Mortification swirled through me, hot and unpleasant. No, he couldn't have. I'd never be able to look him in the eyes again. The image of his face flashed through my mind. His expression as he'd asked if I'd ever thought of him romantically. Tender and curious. With the way I'd sprinted out of his home, I couldn't have left him in any doubt.

Had I finally ruined everything?

Did I still have a best friend and a surrogate family, or would Nate slowly withdraw from me now that he'd realized the truth? It wouldn't be comfortable for him to be around me, knowing what he now did. I couldn't stand his gentle understanding. It would eat me up inside.

I opened my garage with the push of a button as I pulled into the drive. I parked inside and walked into the house in a daze. Duke greeted me with an excited bark, and I bent to pat him. His entire body waggled with the force of his wagging tail, distracting me momentarily from my thoughts. I scooped him into my arms, grunting with the effort.

"You're getting heavy, Dukie."

I carried him to the sofa in my private living space and snuggled on the couch with him, smiling when he scrambled onto my knee and licked my chin. We stayed that way for a while, and gradually, Duke's quiet, loving presence calmed me enough that I began to doubt the version of events in my mind. Perhaps Nate hadn't overheard my conversation—not all of it, anyway—and he'd been asking out of simple curiosity rather than because he knew the truth. Maybe it had just been a "Hey, do you ever think about what it would be like if we were in a parallel universe where we were a couple" kind of question. It wasn't the sort of thing I'd expect him to ask, but it had been a big day, and perhaps he was feeling introspective.

I groaned. Either way, he'd know for sure something was up because of how fast I'd bailed out of there. I'd given him that lackluster story about the dog, but it didn't explain my rapid departure—a fact he'd be well aware of. If he hadn't already guessed, he surely would.

I withdrew my phone from my pocket and found Ryan's

number. After a few seconds of hesitation, I called him. It was late, but not so late he'd be asleep.

"Everything okay?" he asked when the call connected.

"I think I screwed up," I admitted.

"How?" He sounded more alert now. "Are you all right?"

"Physically?" I sighed. "Yeah, I'm fine. Emotionally, I've gotten myself into so much trouble."

I explained the situation to him, and when I'd caught him up, I waited to hear what he had to say.

"Yeah," Ryan said eventually. "By clearing out of there the way you did, you definitely will have made him question things."

I dragged my free hand down my face in dismay.

"But," he added, "I think it's possible you got the wrong idea when he was asking those questions. I doubt he overheard your conversation with Cissy. If he had, he doesn't seem like the type of guy who'd beat around the bush. I don't know him as well as you do, but I get the feeling he'd have just outright told you. He's not a game player, is he?"

"Nooo." I drew the word out, considering the implications. "You're right. He isn't. But if not that, then what?"

"I have an idea," Ryan said. "But I could be wrong."

"Tell me." Whatever he had, it must be better than the possibilities floating around in my head.

"Perhaps he was asking that because he's started seeing you in a different light lately, and he wanted to know whether you might return those feelings."

I touched my mouth. Surely not. "But why would that happen out of nowhere?"

I could practically hear Ryan's shrug. "Who the hell knows? Random shit happens all the time. Maybe he'd never really thought about it until he saw you and me together, and then something in him snapped."

I pondered that. It would explain the unusual vibes I'd

been getting from him lately and the strange way I'd seen him looking at me when he thought I wasn't paying attention. But if that was the case, did that mean he was only seeing me differently out of some perceived sense of competition with Ryan? If he knew I'd always make time for him and Tess regardless of my relationship status, would his interest disappear?

I voiced these thoughts to Ryan. Unhelpfully, he had no answer.

"All you can do is talk to him about it and see what he says," he advised. "Be brave, Grace. You have a chance here. If I had even the slightest shot with Nisha, I'd take it. If you don't, you'll always wonder."

I petted Duke, knowing how easy it was for Ryan to say that when he wasn't in my position. His most important friendship wasn't on the line.

"I'll bear it in mind," I said when it became obvious that he expected a reply.

But honestly, I felt as lost as ever. I had no idea what would happen tomorrow, and part of me wished the morning would never arrive so I didn't have to deal with the fallout.

27

NATE

I'D MESSED up with Grace.

Despite being exhausted, I'd barely managed to sleep after she left on Sunday night. I'd woken before dawn with gritty eyes and a heavy heart. I had hoped she might be open to exploring whether we could cross the line that had always been drawn in the sand, but now I was afraid I'd damaged our friendship irrevocably. After all, the way she'd run from me left little room for interpretation.

I pulled myself together enough to shower, dress, and drop Tess off at school, then I headed to Taste of Destiny and ordered two coffees. I was waiting near the counter when Alice entered wearing a stylish black coat that nipped in around her slender waist, and a beret that few people would be able to pull off. She scanned the line and paused to smile as her gaze landed on me. The barista called my name, and I grabbed my coffees but didn't leave. Alice may have seen Grace this morning. If so, she might know what had happened last night or be able to share insight into Grace's state of mind.

"Morning, Alice," I said after she'd given her order to Eden and stepped aside.

"Good morning." She rubbed her fingers together. "Brr. Is it just me, or is it cold today?"

"It's pretty chilly," I agreed. "Are you getting drinks for yourself and Grace?"

"Yeah." She blew on the tips of her fingers. "You know she doesn't function properly until she's been caffeinated."

I grinned, my mood lightening a little. "Yeah, she could skip breakfast, but god forbid she miss her caffeine fix." I stole a glance at her. "Have you seen her yet today?"

"Just briefly. I popped in on the way over."

I tried to figure out how to broach the subject subtly, but subtlety had never been my strong suit. "How did she seem?"

"Huh?" Alice looked surprised by the question. She shrugged. "Same as usual, I think. She was writing, so I didn't interrupt."

Damn, that didn't help.

"Any sign she wasn't feeling well or might have been upset?"

Alice frowned. "Is there something I need to be aware of? Did something happen to her?"

"No," I rushed to say. "Not at all. Nothing like that. I just worry."

She eyed me warily. "As far as I know, there's nothing to worry about. She has her shit together far more than the rest of us. Beautiful house, cute puppy, adorable rental cottages, and a job she loves that makes bank."

I winced. When she put it like that, Grace sounded way out of my league. All I had to offer was a battered heart and a premade family. "Yeah, you're right. Nothing to worry about."

I excused myself and took the coffees to the Medical Center, hoping my workaholic twin would already be there. I was in luck. Max's blue suburban-dad-style minivan was parked in his usual spot. I carried the coffees to the door and knocked. It took a few moments before he opened up.

"Hey, Nate." He looked surprised to see me. "Come in. I've just been doing some last-minute checks on Cissy before one of her friends from the resort comes to collect her."

"Oh." I hadn't considered he might be with a patient. Stupid since, if I'd thought about it, I'd have realized that of course Cissy would still be here. "Are you busy? I can come back later."

"Nah." He shook his head. "Just give me a few minutes to finish up. Wait in my office."

Soon after, he joined me there. I passed him his coffee, and he sniffed it appreciatively.

"Thanks." He sipped and made a sound of enjoyment. "What brings you by?"

I jumped straight in. "I took a chance with Grace last night. Asked if she'd ever seen us as potentially being more than friends. It...didn't pan out well."

Max frowned. "What do you mean? What did she say?"

I looked at the ground, feeling my cheeks flush with remembered embarrassment. "She made an excuse—something about her dog—and ran out like the fucking devil himself was on her tail."

"Hmm." His thoughts flicked through his eyes, one after the other, but I couldn't pinpoint what they were. Surprise, perhaps. Concern. "Tell me what, exactly, you said to her."

I explained, feeling strangely as if we'd gone back in time and were teenage boys discussing our crushes, except the stakes were much higher. Max listened with his usual focus and didn't interrupt or respond at all until I was done. He seemed to be mulling something over.

Eventually, his expression reluctant, he said, "I don't think Grace is completely uninterested in you, but you took her by surprise. You've been friends for years. Suddenly veering into new territory might have shocked her. You just need to give her some time and show her you mean it."

"You think?"

He was right that I'd just dropped the question on her without any buildup. I'd gone in like a bulldozer once again. Damn it, I had to stop doing that.

"I do." Max hesitated, then reached over and clapped me on the shoulder. "Seriously, man. You and Grace would be a great couple. Don't give up on her because of one rough patch. Give her time to get her head around what you asked and then see if you can broach the topic again. Maybe a little more tactfully this time."

"Tact is not something I'm good at."

He gave me a cut-the-bullshit look. "It might not be something you like, but you're a cop. You deal with the harshest parts of society and have managed not to lose your shit on anyone so far, so you're capable of some control."

I winced. He might be the nice one, but he didn't pull any punches when it came to the truth either. "Fair." I smiled tightly. "I appreciate you hearing me out. I'll do what you suggested. Give her time and try not to treat her differently until she's ready to talk about it."

Hopefully, she'd do the same for me.

28

───────

GRACE

THREE DAYS after I ran out on Nate—and zero conversations with him later—I was in my bedroom, getting dressed for the morning, when I had the creepy feeling that something wasn't quite right. I glanced over my shoulder, half expecting one of those horror movie moments with a masked man standing there holding an ax, but there was nothing. I scanned the room, and everything seemed to be in its place.

I was a tidy person, so it was usually obvious if something was where it wasn't supposed to be. I tiptoed to the closet, feeling ridiculous but unable to shake the niggling fear in the back of my mind. I cracked the closet open and peered in, but again, everything looked normal. I opened it wider and rifled through the hanging items of clothing. They were still organized in the correct order: dresses, shirts, pants, and skirts.

I turned and walked a circle around the room. Duke trotted in and nosed at my leg.

"Hang on, Dukie," I murmured. If someone had been in here, surely he'd have sensed them, or the camera feed would have picked it up. I'd have to check the footage later today.

I was about to leave when I noticed the lid of my jewelry box was slightly ajar. Frowning, I walked over to it. I hadn't put on any jewelry today, so there was no reason for it to be open. I lifted the lid and gasped. The velvet box where I'd kept my wedding ring was empty. I picked up the empty box and checked to make sure the ring hadn't simply slipped out. Then I sifted through my other jewelry. The ring was gone. A thread of concern wove through me. I never wore that ring. Never. I only kept it as a symbol of my friendship with Ryan. It wasn't even the most valuable thing in my jewelry box if a thief had been interested in pawning something for cash.

Someone had taken the ring.

I felt chilled to the core. When had they been in here? How long had it been since I'd worn jewelry? I usually didn't bother unless I was going out to dinner or an event. It could have been days ago, and I might simply not have noticed the box was ajar. For all I knew, someone had taken it at the same time they'd sifted through my underwear.

My heart hammering, I strode through to the kitchen, where I'd left my phone, and called Nate.

"Morning, Gracie." He sounded hesitant, and it occurred to me that we hadn't spoken properly since I'd run out on him, except for a couple of innocuous text messages. "I wasn't expecting to hear from you."

"Someone has stolen my wedding ring." My voice trembled. "I don't know when. I only noticed now, but it might not have been in the last couple of days. I don't wear jewelry very often, especially in winter, so it's hard to say when I last saw it."

"Your ring is gone?" His tone had become businesslike.

"Yes."

"Where do you keep it?"

"In a box in my bedroom."

He swore. "Don't move. I'll be there in a few minutes. Hold tight."

The call ended.

While I waited for him, I sat at the dining table in the living area and opened the camera app on my phone. I fast-forwarded through the footage from this morning and last night. I'd gotten as far back as yesterday afternoon without seeing anyone other than Duke or me when there was a knock at the door. I hurried down the hall and yanked it open. Nate pulled me into a hug, and I buried my face against the side of his neck and breathed in his comforting masculine scent.

"It's okay," he soothed, rubbing my back. "We're going to figure this out."

I drew away, sniffling, and finally realized he wasn't alone. Constable Mehrtens stood behind him, her expression neutral. Embarrassment roared through me. I prided myself on being calm and collected. It was one thing for Nate to see me fall apart, but I'd rather not have Mehrtens witness it too.

"I'm sorry." I cleared my throat, trying to be more businesslike. "Thank you for coming."

"We got here as soon as we could." Nate searched my eyes as though worried I might be about to burst into tears. "Why don't you show us where the ring was? Mehrtens is trained in evidence collection. She can dust for prints and check whether the thief left any trace of themself behind."

I nodded and met Mertens's gaze. The uniformed officer was younger than me and stood ramrod straight, reaching a height of perhaps five foot five. Her sandy-blonde hair was tucked into a tight bun at the back of her head. She held a small kit—presumably to collect the evidence.

"This way." I waved them in.

Duke ran out of the living area and skidded to a stop near my feet. He ignored Nate in favor of barking at Mehrtens, who seemed taken aback.

"Sorry about that." I grabbed him by the collar. "I'll put him in the office until you're done."

I escorted the dog safely to the office and shut him inside with a couple of toys, then returned to the hall and led the two police officers to my bedroom. It was only as they entered that it occurred to me that Nate hadn't been in here before. At least, not for a long time. Suddenly, I felt exposed.

Mehrtens put gloves on and began running through a meticulous process. Nate sat on the end of my bed and patted it for me to join him. I did, hyperaware that the man of my dreams and I were sitting on a bed together. Thank god for Mehrtens or my mind might go places I couldn't afford for it to go.

"So, you noticed the missing ring this morning?" Nate asked.

"That's right."

"But you're not sure when you last saw it?"

I sighed. "No, but probably within the last couple of weeks. I've gone through the security footage from last night and this morning, and nobody had come into the room other than me."

"That's a good starting point," he said. "Do you mind giving Mehrtens access to the recording so she can check further back?"

"Okay." I'd thought he might ask as much, and I was just grateful it would be Mehrtens watching me sleep rather than him. I'd be horrified to discover I said his name in my dreams or anything else humiliating.

"Can you describe the ring?" he asked.

I shrugged. "It's a simple gold band. Just a standard wedding ring."

Was it just me, or did his upper lip curl?

"Has anything else been stolen?" he asked.

"Not that I can tell, but I haven't done a thorough search."

"I'll need you to do that as soon as you can."

"Okay." I'd get onto it when he left. A thought occurred to me. "I've had a couple of other things go missing lately. A blouse and a tube of lipstick. The other day, I thought it looked like someone had gone through one of my drawers."

Nate's cheeks were slowly turning red the way they did when he tried to suppress his temper. I knew he wasn't mad at me, just the situation. "Why didn't you tell me?"

I bit my lip. "I told myself I'd misplaced them. I thought I was being paranoid because of Kennedy's kidnapping. I've been on edge for months, so it made sense it was just an extension of that. And what was I supposed to say about the drawer? Nobody took anything. There wasn't a crime to solve."

"Unlawful entry." He waved a finger at me emphatically. "Disturbing your peace of mind. If that's not a crime, it ought to be."

His miffed attitude brought a small smile to my face. "Yeah, it should be."

He still looked pissed off. "Have any of your locks been damaged? Any windows broken?"

"I don't think so."

He rubbed his temple. "There have been no other reported thefts in town, so either nobody has bothered to file a report or you're being specifically targeted. Could it have been your renter?"

"I don't see how he would have gotten in." I kept the door key well hidden, especially after the incident earlier in the year.

"I'll question him anyway," Nate said. "I need you to think about anyone else who might target you."

A face filled my mind. Ruddy cheeks, watery eyes, and thin lips. Darrel Weich. He'd targeted me. He'd been obsessed with me. But that had been years ago. He'd gone to therapy and turned things around. There was no reason for him to suddenly appear in my life after all this time.

"Grace?" Nate touched my arm. "You okay?"

"Not really," I admitted. But who could expect me to be all right if, as Nate suggested, I was being targeted by someone for god knew what reason?

"We'll get to the bottom of this." He glanced at Mehrtens, who was applying fingerprint powder to my dresser, then dropped a quick kiss on my cheek. "Whoever the hell thought they could get away with scaring you like this has another think coming. I'm going to make sure they regret it."

With his voice so full of conviction, I could almost convince myself he was my partner, not just my friend.

"Thank you," I whispered. Footsteps clomped up the hall, far too heavy to be Alice's. I stiffened.

"Are you expecting anyone?"

"No."

Nate was on his feet in a blink, positioning himself in the center of the doorway. A moment later, Ezra appeared, concern clouding his expression.

"Is everything okay here?" Ezra asked. "Has something happened to Grace?"

"Why would anything have happened to Grace?" Nate demanded belligerently. "Were you expecting it to?"

"Of course not," Ezra said. "But the police don't usually show up at eight in the morning just for kicks, so I thought—"

"Thought what?" Nate snapped, followed by, "Do you often let yourself into other people's houses without asking for an invitation?"

"No." He sounded confused.

"Have you been inside Grace's bedroom before?" Nate demanded.

"Why would I have?"

"That's not an answer." His voice was little more than a growl. "If we check your fingerprints against the ones my colleague is collecting, will we find a match?"

"N-no." The word stuttered out.

"Good to know," Nate said. "Because we'll need to take your prints for comparison and interview you later today. Can you make yourself available?"

"What's this about?"

I rose wearily to my feet and joined them. "I had something valuable go missing. The police are here to investigate."

His eyes widened. "It wasn't me, I swear. I can't believe you had a break-in. Destiny Falls seems so safe."

"Everywhere has crime to some extent," I reminded him. A five-minute web search would show him that Destiny Falls was no exception. Crime may be rarer here than in cities, but we had our share of trouble.

"I'm so sorry." To his credit, he looked genuinely upset. "I'll keep an eye out in case I see anyone around. Please let me know if there's anything else I can do to help." He turned to Nate. "Grace has my details. Just call when you'd like to talk to me."

"You can count on it," Nate's tone had a bite to it.

Ezra backed away, never taking his eyes off me. "You know where I am if you need me."

When he was gone, Nate rolled his shoulders back. "I don't trust that guy."

"Neither do I." I wasn't sure he'd been the one to steal my ring, but he had an agenda, and I still didn't know what it was.

29

———

NATE

I BIT BACK a growl of frustration. If Grace didn't trust that Ezra guy, then why did she continue to let him rent one of her cottages? She didn't need the money. She'd shared with me before how well her books sold, and I knew she wasn't short of funds. So why did she insist? Was it out of sheer stubbornness or because she didn't want to be perceived as weak and afraid? I wish I understood.

I also wished she'd told me about the problems she'd been having. Even if they seemed minor, they'd obviously been preying on her mind. Hell, perhaps they'd bothered her so much that she'd gotten the dog. She'd mentioned pets before but only in a vague sense, never with a concrete plan to get one. I wanted her to feel like she could confide in me, but I didn't know how to get to that place.

I forced myself to walk calmly back to the bed so I could finish getting the background to the situation the way I would if she were anyone else. I asked her when, exactly, the other items had gone missing, and she told me. I couldn't help noting that it was prior to her guest's arrival—a fact I was sure she was also aware of. Perhaps that was why she didn't want to send him on his way. But just because he hadn't made himself known didn't mean he hadn't been around. I'd need to look into him and make sure he'd been where he said he was at those times.

When Mehrtens had finished checking for evidence, she packed her kit away and knelt on the floor nearby. I gave her a quick rundown of everything Grace had told me and then let her and Grace sort out access to the security feed. I took advantage of the opportunity to study Grace. There were dark circles beneath her eyes, and her skin was paler than usual. Some of that would be caused by the stress of the theft and having people in her personal space, but not all of it. Perhaps she'd been sleeping as badly as me. I'd been waiting for her to reach out—hoping she would—but I'd been too nervous to turn up in person and insist we talk it through the way I usually would.

Despite how much I hated the situation we found ourselves in, I couldn't help but be a little grateful for it. This theft had brought Grace and me together again and given us the chance to interact on a professional level. Hopefully, it would help us cut through any personal awkwardness, or at least lessen it. I felt guilty for thinking that, but who knew how long we would have been stuck in a silent standoff without our hands being forced?

Alice arrived a few minutes before we finished, which made it easier to leave. I hadn't wanted Grace to be alone, but Alice would take good care of her.

On our way back to the police station, Mehrtens cleared her throat. "Sarge," she said tentatively. "You know how I'm doing that online criminal psychology course?"

"Yeah." She was a clever cookie, Mehrtens. If she ever

decided to leave Destiny Falls, she could have a big career ahead of her.

She was quiet for a moment, as though choosing her words. "I'm not an expert, but from what Grace said, I think we should treat this as more than a simple theft. It seems someone is focused on her. The things that were taken—a ring and her favorite lipstick and blouse—are very personal. They're not something a run-of-the-mill criminal would take for profit. The ring might net a couple of hundred dollars, but why take that and not empty the entire jewelry box or take the laptop too? Of course, it's possible she lost the lipstick and blouse, but in the context, I'm tempted to say it's unlikely. Whatever is going on, she needs to be careful."

"I agree." Mehrtens had unknowingly verbalized my own thoughts. "I want to know the minute you find anything on those recordings."

"You will."

In the meantime, I needed to figure out how to make Grace understand the danger she might be in without scaring her unnecessarily. Easy, right?

30

GRACE

I WAS MAKING myself coffee when someone knocked on the door. Alice had already left for the day, as had Kennedy, who'd turned up shortly after the police left to comfort me because Nate had clued her in on what had happened. I went to answer the knock, expecting to see Nate on the other side, but it was Ezra. Duke pawed at the floor and released a low growl.

"Hi." Ezra smiled nervously and raised a pair of brown paper bags from Taste of Destiny. "I just got back from the police station." He widened his eyes. "That sergeant is an intimidating guy. Anyway, I have treats. I thought you might like to share something sweet and debrief after your busy morning."

"Oh." I hadn't expected to see him again today after Nate had less than politely shooed him away earlier. "That's really thoughtful of you." I hesitated. He clearly wanted to come in, but I wasn't sure whether that was a good idea. Duke barked, and Ezra backed away. He certainly looked harmless, and he hadn't been here when things first started going missing. I mustered a smile. "Come in. I was just making coffee. I have enough for two, if you'd like."

"Yes, please."

He followed close on my heels as I walked to the kitchen, visibly worried that Duke might take a bite out of him. I fixed us each a cup of coffee and carried them to the dining table, then brought over a large plate for him to place his treats on and two smaller ones, in case we'd need them. Duke barked again, shoving against my shins as though trying to get my attention.

"I don't think your puppy likes me," Ezra said.

"He's slow to warm up to people," I lied. "Sit on your bed, Duke."

Shoulders hunched, Duke slunk to his bed and flopped, watching us with narrowed eyes.

Ezra opened one of his bags and slid the contents onto the plate.

"Savory scones," he explained.

"Oh, yum. The rosemary ones?"

"Exactly." He opened the other bag to reveal a pair of what looked like chocolate truffles. "They're gluten-free vegan peanut balls dipped in dark chocolate. I forgot there's a chance you might have a nut allergy until I was already halfway here." He ran his hand through his hair, expression sheepish. "Hopefully they're okay for you."

"They both look great." I smiled. "I don't have any allergies."

He took a scone, so I did the same. I hadn't thought I was hungry, but my stomach rumbled, reminding me I hadn't eaten since lunch, and I'd barely managed to get anything down then. The scone was still warm, and I devoured it embarrassingly quickly, but Ezra didn't seem to mind. Duke whined, and I tossed him the last mouthful, hoping he'd behave himself for a while longer.

"So, what was stolen?" he asked, his mouth stuffed with scone. "They wouldn't tell me at the station. I hope it was nothing too important."

I debated whether to be truthful, but with the way the Destiny Falls gossip mill worked, I was sure he'd be able to find out from someone else if he wanted to. "My wedding ring."

His eyebrows flew up, and he choked on the scone in his mouth. He swallowed with a wince, then drank coffee and coughed to clear his pipes. "I had no idea you were married."

"I'm divorced, not married."

"Oh." He popped the last piece of his scone between his lips and reached for one of the peanut balls. I took the other. "Me too. I work as a physio for the New Zealand women's hockey team and ended up marrying one of the players. Once she retired from professional hockey, she expected me to give up my job on the team as well, but I couldn't. I love it too much. She ended up resenting how often I was away, so things fell apart."

I bit into the peanut ball, uncertain why he was sharing so much with me.

"Sorry." His cheeks colored as if he'd read my mind. "I'm oversharing. It was recent, and I'm still working through some things, especially since I didn't have much mental space to do that at the time."

"Why's that?" I asked against my better judgment.

"My father had cancer. I was helping Mum care for him during my divorce. He only passed recently."

"I'm sorry." I felt a pang of sympathy. "That must have been hard. How's your mum?"

"Hanging in there. Keeping herself busy with volunteer activities."

"That's good." At least she had something to take her mind off the loss. "Where does she live?"

"Wellington." He licked his fingers clean. "It's strange that someone would only take your wedding ring. It couldn't have been your ex, could it?"

Despite myself, I laughed. "God, no. Ryan is the last person who'd do something like that. We're still friends."

He gave me a dark look. "Can you ever really be friends with an ex?"

"Yes," I insisted. But then, I supposed Ryan and I weren't a typical divorced couple. We hadn't been in love when we married, and while we had grown to love each other, it wasn't in that way. "Trust me, it wasn't him."

"If you say so."

His tone said he wasn't convinced, but I ignored it. I didn't owe him an explanation.

Duke's ears pricked up. I listened and heard the faint noise of a vehicle outside. He didn't race to the door, which made me think it was likely to be someone whose vehicle he'd become familiar with. Nate, perhaps. I glanced at the time. It was just after three, so the school would have let out for the day, and his shift had also ended.

"I'll be back in a moment," I said, standing up.

Ezra stood too. "Sounds like you have company. I'll head back to the cottage, but come over later if you'd like to talk more. I can make you a coffee or cup of tea, whatever you prefer."

"I might, thanks." I absolutely wouldn't. While our conversation had reassured me that he was at least partly normal, there was still something off about the guy, and I wasn't about to put myself in a vulnerable position.

I escorted him to the door and opened it to see Nate and

Tess on the other side. Nate's gaze quickly cataloged my features, then flicked to Ezra. He bristled.

Don't make a scene, I warned with my eyes.

He seemed to get the message, giving the other man a brusque nod as he passed by. When Ezra was out of the house, Nate closed the door behind him.

"What are you thinking, having him over here?" he hissed. "We haven't got the results of his fingerprint comparison back yet. He could be the one causing your problems."

I grimaced. I hadn't thought about the fact those results might take a while to receive. I'd assumed that because the police had let him go, they didn't have anything tying him to the crime.

"I didn't realize. He turned up with food, and I didn't want to be rude. Not to mention that he wasn't in town when the first incidents happened."

"So he says," he grumbled.

My breath caught. "Is he lying?"

"We're not sure yet." He looked uncomfortable. "But take anything he tells you with a grain of salt. He's still a person of interest as far as I'm concerned."

"Okay." I rubbed his shoulder in a way that usually calmed him down. "I'll be more careful."

"Good." He glanced down at Tess, who was clinging to his side, well aware of the tension between them. "Tess and I would like to invite you over for dinner later."

A knot in my chest loosened. Despite putting on a good act, I hadn't wanted to be alone tonight. If I visited with them, I could stay until after Tess's bedtime. "I would love to."

31

NATE

ON FRIDAY, I collected Tess after school, and she lazed on the couch with a book while I once again read the threadbare report on the evidence collected from Grace's house. There had been no fingerprints, but the presence of smudges indicated that the perpetrator may have worn gloves. Whether that had been a precautionary measure or simply because it was cold, I didn't know. There had been no other useful information gathered. The only fingerprints on the dresser itself had been Grace's, and when Grace had gone through the contents of her jewelry box and cabinets, she'd let us know that nothing else seemed to be missing. All of which meant that we had absolutely zero to go on. We couldn't arrest Ezra or rule him out, and unless we found something else or Grace's thief acted again, we might never know for certain who'd taken the ring.

I huffed in frustration and rubbed at my buzzed hair. Damn it, why couldn't we have gotten a lucky break? It would be so nice to have a great big sign pointing to the culprit, but unfortunately, real life was rarely that tidy.

"Everything okay, Dad?" Tess asked distractedly.

"Fine," I replied. Even if I explained the whole situation—which I wouldn't do with my eight-year-old daughter—she had her head buried too deeply in her book to take any of it in.

The doorbell rang, and I went to answer it. Tess didn't budge from her comfortable position.

"Hey, Maddy," I said as I opened the door and smiled wearily at my ex.

Maddy scanned me from head to toe, and her fair eyebrows knitted together. "You look like shit."

"Well, thanks, darling." I knew I sounded sarcastic, but I couldn't help it. It wasn't even as if I could retort that she'd seen better days herself because honestly, Maddy looked good. She'd been a pretty girl, and she'd grown into a stunning woman. Ever since she'd gotten together with her fiancé, Steve, she practically glowed with happiness. Seeing that had been a punch in the gut initially. Not because I was jealous of their relationship, but because I'd realized she'd never looked like that with me. I hadn't made her happy.

She rolled her eyes. "You know what I meant, Nate. Is something wrong?"

I sighed. "Just some things going on with Grace. Someone is stealing from her. It might be more than that, but we're not sure yet."

"Ah." Her tone said she understood. "Of course it has something to do with Grace." Her eyes narrowed. "But you're not telling me everything, are you?"

I hesitated, unsure whether to confess the thoughts I'd been having about Grace to my ex. It probably wasn't something she wanted to hear, but if Grace was going to become a bigger part of my life, Maddy would need to be on board with that. We had the co-parenting thing worked out pretty well, and I'd like to keep it that way.

"Grace and I might be going through some changes in our relationship," I said slowly.

"You are, huh?" She put her hand on her hip and arched an eyebrow. "Does Tess know?"

"Not yet."

"Hmm." She somehow managed to make the sound disapproving. "Have you considered how it will affect her if it doesn't work out? You know she dotes on Grace." She grumbled something else that could have been "More than I'd like her to", but it was impossible to be sure.

I rubbed my temples. They were already beginning to throb. Maddy tended to have that effect on me. "We won't tell Tess until we're sure it's going to last. Come on, Mads. Grace and I have known each other forever. You know we wouldn't cross that line unless we thought it was worth the risk."

She rolled her eyes. "You've had a thing for her for a long time. I think you'd take any chance you got."

"What?" I asked, poleaxed. "No, I haven't. This is new. Except for once or twice in high school, I only ever saw her as a friend."

"Uh-huh." She held my gaze for a long moment. "Whether you're lying or not, you've always put Grace on a pedestal. Even when you claim to only ever have thought of her as a friend, no other woman could live up to her in your eyes."

"That's not true." My denial was automatic, but I realized it wasn't entirely truthful when I paused to think about what she'd said. Yeah, maybe I hadn't seen Grace as a romantic option, but I'd definitely compared women to her, and they'd come up short. "Oh shit."

"Yeah." She gave a short laugh. "She's always mattered

more to you than is normal, even for a close friend. When she moved away, you were lost without her. You blamed your stress on being a new husband and a new dad, but there was more to it than that. You missed her. It didn't matter what I did or how far away Grace went, nothing could change it." Her expression turned wry. "I probably wasted more time than I should have holding onto the hope that eventually you and I would connect like that. I refused to see the writing on the wall."

"But I didn't.... I never...."

She patted my shoulder. Her expression wasn't angry, but I could sense a hint of bitterness lingering beneath her smile, and I couldn't blame her. What woman would want to be married to a man who—even unknowingly—didn't value her the way he should have? A man who'd put another woman on a pedestal?

"Shit, I'm sorry, Maddy. I never meant to make you feel that way."

"Yeah, well, it happened." She smiled tightly. "It's the past now. I've come to terms with the fact that whether you were conscious of it or not, your heart was already taken. No one else had a chance, including me."

"Why didn't you ever say something?"

She shrugged. "Why bother? If it came down to a choice between Grace and me, I was never going to win. Anyway." She shifted from one foot to the other, obviously uncomfortable with the direction the conversation had taken. "Can you get Tess?"

"Sure." I left her reluctantly, wanting to ask more about her thoughts on the matter of Grace and me but knowing that we'd exhausted her willingness to talk about it. I didn't blame her. In her shoes, I wouldn't either. But I had to wonder, if she'd seen it, and my siblings seemed to have seen enough not to be surprised by my interest in Grace now, then how blind must I have been for all these years? Weren't cops supposed to be observant? If I'd been this stupid in police school, they'd never have let me head up a small station on my own.

How had I gotten myself into this mess? And how could I get out of it?

32

———

GRACE

I woke up buzzing with excitement. It was book release day. I didn't even manage to wait until I'd gotten out of bed before checking the reviews. A few had already come in from my review team prior to release, and they were all positive, but I'd no doubt spend the entire day obsessively checking and rechecking. I opened a search browser on my phone and typed in the book's title. As soon as I clicked on the first retailer link, I knew something was wrong. Yes, the early positive reviews were there, but many of the new reviews were one and two stars, dragging the average down in a way that made my stomach drop. How could the difference between the early reviews and these ones possibly be so different?

I scrolled down the page and skimmed through the reviews. The most recent ones cited poor editing, spelling and grammatical errors, and frequent typos. I shook my head in disbelief.

No.

It wasn't possible. I'd done a last check through the manuscript myself before it had been uploaded. Everything was fine then, and none of my early readers had flagged problems. The book had been through two editors, a proof-reader, and several dozen early readers. It simply wasn't possible that so many errors would have slipped through unnoticed. Something must have gone wrong in the back end of the retailers.

My phone rang. Alice.

I answered.

"Have you seen?" Her tone was panicky. "I've been going through everything, but I followed your instructions to the letter. All I can think of is that there was a glitch in the system, and they accidentally sent out an older, unedited version of the story to readers."

"Damn." I didn't usually swear, but times like this called for it. "Have you contacted anyone about it?"

"I've typed an email to go to the distributor, but I wanted to check with you before sending it. It should be arriving in your inbox any second now."

"Thanks." I switched the phone onto speaker and checked my inbox. A new email from Alice popped up, and I read it quickly. "Yes, send it. The sooner we can get this fixed, the better. Thousands of people preordered that book."

"I know." She sounded miserable. "I'm so sorry this happened. We'll have to contact your readers and let them know we're dealing with the problem, then we'll need to arrange to send everyone who ordered the book a free replacement copy and figure out if we can somehow get the negative reviews removed once it's fixed. Ugh, this is a nightmare."

"Tell me about it." This was my third book release since I'd hired Alice as an assistant, and the first two had gone off seamlessly. Waking up to this must have shocked her nearly as much as it did me. "Don't worry, we'll get it sorted. Nothing is unfixable."

She exhaled loudly. "Yeah. I keep telling myself that. I'll be there as soon as I can. It'll be easier to work from the computer in the office."

"Get coffee on the way. I have a feeling we'll both need it."

"Will do, boss. See you soon."

Two hours later, Alice and I were hard at work on damage control. I'd contacted my readers and been on the phone with a representative from the distributing company, who'd assured me they were doing all they could to remedy the situation. Alice had barely raised her eyes from the computer since she'd arrived other than to give me a brief hug and pass me a coffee.

A faint knock sounded. I paused what I was doing and listened. Another knock. Someone must be here.

"Ignore it," Alice growled.

I thought about doing just that, but it might be something important. "I'll be back in a second."

I hurried down the hall and opened the door just as Kennedy raised her fist to knock again. She jolted in surprise, then hauled me into a bone-crushing hug.

"I saw what's happened," she said. "I checked out your new book. Something went wrong, didn't it?"

"Yeah." I spoke into her hair. "Looks like a glitch in the distributor's system. They published an old version of the file."

She squeezed me even tighter, then let me go. "I thought you might like company. I brought cookies." She back-tracked onto the doorstep and picked up a paper bag and an envelope from on top of the railing. "That reminds me—you have mail. I grabbed it on the way in."

"Thanks." I took the letter and stepped aside to let her in.

She dug into the paper bag and pulled out a chocolate chip cookie. "Have this. You probably need it."

I accepted the cookie gratefully and led her to the office. "I'm sure Alice would appreciate one too, if you have enough."

"Of course." She darted into the dining area and returned with a chair. "You guys do whatever you need. I'll make sure you have coffee and sugar."

"You're the best."

When Kennedy had turned up on my doorstep last year, I never expected we'd end up so close. She'd burned a lot of bridges when she left over a decade ago, but she'd managed to mend a lot of that damage when she won back her first love, Liam.

I finished the cookie and wiped my fingers on my jeans, then dropped into my office chair. I tore open the letter Kennedy had given me and pulled out a single piece of paper from inside. The page was all white with one sentence printed on it in stark black letters.

Your life is mine.

I gripped the paper so tightly, it crumpled between my fingers. A wave of dizziness swept over me, and I was relieved I was sitting because I might have fallen.

Kennedy noticed my reaction first. "What is it?" she asked.

I held the paper out so she could see. "Don't touch it," I warned. "There might be prints."

I didn't know a lot about police procedures, but I knew that this letter would be considered evidence of stalking or harassment, so I should limit how many people got their hands on it.

My stomach rolled. What did the note mean?

Your life is mine.

Did the person think I owed them, for some reason? Were they delusional and claiming me as their soulmate? Or was it something more sinister.

I shivered. Perhaps they meant they intended to take my life. My free hand flew to my lips, and I stifled a sob. The envelope fluttered to the floor at the movement, and Alice bent to pick it up.

"No!" Kennedy exclaimed.

Alice stopped, startled.

"Don't," Kennedy said. "We need to not touch anything and call the police."

I carefully showed Alice the note, then put it on the desk. She stared at me, wide-eyed and pale.

"This is bad," Alice said, echoing what we were all thinking.

"Yeah." I buried my face in my hands and yanked at my hair. What were the chances that I'd gotten this note on the same day my book release had gone wrong? Was the universe messing with me? I straightened and composed myself. "I'm going to call Nate. Alice, keep working on the problems with the book. Kennedy, will you stay for a while?"

"Of course." Kennedy reached over and squeezed my hand. "I'm not going anywhere."

33

NATE

As soon as I answered the call from Grace and heard the slight hitch in her breathing as she said my name, I knew she was in trouble. I forced myself to wait until she gave me enough details to make an informed decision before rushing over there, and when she'd finished, I pocketed the phone and turned to gaze across the open-plan room my officers and I used as our base of operations.

"Mehrtens!" I barked. "Get your gear. We need to get to Grace's place ASAP."

"Yes, sir." The young officer leaped into action, grabbing her kit—which was always prepared, just in case—and a couple of other necessities. I met her at the door, and we loaded into my police cruiser. Tempted as I was to break the speed limit, Grace wasn't in imminent danger, so I settled for white knuckling the steering wheel and muttering under my breath.

"What happened?" Mehrtens asked. "Another theft?"

"Someone delivered a threatening letter," I told her.

I braked outside Grace's house and lurched to a halt near the drive. I jumped out, slammed the door behind me, and strode down the path. Ezra's cottage caught my eye, and I glared, mentally willing him not to interfere. His face appeared in the window, but he vanished from view a few seconds later.

"Stay gone," I said. If he put himself in front of me, I wasn't sure I'd be able to remain professional. For all we knew, he could be the person responsible for the note.

"Excuse me, Sarge?" Mehrtens queried, puffing as she hurried after me.

"Nothing." I reached the door and let myself in, expecting Duke to greet me, but the hall was empty. I made my way to the private living room, where Grace had said she'd be waiting. She and Kennedy were side by side on the sofa. Kennedy had an arm around Grace, and Duke was sprawled across them. The puppy's head was resting on Grace's thigh, and he didn't look like he intended to move any time soon.

"Gracie." I wanted to hug her. To kiss her soft lips and tell her everything would be fine. Instead, I stooped down in front of her and asked, "Where's the letter?"

She gestured to the coffee table. I glanced over and noticed an envelope in a sealed Ziplock bag on the clean glass surface.

"Kennedy and I have both touched the envelope," Grace said. "She brought it inside. I opened it, and when she saw what the letter said, Kennedy stopped Alice from touching it, and then I called you. Hopefully we didn't contaminate the evidence too much."

"You did good," I assured her, subtly giving Mehrtens the nod to start. "Talk me through what happened."

Grace's eyes filled with tears, and she clutched Duke closer. The little guy cuddled against her chest, giving her the comfort I couldn't. I was glad she had him and her friends and hadn't been alone when she'd opened the letter. I hated to think how much more scared she might have been.

"I have a book release today, but there have been some problems with it," Grace said. "Alice and I were in the office, trying to deal with as much of it as we could when Kennedy arrived."

"I saw what was happening online," Kennedy chimed in. "I wanted to be here for moral support. I checked the mail on the way inside and saw the envelope there, so I brought it in."

"I opened the envelope," Grace said, picking up the story. "I expected it to be a bill or something from the government, since the name and address are typed and it looked official, but there was only one piece of paper inside." She shuddered. "It says, 'Your life is mine.'"

Something wrenched in my gut. The note was a threat, no doubt about it. Whoever this mystery person was, they were trying to scare my Grace, and that wasn't acceptable. I was going to hunt them down and make them regret it. Well, within the confines of the law because I was a police officer and couldn't always indulge my dark revenge fantasies.

"There's no postmark showing the city of origin," Mehrtens said. "It could have been missed, but that might also be a sign it was delivered by hand."

Grace's lips parted and a puff of breath escaped them. She was spooked.

"Kennedy, can you get one of Grace's jackets?" I asked. "The last thing she needs is to get cold when she's had a shock."

"Sure." Kennedy left the room, throwing a supportive smile over her shoulder at Grace.

With gloved hands, Mehrtens opened the Ziplock bag

and extracted the envelope. She eased it open and withdrew the note, showing it to me. As Grace had said, the words "Your life is mine" were printed in a standard font on the center of the page.

"I'm going to need to process this properly at the station," Mehrtens said. "It might be a good idea to get a second opinion from an expert too."

I nodded. "We'll head down there now. Grace, are you okay to come down and make a formal statement?"

"Yes." Her voice was nearly a whisper. Despite the minor thefts, she clearly hadn't expected anything like this to happen.

Kennedy returned to the room and handed Grace a jacket and a bright pink knitted beanie—presumably one of Desdemona's creations.

Grace took them silently, then eased Duke off her lap and got shakily to her feet. "I'll ask Alice if she can stay here to keep working on the book issue while I'm gone and make sure Duke behaves."

"I'll come with you," Kennedy said.

"Thanks, but you should go home." Grace's expression was strained. "I don't know how long it will take."

"It doesn't matter how long it takes." Kennedy's expression was fierce. "You need me, and I'm going to be there." She hesitated, then added, "Nobody knows what you're feeling as well as I do."

Grace embraced Kennedy and said something to her quietly.

"Okay," Kennedy said. "It's decided. Let's go."

The four of us headed for the police cruiser. I noticed Kennedy's car was parked in the drive. I'd been too distracted to pay attention earlier. She went to her car and indicated that she'd follow us. In the cruiser, I drew in several long breaths and released them slowly, knowing I needed to calm myself.

"You should come and stay with me tonight," I said to Grace. "I don't want you home by yourself. Or I could come there if you'd rather. Tess is with Maddy this week."

"I'll come to your place."

Grace's easy acquiescence both surprised me and made me uneasy. My friend may not be particularly assertive, but she was no pushover and she had a spine of steel. The fact that she was willing to concede on even a small point like this said a lot about how freaked out she was. I didn't like her fear, but I had to admit, I was relieved she hadn't argued.

"Good."

When we arrived at the police station, I sent Mehrtens to process the evidence and summoned Patton, a constable with a wisp of a mustache who was not long out of school, to take notes during the interview. The audio would be recorded, but we also needed a written record for our files.

"You can wait out here," I told Kennedy, gesturing to one of the chairs outside the interview room.

"Can't I come in to support Grace?" she asked.

I glanced at Grace. "Up to you, honey."

She drew in a deep breath and gave Kennedy a look of gratitude. "I'd appreciate that."

"No problem."

I guided Grace and Kennedy inside, making sure Grace took one of the seats usually reserved for myself or my colleagues because I didn't want her to feel like she was being treated like a suspect. I sat opposite and waited until Patton had returned with a coffee and a packet of M&Ms for Grace before beginning.

"For the recording, please repeat what you told me this morning," I said.

Grace complied, giving a basic rundown of the chain of events that had led her here.

"Do you know anyone who might want to harm you?" I asked, resting my forearms on the table as I leaned across it so I could read every flicker of her expression.

"No," she said, but her eyes darted to the left.

"No ex-lovers, former friends, or guests who took a dislike to you?" She'd had a thought. Something important. But she was keeping it to herself.

"No scorned ex-lovers, and I haven't had a major falling out with any friends." She interlaced her fingers around the mug of coffee as if warming them. "As far as I know, I haven't had any unhappy guests. My online reviews are all good."

"Any other enemies?" I prompted. "Anyone at all? It could have been the slightest thing that set this person off. It might not have been something that happened recently."

Grace squeezed her eyes shut as if she was in pain. I wanted to reach for her, but I couldn't. She opened her gorgeous hazel eyes, and they seemed to have lost a little of their light. "I used to have a stalker."

34

GRACE

"You *what*?" Nate looked like his head was about to explode.

I winced. "I used to have a stalker back when I lived in Auckland. His name was Darrel Weich."

His expression twisted into something that just about broke my heart. Defeat. "Why didn't you tell me?"

I heard his unspoken question too. *Do you ever tell me anything anymore?*

This was just one thing in a long list of secrets I'd kept. Not out of any sense of malice, but to protect myself. If he'd known about the incident with Darrel when it had happened, he'd have come straight to see me in Auckland, and then I'd have had to explain why I was living with a husband he didn't know I had while also trying to keep my heart safe from him. Because if there's one thing I couldn't resist, it was when Nate got protective of those he loves. If he'd gone all overprotective alpha male on me, I'd never have been able to convince myself to keep my distance.

Before I knew it, I'd have been back in Destiny Falls, watching him live the happily ever after I longed for, with another woman.

But no matter the reason, I'd lied to him. That had to hurt.

"I'm sorry." I didn't offer an explanation because I didn't have one that would appease him. "It didn't last for long. A few weeks, that I know of, but I only learned that after it all came to a head. I was married to Ryan at the time, so he helped me through it, and I tried not to think about it after."

"I see." Nate's teeth were gritted. He glanced at Patton, who was studiously jotting notes. "What happened with Weich?"

"He was a fan of my books, but I don't think I ever interacted with him personally. He convinced himself that we were in love and that the weekly newsletter I send my readers included hints about how much I missed him and secret clues to indicate I was being held against my will." I breathed out slowly, hoping to calm my racing heart. Even thinking of him stressed me out. "I've done some research since then, and it seems it's not uncommon for people with particular mental traits to fixate on someone in the public eye—even peripherally, like me—in that way."

Nate nodded briskly and gestured for me to keep talking. I psyched myself up for what came next.

"One day, I was working from home, and he threw a brick through the back window. I thought he was just a vandal at first, but then he came into the apartment, shouting my name. He kept saying that he was there to free me so we could be together. Our closet had a trapdoor that went beneath the house, so I hid there and called the police. They arrested him for breaking and entering and helped me file a restraining order."

"Breaking and entering?" Nate sounded pissed. "That's all they could get him on?"

I shrugged. "He had no weapons, other than the brick he threw through the window, and I don't think he intended to harm me. He honestly thought that Ryan was holding me captive."

Nate pinched the bridge of his nose and growled in frustration. "Only you could find the good in a man who broke into your house and probably planned to kidnap you so he could enact his twisted fantasies. Did he serve any time?"

"No." I looked at the table, not wanting to see the fury I knew would be blazing in his eyes. "I agreed not to press charges if he went to mandatory counseling until a psychiatrist was willing to say he wasn't a danger to anyone."

"Oh, Grace." He sighed, long and low. "You have such a big heart, but where's your sense of self-preservation?"

I straightened my spine. "I moved house and made sure our new place had a security system. I also put measures in place to ensure that nobody would be able to use my books to track me down again."

"That's something," he allowed. "Do you know where Weich is now?"

"The last I heard, he'd gotten a job in Auckland and seemed to be on the straight and narrow, but that was years ago. Honestly, this whole thing was so long ago that it seems unlikely he'd be involved. Even if he were to regress, surely I'd have heard something before now."

"Maybe. Maybe not." Nate caught Patton's eye and added, "As soon as we finish this interview, I want you to find out where this Weich guy is and what he's doing. If he's gotten so much as a parking ticket since the restraining order was filed, I want to know about it."

Patton nodded. "Yes, Sarge."

Nate turned back to me. "Have you learned anything

else about Ezra? He seems suspiciously interested in you, and he would have had plenty of opportunity to deliver the letter."

A chill ran through me at the thought that I could be harboring a villain under my own roof, but even though Ezra was odd and made me nervous, he hadn't been hostile or come onto me. "I discovered that he's newly divorced and his father died of cancer recently."

"So, he's had a lot of upheaval in his life," Nate commented.

"Has he made any untoward advances toward you?" Patton asked, earning a scowl from Nate, who clearly wanted to take the lead on questioning.

"No." I thought back through my interactions with him. "I don't know that he reads social cues very well, but he absolutely hasn't flirted with me. It's more like he's a nosy neighbor who doesn't know when to back off."

"Has he ever said or done anything threatening?" Nate asked.

"Not exactly, but I have to admit, it made me nervous when I caught him around the side of my house that time I was coming over for brunch at your mum and dad's place."

"It's possible you interrupted him trying to figure out how to get into the house," Nate pointed out. "Was the ring there at that time?

"I don't know." I felt useless, not being able to offer more information. "It could have been. I'm sorry, I really don't remember when it disappeared."

"It's okay." He patted my hand briefly, and Kennedy scooted her chair closer. "Patton, digging into Ezra Mendel is priority number two."

"Got it, boss."

Nate searched my eyes as though hoping he might find all the answers he needed inside them. He could search for as long as he wanted, but I doubted he'd ever see what he was looking for. "I know we already talked about friends and exes who might hold a grudge after the ring was stolen, but I have to ask again. Is there anyone you could have forgotten? Even something as simple as a bad blind date could trigger the wrong person."

"Nate." I sounded as exasperated as I felt. "I don't even remember the last time I went on a date. I hate online dating, and it's not as if there's a thriving singles scene in town. I might have met up with a guy in Queenstown a year or so ago, but I doubt he'd remember my name now."

"We'll need that information anyway." He pursed his lips. "I know it's a nuisance, but we've got to cover the bases."

"Yeah, fine." I sighed. "I'll try to find the details."

"Thanks. We appreciate it." He thought hard for a moment. "How about readers or other authors? Are there any who have made you uncomfortable?"

I pulled a face. "I doubt it. They're pretty great, and I don't think there are any who've raised red flags in the past few years, but I'll check with Alice. She manages a lot of my communications, and she might have deleted anything like that before I saw it."

"Can you get her to do that today? We'd like either electronic or print copies of anything she can think of that might be worth investigating."

"I'll ask her when I get back." Considering the massive mess my book release had become, hopefully she wouldn't mind working overtime.

Nate asked a few more questions before releasing me—but only after I'd promised to go to his place as soon as Alice finished work so I wouldn't be alone at home. When we left the police station, Kennedy wrapped me in a hug.

"Oh, honey." She pulled me close. "I've got you."

"Thank you," I hiccupped.

"Come on." She eased away but kept an arm around my back. "Let's get you something to eat, and I'll help you pack a bag."

I gave a watery laugh. "Thank you."

"I know how you're feeling. I've been there." Her tone was gentle, and I thanked the universe that I had her there to help me through the day from hell. "We're going to figure this out."

35

NATE

I WANTED TO PUNCH SOMETHING. I needed to get home and lay into the boxing bag in the garage. The thought of some asshole terrorizing Grace made me madder than I'd ever been before—and that was saying something. I practically vibrated with fury, and it was only thanks to years of training that I forced myself to follow proper police protocol. It didn't help matters that I'd had to ask her questions I should know the answer to already. I wanted to simultaneously kick my own ass for not paying enough attention to her and grump at her for not being honest with me in the past. We were caught in such a quagmire of lies and half-truths that I hardly knew what "facts" I could rely on and which I couldn't.

While Patton tracked down Darrel Weich, I looked into Weich's criminal history. He'd been arrested for being drunk and disorderly a few times and for driving under the influence, but there were no major blemishes on his record. The nastiest incident was a bar fight where he'd punched someone who'd been hassling a female patron. Clearly, he had it in him to be violent, but I didn't see any evidence that he made a habit of stalking women. Grace's was the only restraining order against him. Of course, that didn't necessarily mean he'd never stalked women before, just that no one had made a formal complaint or filed any kind of protective order. Perhaps I should ask Mehrtens to question his ex-girlfriends and women from his workplace to see if he had a history of harassment when she was done cataloging evidence from this morning.

"Sir." Patton appeared in front of me, his wisp of a mustache twitching. "I just got off the phone with Weich's manager. Weich is currently at work and has been there for all of his scheduled shifts for the past month."

My stomach sank. It would have been so convenient if Weich was behind Grace's problems because he was a known quantity. I could have had everything wrapped up and Grace out of danger by nightfall.

"Thanks, Patton." Weich's presence at work didn't mean he wasn't responsible—I'd learned during the investigation into Kennedy's stalking that letters could be delivered by intermediaries—but if Weich was the culprit, he was being clever about it. "Can you call the manager back and ask for the names and contact details of any women who have worked closely with Weich since he started?"

Patton hesitated. "We don't have a warrant."

"I know." I grimaced. "Just ask. They're not obligated to give us anything, but if you share the context with them, they may be willing to offer us a name or two."

"Okay. I'll do that now."

The investigation continued in the same vein until I finally decided to call it quits for the night. Weich's car hadn't been seen in the area. Ezra Mendel appeared to be exactly what he said he was: a divorced man who'd lost a parent and taken a temporary leave of absence from work to stay in Destiny Falls. Perhaps the reason he pinged on my radar as someone to be wary of was that he was on the verge of a breakdown. There wasn't necessarily anything sinister about it. His employer had only good things to say and had laughed his ass off when I'd asked whether I thought Ezra was capable of stalking a woman. He'd told me the man had a reputation among the hockey players as having the hands of an angel. He was gentle and kind.

Supposedly.

I wasn't convinced. After all, everyone thought Ted Bundy was charming.

My need to hit something waned as the day wore on, and by the time I drove home, all I could think about was how lovely it would be to flop on the couch with Grace, drink a beer, and start rebuilding the connection that had somehow frayed between us over the years.

I parked behind Grace's car and strode up the path to the front door. When I turned the handle, I was pleased she'd locked it. I let myself in and was greeted by a bouncing Duke.

"Sorry!" Grace appeared behind him, flustered. "He's excited by all the new smells. It's taking him a while to calm down."

I bent to pet Duke, dodging out of the way as he leaped up, narrowly avoiding a face-to-face collision. "It's no wonder he's energetic." I straightened. "It's been a big day for all of us."

She nodded, and I couldn't help noticing how tired she looked. Not just like she needed a decent night of sleep, but as if she was exhausted on a bone-deep level. Today's events had taken a toll on her.

"It has. I started making a curry," she said. "You didn't have much in your fridge I could work with."

"Sorry. I'm hopeless on weeks when Maddy has Tess. My healthy eating goes right out the window."

She narrowed her eyes. "You've got to take care of yourself, Nate Braddock. Nothing is allowed to happen to you."

When she said things like that, she felt like my best friend again, even if things were beginning to change between us.

I pulled her into my embrace and hugged the crap out of her. "Nothing is going to happen to me," I murmured in her ear. "Just like nothing is going to happen to you. You hear me?"

"Yeah." The word was shaky.

"Whoever is trying to cause trouble, they're not going to get away with it." I closed my eyes, wallowing in the sensation of how perfect she felt in my arms. Holding her like this, I knew in my gut that I wanted more than friendship with her. I could no longer be happy with what we've shared all these years. Seeing her in a new light, as a woman who had secrets and a life separate from mine, made me realize just how much I wanted to intertwine our lives and know everything there was to know about her. I wanted all our truths—ugly and beautiful—out in the open, and I wanted her to turn to me when she needed help.

Not Ryan. Not Kennedy. Not even Desdemona.

Me.

Being Grace's friend was great, but I wanted more.

She disentangled herself from the hug and swiped at the moisture glistening on her eyelashes. "Thanks. I feel a bit silly. It's just a nasty note and a couple of missing things. It might not be anything serious, but I'm really scared."

Whoever was behind this, they'd pay for that.

"I'll keep you safe," I promised. "Between me and my brothers, the police force, Kennedy, Alice, and Desdemona, we're not letting this guy anywhere near you."

She held my gaze. "I hate not knowing what's going on. With Darrel, I didn't realize he'd been watching me until the police found evidence of it afterward. It just seemed like a blitz attack out of nowhere, and then it was done. This is different. I can sense this malicious presence, but I can't tell where it's coming from, and I don't know what I'm supposed to do."

"We'll figure it out together." I took her hand, a gesture that I'd made hundreds of times, but this time it carried more weight. Because this time, I finally understood how much Grace meant to me. I was completely, stupidly in love with her. It was just as Maddy had said. Whether I'd been aware of it or not, Grace had always had my heart, and I wasn't going to lose her just as I'd finally wised up to the fact.

36

____

GRACE

Even though it had been an awful day, holding hands with Nate comforted me. I sensed in my soul that I was meant to be here with him. Perhaps it wasn't the best time or the most romantic setting, but the universe had brought us here for a reason. Nate was everything I'd ever wanted. Protective. Reliable. Kind-hearted. Sure, he was gruff on the outside, but on the inside, he was gooey as a marshmallow. He would never let me down. If he said he'd keep me safe, I believed him.

As if drawn magnetically, I moved closer and laid my head on his shoulder. He wrapped his arms around me. It felt wonderful. His body was strong and steady against mine. His heart thumped a reassuring beat. I softened into him, mentally letting go and allowing myself—for just a few seconds—to imagine this man belonged to me in every way. A smile curved my lips. He smelled faintly of lemon, as if he'd been sucking the lemon drops he kept hidden in his desk drawer at work and in the glove compartment of his car.

His breath hitched, but I didn't let it pull me from the fantasy. I imagined I could feel his body responding to my nearness. His breathing becoming irregular. His muscles tensing. But it must be in my head, right? It wasn't real. It couldn't be.

"Gracie." His voice was husky.

"Yeah?" I couldn't seem to bring myself to let him go. Hopefully he'd put it down to the emotion of the day.

"We need to set some things straight."

His words were like a splash of cold water to my face. I jerked backward, putting space between us. His jaw was tight, his eyes blazing. Shit. I'd overstepped and he was going to call me on it.

"Let me just—"

"No." He grasped my wrist and held firm. "No running away this time."

My pulse thundered in my ears. "Okay, but let's sit down."

I'd need to be seated for whatever horror show was about to come.

He led me by the wrist to the living room and guided me onto the couch. We sat side by side. Duke watched us intently, perhaps sensing my unease. He growled, but Nate released me and offered his hand to the dog to sniff. Apparently satisfied, Duke curled up at our feet.

Nate angled his body toward mine. "We're overdue for a conversation."

"About?" I squeaked. Of all the days for us to finally have this confrontation, why did it have to be today?

"Us." He drew in a slow breath. "I've come to realize over the past few weeks that I care for you more deeply than I ever would have guessed." His deep blue eyes seared into mine, warming me to my toes. "You didn't seem interested when I tried to bring it up the other day, but I have to say this or I'll always regret it. I want to date you. Gracie, I want everything with you."

Wait, what?

I stared at him. "Hold on, I just want to make sure I heard you right. You want to *date* me?"

"Yes." His gaze didn't waver, and his tone sounded 100 percent certain.

"Me?" I repeated in disbelief.

One side of his mouth hitched up. "Yes, Gracie. You. My best friend. The one woman who's always meant more to me than anyone else—besides my mother, of course."

"But...." My mouth opened and closed soundlessly. "You never...."

I didn't understand what was happening. I'd been sure he was about to tell me he knew how I felt and that I needed to get over it. I never could have seen this coming.

"Wait a sec." I held up my hand as if I were directing traffic. "What do you mean, I didn't seem interested when you tried to bring it up?"

He shifted in place. Cleared his throat. "Uh, well, you ran out of the house. I'm not sure how else I was meant to interpret that."

"Oh my god." One by one, things began to fall into place. "I thought you'd overheard my conversation with Cissy."

He frowned. "What conversation?"

"Um." I clapped my hand to my mouth. *Way to out yourself.* "I told her something personal. I thought you were going to ask me about it, and I was embarrassed, so I left. I'm sorry."

His smile began to widen. "No harm done. So does that mean you might be open to the idea?"

I looked down, suddenly feeling shy. "Yes." It felt like a

massive confession. "But this seems to have come out of nowhere, and I don't want to lose you if things become awkward. This isn't a misguided reaction to me being in danger, is it?"

He moved closer, and the weight of his hand settled on my thigh, his palm hot against my skin even through a layer of fabric. "It might seem like it's come out of nowhere, but I've been thinking about it for a while. I know my own mind, and I know what I want." He tipped my chin up. "That's you."

I kissed him.

I couldn't say who moved first, but I found myself on his lap with his arms around me while we tentatively explored each other's lips. His were softer than I'd expected. As our faces brushed together, his stubble rasped pleasantly against the skin of my cheek.

We took our time. The kiss wasn't rushed, but gentle and sweet. Almost chaste. It was, without a doubt, the best kiss of my life because Nate Braddock was attached to the lips that were on mine. Nate, whom I'd loved forever. Nate, with his gorgeous blue eyes and rugged good looks. His gruff demeanor and hot temper only showed how much he cared.

We drew apart, our mouths separated by an inch, exchanging breath. It was more intimate than any sexual encounter I'd ever had.

"Wow," I breathed.

Nate brushed his lips over mine again. "You're incredible, Gracie. Exactly like I knew you would be."

I kissed him again, just because I could. Because after years of holding myself back, I was finally allowed to touch him and kiss him the way I wanted. Emotion swelled in my chest, robbing me of my ability to speak.

Don't get ahead of yourself, I told myself. *He asked you on a date, not to marry him. One step at a time.*

But this one step had been a long time coming, and a girl was allowed to dream, right?

37

———

NATE

WAKING with Grace in my arms felt like heaven. After we'd eaten dinner, we'd fallen into bed early, but nothing had happened except sleep. We were both clothed, and our snuggling was purely for comfort and to enjoy being close to each other. It was innocent. Still, we'd never have done this as friends. We might have shared a bed if the need arose, but we wouldn't have cuddled. We'd have each done our best to pretend we were alone.

I liked holding her against my body, listening to her soft breaths, and inhaling her sweet scent. She murmured something in her sleep, and I smiled at the intimacy of this shared moment. I dropped a light kiss on her shoulder and closed my eyes. I'd need to get out of bed soon, but for now, I wanted to remain cocooned and pretend the rest of the world didn't exist.

I wasn't sure where we went from here. It wasn't as if we were two strangers who'd started dating from scratch. We had years of history. Did that mean the normal dating timeline didn't apply, or should I treat dating as something separate from our friendship?

"Why are you thinking so hard?" Grace asked sleepily. She rolled toward me and rested her forehead against mine. Her eyelashes fluttered as she cleared the sleep from her eyes.

Seeing her like this, my heart felt too big for my chest. It was astounding that I hadn't noticed what an entrancing woman she was until recently. Now, it seemed like the most obvious thing in the world.

I kissed the tip of her nose. "Come out to dinner with me."

Her forehead crinkled with bemusement. "Of course."

"Tonight," I prompted. If I wanted to clear up any confusion about where we stood, it was best to act now. "On a date."

Her expression softened. "I'd like that."

"So would I."

I kissed her again, this time on the mouth. A sigh eased from her, and she parted her lips and melted against the bed, her entire frame turning languid. I cupped her face with one hand and rested the other on her slim hip as I deepened the kiss. It was slow and purposeful. I poured forth every bit of my need for her, but I didn't let my hands wander. There was no need to rush. We'd have plenty of time to get to know each other in this new way as well as we did in every other.

When we broke apart, we were both breathing heavily. My phone buzzed, reminding me I needed to get to work.

"We'll finish this later," I promised, rolling away from her delectable self.

She flashed me a coquettish smile. "I look forward to it."

I shook my head, stunned once again by the contrast

between the Grace I was seeing in my bed and the one I'd been friends with since we were teenagers.

We were in perfect sync with each other as we prepared breakfast and ate in the living room. We'd shared so many meals before that it felt natural.

"Are you going back to your place today?" I asked as we cleared up.

"Yes." She pursed her lips. "Alice will be with me, and I promise to leave when she does and come back here. I can do most of my stuff remotely if I have my laptop. It's just easiest working with her at the office because it's set up for both of us."

"Okay." I grabbed my gear and kissed her cheek. "I'll see you later. Don't forget, we have a date."

Her answering smile made me forget about how much messed-up shit we were dealing with, at least until I entered the police station and was met by an eager Patton, who looked like he'd already been here for a while.

"Sarge," he said, thrusting a mug of coffee into my hand. "I've managed to confirm Ezra Mendel's alibi for when Grace's blouse and lipstick went missing. He was on the other side of the country. That doesn't mean he's not involved, but if the incidents are all connected, it's possible he's not our guy."

Just like that, my mood deflated. I supposed that having more information was a good thing, but the more we learned, the less idea we seemed to have about who had actually sent Grace that threatening note.

"Thanks, Patton." I sipped the coffee and grunted approvingly. Black, no sugar. Just what I needed. "We'll have to widen the net. Alice sent over a couple of emails last night that she thought might be cause for concern, so let's see if we can uncover anything useful from those."

"Yes, sir." He bobbed his head.

I made my way to the desk, thinking about how strange it was that the parts of the job that most excited cops inevitably involved someone else's misfortune. We were trained to be problem solvers, but I always woke up hoping for a boring day because it would mean nobody had been hurt or endangered.

The hours slipped by, and before I knew it, it was time to head home. Grace was already there, having messaged thirty minutes ago when she and Alice left her place. I spent the drive trying to breathe through my frustration. We had our date tonight, and I didn't want my irritation over how slowly matters were progressing to impact Grace's enjoyment of the night. Still, I didn't breathe easy until I'd dumped my bag on the living room floor and swept her into my arms. I held her tight, and the tension dissipated from my shoulders like magic. Damn, she felt perfect.

I breathed in the scent of her hair that smelled like peaches and sunshine. Her breasts were pressed to my chest, and my cock started to thicken against the seam of my work pants. Nerve endings that had been dormant flickered to life. It was as if my libido had been sleeping, but she'd woken it up. God, I'd been celibate for a long time. If she brushed against me the wrong way, I might embarrass myself. I drew back from her and kissed her forehead.

"Hey, Gracie. How was your day?"

She shrugged and pulled a face. "I mean, it wasn't the best, but compared to how awful it could have been, it wasn't bad."

"That's good." It was something, at least. "I'm going to change into a tidier outfit for our date. Why don't you tell me all about it at the restaurant?"

38

───────

GRACE

MY EYES WIDENED as Nate emerged from the direction of his bedroom into the living area. When he suggested that we go for dinner this morning, I'd expected it to be much like any other meal we might have shared together. We'd eaten out together plenty of times over the years. But he'd never dressed like this, in mouthwatering dark jeans and a form-fitting jacket over a button-down shirt. He'd pulled out the big guns. I couldn't take my eyes off him. He sent me a smile that was two parts cocky to one part hesitant, and it melted me inside. I realized I wasn't seeing the version of my best friend I was used to. I was seeing the version of him who wanted to impress a woman.

I loved it.

"Should I have worn something nicer?" I asked. I'd opted for jeans and a cashmere sweater that flattered my complexion, but if I'd known what he was wearing, I might have chosen a dress instead.

188

"No, you're perfect." He kissed my cheek and placed his hand on my lower back to guide me to the door.

Behind us, Duke whimpered. I blew him a kiss over my shoulder. "We won't be too long, Dukie," I promised. He settled down.

Outside, Nate opened the passenger door first and held it while I lowered myself into the car. A crazy grin spread over my face. He was trying to romance me. I could squirm with delight.

Still, as he sat behind the steering wheel, I said, "You know you don't need to woo me or pretend to be anything other than what and who you are. Don't forget, I know you better than anyone."

He glanced over at me, his eyes seeing more than I liked. "Perhaps I don't need to woo you," he said, "but I want to. You deserve to be taken out properly and treated right. You're special, Gracie, and you deserve more than a grumpy single dad with a chip on his shoulder, but I'm going to do the best I can to be worthy of you anyway."

Tears filled my eyes. I took his hand. There was nothing I could say to that.

"Is this real?" I whispered.

"Yeah, honey." He kissed the back of my hand. "I promise you, nothing could be more real."

Don't cry, I warned myself. Usually, I had no problem keeping my emotions under wraps, but everything was near the surface right now, and I didn't want to have to explain that my tears were happy ones.

"So, where are we going?" I asked to distract myself.

Nate switched the engine on and pulled away from the curb. "At first I thought of the resort, but there's a chance we'd get stuck and not be able to come down again, so I decided we're better off avoiding that. That leaves the pub and the cafe." He glanced at me. "I'd rather not have either of my parents at our first official date, so the pub is out."

I frowned. "But the cafe won't be open."

He waggled his eyebrows. "Wait and see."

"What does that mean?"

He pulled up outside Taste of Destiny but stopped me when I started to get out. "Wait a moment."

Eden hurried out of the café, and Nate met her halfway between the car and the door, taking hold of the basket she carried. I watched them, intrigued. When Nate got back into the car, he passed me the basket.

"Dinner," he said. "I asked Eden to pack a selection of sweet and savory food before they closed for the day."

"A picnic?" It hardly seemed the weather for picnicking.

"Sort of."

I stayed quiet while Nate drove again. After a few minutes, I realized where we were going. The lookout point just out of town. A spot I'd told him was one of my favorite places to visit when I needed reminding of why I loved Destiny Falls so much—usually during the harshest parts of winter. He parked, the headlights bright in the descending darkness, and shut off the engine.

"Here we are." He took the basket from me and lifted the lid. "Sorry, I know it's not fancy, but it's the best I could come up with on short notice."

I beamed. "It's perfect. Thank you."

"I'm glad you like it. "

He handed me a paper plate and tilted the basket so I could view the options. There were salad sandwiches, muffins, a couple of wrapped items that smelled like pie or quiche, and on the side, a cupcake with a pink heart frosted on top.

We talked while we ate. The evening felt both new and familiar at once. Conversation came as easily between us as it always had, but there was an electric undercurrent that thrilled me. Each brush of our hands or graze of our legs sparked a longing for more, and I knew I wasn't the only one affected. Our glances caught frequently, and a sizzling tension seemed to zing between us. When I reached for the cupcake at the same time he did, our fingertips connected and our gazes locked. I felt frosting squish beneath my thumb, and I raised it to my mouth and licked it clean, still holding his gaze.

Nate's eyes flared hot, then he cleared his throat. "That's it. We're going home."

39

NATE

WE TRIPPED through the front door, separating briefly for me to kick my shoes off and for Grace to unzip her boots, then we came together again, our mouths clashing. I backed Grace against a wall, hardly able to believe it was her lithe body against mine, her long leg hitched around my hip.

When I'd been younger and had wondered whether I should ask Grace out, I never realized how much passion she concealed beneath her demure exterior. If the men of Destiny Falls knew what I'd just discovered, they'd be lining up outside her door.

No. I growled at the thought. *Grace is mine.*

I curved my hand around her tight ass and rocked against her, pleased when she whimpered into my mouth. I wanted to take her to my bedroom, strip her naked, and slide inside her, but something held me back. I stilled, panting into the side of her neck.

"What's wrong?" she asked, her pliant form beginning to stiffen in my arms.

"Nothing." I breathed in, got a lungful of her delicious scent, and shuddered. "I don't want you to think this is just about sex."

She rolled her eyes, an expression so foreign coming from her that I almost chuckled. "I know that." She arched her back, rubbing herself against me. "But sex is great, and if you give me orgasms, I promise not to think you just wanted to get some."

"Thank fucking god." I wrapped my free hand under her other thigh and lifted her. She wrapped her slender legs around my hips and held on tight while I carried her through the house to my bedroom. I barreled inside and deposited her on the bed.

I forced myself to slow down, slowly stripping off my jacket, then my shirt, before crawling on top of her. Grace hadn't moved, too busy watching me with eyes that rapidly darkened.

"I've been sneaking peeks at you for half my life," she said breathlessly. "Now I can finally look my fill."

I paused above her, letting her sweep me with her heated gaze. I wasn't the prettiest Braddock brother or the most muscular, but I had strong arms and a thick chest, and I trusted that she wouldn't find me wanting.

When her eyes met mine again, I grinned wolfishly down at her. "My turn."

I grabbed the hem of her cardigan and tugged it up. She lifted her weight off her back, and I stripped the cardigan over her head, leaving her in a pale green blouse. That went too, and then I sat back on my haunches to study the expanse of gorgeousness I'd revealed. Grace's stomach was taut, her breasts spilling out of a black silk bra that would have been conservative if not for the fact that it was cut so low that it barely covered her nipples.

"You take my breath away," I whispered.

Her smile was shy. Captivating.

I dipped down to kiss her abdomen and trailed soft kisses up her ribcage and over the exposed tops of her breasts. I eased the straps of her bra down and she reached beneath herself to unclip the back. When her upper half was completely naked, I used my tongue to toy with her rosy nipples until they formed stiff peaks.

She sat up and pushed my shoulders, then straddled my lap and traced the tip of her tongue from the crook of my neck to the lobe of my ear. She bit the earlobe softly. Teasingly. She rubbed one of her thumbs over my left nipple, and I grunted, feeling it in my dick. She smirked and repeated the movement with the other nipple, then let her hands dip further down my body, over my firm stomach, slipping around to draw a line down my spine, then dropping to the waistband of my jeans. Her touch was gentle but confident, and completely addictive.

I wrapped my arms around her and rolled us so that I was on top again. She squealed in surprise, then laughed. Her laughter stopped when I unzipped her jeans and peeled them down her thighs. I held her gaze as my fingers skimmed her smooth skin, leaving goosebumps in their wake. Her face was so expressive. Everyone thought she was so self-contained, but here with me, she let me see everything. How much she loved my touch. How badly she wanted me.

It was heady. I'd never experienced anything like it.

Determined to give her everything she wanted, needed, and deserved, I explored her thighs with my mouth, working my way down to her calves. I paused at her feet to give each of them a quick rub, then got off the bed and stripped off my remaining clothes. In a few seconds, I was naked, and Grace was clad only in sheer black panties that matched her bra.

"Gorgeous." My voice was a rasp. "Absolutely fucking divine."

She raised herself up on one elbow, giving me a questioning look.

"You are," I told her. "You're a goddess, and I'm going to worship you like one."

I buried my face between her thighs and rubbed my mouth against the silk of her panties. She threw her head back and gasped, her hips bucking toward me, seeking more. I pinned her down, an arm over each thigh, and licked at the dampness soaking through the delicate fabric. Her arousal tasted as addictive as she was. I groaned against her, hungry for more.

"Please, Nate," she panted. "Oh, please."

I grabbed the sides of her panties and yanked them down, barely clinging to enough presence of mind not to tear them. I plunged my tongue into her folds, holding her hips down as she cried out and arched her back.

"Is this what you need?" I asked, licking her like my favorite ice cream.

"Yes. Oh god."

I tongued her clit, gently working a finger into her, and growled as she spasmed around it. Everything about her was pretty, pink, and perfect. I took my time with her. Enjoyed her. When she was wound tight, I pulled away, then froze.

"Do you have a condom?" I asked, scarcely daring to breathe. I'd been so busy today, it hadn't occurred to me to pick some up, and honestly, it'd have been presumptuous to think we'd just fall right into bed anyway.

"In my purse," she replied.

Jealousy flared through me for a brief moment as I wondered who she'd been thinking of when she'd packed that condom, but then I got over myself and focused on being grateful she was prepared.

I found the condom and rolled it along my length. Grace parted her thighs and offered herself to me. I paused to feast my eyes on the vision she presented, then moved forward and slowly pushed into her. She was tight, so I waited for her muscles to ease before drawing back and thrusting again. She wrapped her legs around me and crossed her ankles at my lower back, bringing me even deeper inside her.

My eyes rolled back. "God, Gracie. It's like you were made for me."

"I'm yours." She clasped me tight, rocking her hips in time with the rhythm I'd set. "Always have been, even if you didn't know it."

"Mine," I agreed. "And I'm yours."

Her breath stuttered and she contracted around me. I gritted my teeth, determined this wouldn't end too soon. I gathered her close. Kissed her. Wrapped her silken hair around my fist and gently guided her head back, exposing her throat and the rapid pulse that beat within. I latched onto the tender skin and sucked. She whimpered in response. I released her hair and plunged into her, unable to think of anything but how perfectly we were matched. With every stroke, she met me halfway. Her eyes caught mine, flecks of emerald sparkling in their depths. Her lips parted. My own stark desire reflected back at me along with something else. Something more.

But before I could identify it, she cried out, clamping down around me. I jerked inside her. She felt so good. Her channel rippled around me, tugging me under, and I buried my face in her hair as pleasure tore through me.

We stayed where we were for several minutes, catching our breaths until Grace finally gave me a little shove.

"You're too heavy," she complained. "I can't breathe."

I laughed, flopping onto my side. "I just had the best sex of my life, and you're moaning about my weight? You know how to stroke a man's ego."

She smiled, her eyes telling me everything her words didn't. This meant every bit as much to her as it did to me. "You know I didn't mean it like that."

I disposed of the condom and tucked her against my side. She rested her cheek over my heart. It felt like she belonged there. As though I'd bear an impression of her on my skin from this moment forward, just waiting for her to return.

"This is really happening." She sounded like she was only just beginning to believe it, but I'd make sure she didn't have any reason to doubt.

"It is, and I couldn't be happier."

40

GRACE

DESPITE THE NOTE, the ring theft, and temporarily moving out of my home for my own safety, the next two days were among the best of my life. I stayed with Nate, and he and I couldn't keep our hands off each other. We made up for lost time, and now my body was pleasantly sore from making love with him over and over again.

During the quieter moments, we just cuddled with each other—and Duke—and talked. It was so close to the life I used to dream about that I had to remind myself not to get caught up in it. Nate and I were together, and we were committed to seeing where this change in our relationship led, but I was in love with him, and he hadn't given any indication he felt the same. He cared for me and was attracted to me, but this could still implode, and I needed to be mentally prepared in case it did.

I was in my office on Friday morning, working on Rocky and Jewel's story, when my phone pinged. I considered ignoring it, but I'd hit a paragraph that needed a bit more thought, so I checked the phone and frowned. It was a notification from the bank that my everyday account had gone into overdraft. But how was that possible? I hadn't made any transactions this morning, and I earned plenty enough that the days of going into overdraft in order to pay one of the bills were long behind me.

I opened the mobile banking app and my stomach hollowed out with shock. Last I'd checked, there had been over a thousand dollars in my account, but now it was one hundred dollars overdrawn. I tapped the screen to open the transaction details.

What on earth?

There were a series of withdrawals from the local ATM, each for $200, the maximum that could be withdrawn at a time.

My fingers trembled. I glanced over at Alice, who was engrossed in something on her computer. I looked back at the phone, but the text on the screen hadn't magically changed while I'd been looking away.

Perhaps there was a reasonable explanation. I separated business finances from personal finances, but it was possible Alice had taken the wrong card when she needed cash out for something related to the business. It would be unusual for her to use cash or to make a withdrawal without consulting me, but it could have happened.

"Alice," I said tentatively. "Have you used my debit card today?"

"Huh?" Alice glanced up, her bemused expression showing she hadn't heard me properly.

"My debit card." I forced myself to be calm. "Have you used it today?"

"Um, I don't think so. Just let me check what I've done this morning." She returned her attention to the screen, clicked, scrolled, and shook her head. "Nope. Why's that?"

My insides knotted. "You haven't visited an ATM today?"

"No." She finally gave me her full attention. "What's going on, Grace?"

I showed her my phone. "Someone has withdrawn twelve hundred dollars from my personal account at the ATM on Centennial Street."

Her hand flew to her mouth. "Oh my god." She scanned the details. "Could it be one of those scams where they have a device that records your card details if they can get close to you?"

"Good question." That hadn't even occurred to me. "Let me check if my card is in my purse."

I stood up. Duke's ears perked up as I passed him on the way to my bedroom to get my purse. He trotted after me. When I checked my purse, I discovered that my personal debit card was missing. I slumped onto the edge of the bed, stunned. Duke jumped up beside me and laid his head on my lap, whining. I patted his head absently.

How could someone have gotten access to my card? Apart from when I used them, my cards all stayed in my purse, and my purse remained either in my bedroom, my office, or with me at all times. That meant whoever took it had been close to me at some point.

The temperature seemed to drop ten degrees. I shivered. Was this theft related to whoever had sent me the note? Nate had shared that Darrel Weich was unlikely to be responsible unless he was using an intermediary. Nate had also reluctantly admitted that Ezra seemed to be on the up and up. If anything else had been taken, I would have immediately thought it was related to the note and the previous thefts, but a debit card wasn't like the other things that had gone missing. It had financial value. Any thief might be interested in it, not only one who was obsessed with me.

I glanced back at the purse and stilled. My debit card

wasn't the only thing missing. My driver's license was gone too. There was no reason I could think of for someone to take that unless they either were hoping it would have useful information for guessing the debit card's pin number or they intended to impersonate me—presumably online, since a quick glance at the photo would show anyone in real life that the person wasn't who they were claiming to be.

Duke whimpered, and I realized I'd stopped petting him. He looked up at me, eyes wide with concern. No doubt he could sense my distress.

"It's okay, boy," I whispered. But honestly, I didn't know if it was. If someone could get close enough to me to access my cards, what was to stop them from taking that next step and doing something to me?

Perhaps they'd taken the card before I moved to Nate's place, back when I was being less cautious. I wracked my mind, trying to recall when I'd last used either the debit card or the driver's license, but I came up empty. All I knew was that it hadn't been since Wednesday. I'd been lying low, only moving between Nate's place and my office.

I sighed. I needed to call Nate and update him. He wouldn't take this well, but at least it might provide them with a new lead.

41

NATE

I GRITTED my teeth as Mehrtens and I returned to the police station from the scene of a traffic accident on the side of Destiny Peak. It had been a one-vehicle-car-versus-railing crash, where a group of friends who'd spent the day skiing had taken a bend too quickly, slid on the icy road, and slammed into the protective railing that wrapped around the edge of the corner. The momentum of the crash had partially torn out the railing, and now repairs would be needed, but everyone in the car would be all right. The driver had bruises from the airbag inflating, and one of the passengers was suffering from whiplash, but the paramedics hadn't been too concerned. I felt for the passengers, who'd been badly shaken, but I couldn't help thinking that every avoidance incident like theirs I had to deal with meant less time I could focus on who had it in for Grace, which meant more possibility of the stalker becoming dangerous the way Kennedy's had.

I parked, and Mehrtens threw the door open and

leaped out before I'd even turned off the engine, as if she couldn't wait to get out of the car with me. I didn't blame her. My mood had been foul since we'd struck out on every single lead we had for Grace's case. I tried not to take it out on the team, but they could sense my frustration, and Mehrtens wasn't the only one tiptoeing around me.

She waited for me to join her, and we headed inside. We were halfway up the steps when my phone rang. I dug it out of my pocket and answered without checking Caller ID.

"Sergeant Braddock speaking."

"Nate." It was Grace. "Is now an okay time to talk, or are you in the middle of something?"

"Now is fine." I paused and gestured for Mehrtens to go ahead. She left me alone outside the station's entrance. "What is it?"

"My debit card and driver's license are missing," she said. "Someone withdrew twelve hundred dollars from my account from the ATM this morning."

I closed my eyes and pinched the bridge of my nose. Damn. The situation was escalating. "Are you alone? Do you know when they were taken?"

"I'm not alone. Alice and Duke are with me. I'm not sure when they were taken." I could hear the distress in her voice and hated it. "I'm sorry, I know that's unhelpful."

"It will be fine," I assured her. "This might actually be a good thing. ATMs have cameras. If we can get a warrant for the camera footage, we might be able to identify the perpetrator."

"Really?" Her tone lifted. "Then it could all be over."

"It's possible." I wanted her to keep her optimism but not pin all her hopes on it. "I'll put in a request for a warrant. In the meantime, stay with Alice or someone else you trust. I don't even want you going to my place alone. If the stalker is in town, that means you're in danger. You need to take every precaution."

"I will." Grace sighed. "But it annoys me that I have to be so careful. I know that's just the way it is, but I should be able to live my life without thinking of whether what I'm doing might expose me to someone dangerous."

"I know, honey. It pisses me off too. It's not fair that you have to make changes because of someone else's problems, but your safety matters more to me than what's fair."

"I know it does." She huffed. "I promise I'll be careful. It just makes me angry."

"Hold onto that anger," I urged. I'd rather she felt mad than scared as long as she didn't do anything reckless. "Channel it. Don't let it overwhelm you."

She snorted, and I could picture her rolling her eyes. I got it. I could hardly lecture people about how to deal with their anger.

"Do you have any idea when somebody could have accessed your cards?" I asked, turning my mind to the information I'd need to hunt down her stalker.

She was quiet for a moment, presumably thinking. "The only time I don't have my purse on me is when I'm at home or your place and leave it in another room. Although I guess I leave it in the house while I play outside with Duke sometimes too."

"Nowhere else?"

"Not that I can think of."

I didn't like it. That meant whoever had done this had access to Grace despite the additional security measures we'd put in place.

"Have you reviewed your security footage?" I asked.

"No," she replied. "But I should have been alerted by the new security system if anyone entered the house while I was gone."

"I'll get Mehrtens to check it anyway." Security systems were useful, but all computer-based programs had weaknesses. Perhaps someone had hacked them or otherwise skirted around the system to avoid setting it off. The other possibility, of course, was that the theft had occurred at my place. I didn't want to believe it, but the fact was, my house didn't currently have security in place beyond the basics. The main benefit of having her stay there was that most people would assume she was at home, and anyone outside of her daily life shouldn't know who I was or where I lived. If they'd found us, it was because they'd been watching her and followed her there.

"I'll look too," Grace said. "I'm not in the mood to work now. I can't stop thinking about how close they might have gotten to me." Her voice dropped. "I'm scared, Nate."

"Whoever this is, they won't get to you." My chest filled with deep certainty. I'd do everything I could to protect Grace.

"I hope not." Her voice was strained. "But nothing we've done so far has stopped them. This almost feels like showing off. As if they're just proving they can do whatever they want."

"They can't," I bit out. "We'll find them, and we'll stop them from doing anything like this again."

"I really hope so," she whispered. "Do you need me to come in and make a formal statement?"

"Yes, but don't come alone if you can help it. Bring Alice for support." And to deter anyone who might be watching her from making a move.

"Okay, we'll be there soon."

THE HOUSE SECURITY footage revealed nothing, and while I got a warrant approved for the ATM camera, the bank advised that they wouldn't be able to provide the recording until Monday. I drove home at the end of my shift in brooding silence. Each time I failed to identify Grace's stalker—or even find a clue to their identity—the worse I felt about it in my gut. It reminded me of how badly I'd failed Kennedy. We hadn't figured out that the biggest threat to her safety was right under our noses until it was almost too late, and she hadn't escaped unscathed. She'd been shot, and we'd almost lost her. I couldn't let the same thing happen to Grace.

At the end of the day, I pulled up her drive and jogged to the front door. I knocked and waited. A few moments later, she emerged with Duke at her heels and both Alice and Kennedy close behind. She must have called Kennedy for support, since I hadn't spoken to any of my brothers in order for the word to get back to her that way.

"Any luck?" Alice asked.

"Not yet."

She grimaced. "How long is this person going to get away with causing trouble? It isn't okay."

"I know. I wish I had a different answer for you, but whoever it is, they're careful, and following up leads takes time."

"Sorry. I didn't mean to insult you or your officers," she said. "I'm just frustrated."

"So are we," I said. "Ready, Gracie?"

"Yeah." She tried to smile but it was tremulous. She said a quick goodbye to Alice, then turned and gave Kennedy a fierce hug. Kennedy murmured something to her too quietly for me to hear and kissed her cheek. When they parted, Grace and I loaded into my car. Duke nosed the window, and I wound it down a crack for him. Grace stayed quiet until we arrived at my place and had gone inside.

"Did anything else happen today?" I asked. Her silence was worrying me.

"No." She dragged her hand down her face, her expression so weary, I ached to comfort her. "I'm just tired of this. I feel like I'm always looking over my shoulder, but somehow this person gets what they want anyway."

I pulled her into my arms and held her close. "We'll find them."

Somehow, someway, I would find them and make them regret causing Grace even an ounce of discomfort.

She rested her cheek on my shoulder. "I believe you. I just wish we had more to go on."

"Me too." I kissed her forehead and gently tucked a strand of hair behind her ear. "But when we get the ATM footage on Monday, it might be game over. If we've got their face on camera, we'll nail them." I just had to hope they weren't savvy enough to have thought of the camera ahead of time.

A pair of paws hit the back of my thighs, and I lurched forward, stumbling, and nearly taking Grace with me. I caught myself before falling over and whirled around. Duke stood there, eyes wide, his body language screaming of guilt.

To my surprise, Grace laughed. "I don't think he likes being ignored."

"Needy dog," I grumbled, stooping to give him some love.

"Have you eaten?" Grace asked.

"Not yet. I thought we could cook something together, then perhaps watch *House of the Dragon*."

"Sounds perfect."

We cooked a simple meal of vegetables and chicken, then curled up on the couch together after we'd tidied the dishes away. Duke joined us, burrowing into a spot between me and Grace before falling asleep almost immediately. When the episode we were watching reached a particularly passionate scene, I glanced at Grace and found her watching me steadily, her pupils dilated with need.

"I think we should go to bed," she said, her voice low enough not to disturb Duke.

I liked the wicked glint in her eye. "You sure?"

"One hundred percent."

We slipped off the couch, leaving the dog behind, and raced to my bedroom. Once inside, we each shed our clothes and reached for each other. Our mouths clashed in a heated kiss. Hands fumbled and stroked. Our breaths were sharp in the air between us. We came together in a blaze of fierce desire and emotion. I groaned as I pushed into Grace, feeling like a man possessed. I was desperate to make her fall apart. To get closer and closer to her until we were one. It felt as though if I let her go for even a moment, I might lose her.

We moved together, gasping and writhing. I grabbed Grace's hips and angled her until I hit a sweet spot, and she cried out. I thrust into her mercilessly, over and over, making her mine in every way. When she started growing taut in my arms and arched her back, I knew she was close. I kissed her, relishing her taste, knowing there would never be another woman for me. She moaned and clenched around me, pulling me with her into oblivion.

Still, I didn't let her go. I knew in my heart I never would.

42

———

GRACE

SPENDING a weekend with Nate had been wonderful, but I was grateful to return to work on Monday without him. He'd been glued to my side every minute of the day, as if afraid to let me out of his sight. It was sweet, but I was used to having time to myself. Nate's hovering could be exhausting.

I was sitting at my desk, reviewing what I'd written last week, when Alice entered the office, bringing with her the smell of coffee. I greeted her with a smile. "Have I told you you're the best assistant ever?"

She rolled her eyes. "Almost every time I bring you coffee."

"Well, it's true." I took a cup from her and inhaled the scent. "Delicious."

"It's just as well it wasn't your business account card that was stolen," Alice said. "Could you imagine if someone had emptied that account? You might not be able to afford me, and then you'd have to get your own coffee."

"Oh, the horror." My jaw tightened. I knew she was trying to lighten the mood, but I couldn't help thinking that she had a point. If the thief—the *stalker*—had taken my business debit card instead of my personal one, I could have been in a lot of trouble. While I kept some of my money in a savings account and I had investments, I'd struggle without my business funds.

"Sorry." She winced. "I didn't mean to be insensitive. I was trying to look on the bright side. It could have been worse."

"That's true." I drew in a slow breath and considered her words. She was right. As things went, the damage had been limited. It seemed worse in my mind because of the sense of being violated, but the actual ramifications were minor. "Thanks. I needed to hear that."

"That's what I'm here for." Alice's expression softened. "I'm sorry for what's happening, Gracie." She put her coffee down and rolled her chair over to hug me with one arm. "I can't even imagine how it must feel."

"It's not the best, but you're right, it could have been worse."

We separated, and I turned back to my document.

"So...." She drew the word out.

I glanced over my shoulder at Alice. "Yes?"

"You and Nate, huh? What's going on there?"

I grinned and my shoulders relaxed. I swung back to face her. "We're dating."

"Finally!" She clapped excitedly, looking as thrilled as I felt. "So, who made the first move?"

I shrugged. "Him, if you can believe it. The timing isn't the best, but I'm so happy we've ended up where we are."

She winked one beautifully made-up eye. "I'm glad. You deserve it."

"It's still early days," I added, that voice of caution in my head warning me not to oversell our budding relationship. "I'm not sure if it will go anywhere."

"It will," Alice said confidently. "That man has finally realized what a catch you are. He's not going to let you slip away now."

A smile tugged at my lips. "I hope not."

"Trust me." Alice patted my knee. "It will all work out."

43

NATE

WHOEVER WAS STALKING GRACE, they were smart. The bank sent us their security footage from the ATM as promised, but the person who'd withdrawn cash using Grace's debit card had worn a hat, sunglasses, and a dark jacket that covered everything. They hadn't looked at the camera, and from the angle of the recording, it was impossible to tell the length of their hair. All we could ascertain was that they were white and stood somewhere between five eight and six feet tall—either a tall woman or a man.

On the way home, I dropped by Maddy's place to collect Tess for her week with me. I knocked at the door and waited until Steve answered.

"Nate, hey." He flashed me a grin. "Maddy is just helping Tess pack. We went shopping over the weekend, so she has a few new wardrobe items she'll probably want to show you."

"I'm sure she loved that." I was glad Maddy had taken her shopping. I'd do it when needed, but I avoided it whenever possible. Shopping wasn't my forte. Fortunately, Tess was a pretty low-maintenance kid—with the exception of her book obsession.

"They had a great time." Steve stood aside. "Come in while you wait. They won't be long."

I stepped into the foyer just as Maddy and Tess came into my line of view. Maddy looked harried. She passed Tess a backpack and kissed her forehead.

"Bye, baby," she said. "I'll see you next week, but I expect to hear from you on the phone before then."

"Yes, Mum," Tess said dutifully.

"I love you, Tessie."

"Love you too."

They hugged and Tess crossed from her mum to me. I pulled her into a firm embrace, breathing in the sweet strawberry scent of her hair. God, I missed my daughter while she was away. I didn't know how I'd have coped if I'd ended up with a custody arrangement that gave Maddy weekdays and me weekends or the odd day here and there. I needed a good chunk of time with her.

I passed Tess a key. "Why don't you head out to the car? I'll be there in a minute."

She took the key and waved at Maddy and Steve, then ducked out the door.

"She's had a busy weekend," Maddy told me, her shoulders slumping now that Tess was out of sight. "She might want an early night. God knows I need one."

I chuckled. "Thanks for the heads-up. I'll keep an eye on her. Any problems?"

"Nothing worth mentioning."

"Good."

"I've heard a bit around town about Grace's problems." Maddy sounded cautious. "Tess won't be in danger by staying with you, will she?"

I grimaced. "We'll make sure she's never alone, and

whoever is harassing Grace hasn't given any indication that they'll turn violent."

"They'd better not." Maddy's eyes flashed with temper. "If there's even the faintest hint that she isn't safe with you, I want her back here with me, okay? Your priorities might be torn, but mine are completely clear. Keeping Tess safe is the most important thing."

"My priorities are not torn," I growled. "I'd never do anything to knowingly endanger Tess, you know that, but my job has risks."

"It isn't just about your job though," she said. "It's about Grace, and you're not rational where she's concerned."

I ran my hand over my hair and blew out a frustrated breath, knowing I needed to take a few seconds or I'd say something I regretted. "If there's any sign of physical danger, I'll bring her to you."

She nodded curtly. "Thanks."

"See you next week, if not sooner."

She said goodbye, but I was already getting the hell out of there. I knew Maddy had a point and was only concerned for Tess's welfare, but I didn't like the implication that I didn't care as much as she did.

Tess sat in the passenger's seat, her feet propped on the dash and a book balanced on her knees. I forced myself to calm my breathing and smile at her as I dropped into the driver's seat.

"I hope you don't mind, Grace is staying with us this week." I watched closely for her reaction. Unlike Maddy, I didn't think she'd be bothered, but if she got wind of the fact my relationship with Grace was changing, she might have something to say about it. She loved Grace, but it was impossible to know how she'd react to a change in the status quo.

"Okay." She sounded unconcerned. "All week?"

"We're not sure yet. We're sorting out some stuff for her, so it will depend on when her problems are fixed."

She looked up from her book and frowned at me. "What kind of problems?"

"The type you don't need to worry about."

She huffed but turned her attention back to her book.

When we arrived home, Duke bounded out to greet us. Tess cuddled him with a level of enthusiasm she hadn't shown me, but I could hardly complain. The dog was much cuter than I was. We found Grace in the kitchen, cooking something that smelled amazing.

"What are you making?" I asked.

"Fish kofta with rice and flatbread. One of Desdemona's recipes." She glanced over and, catching sight of Tess, smiled. "Hey, you."

"Hi, Grace." Tess went to the stovetop and peered into the pot Grace was cooking the kofta in. "Is that for dinner?"

"It is. If you're willing to give it a try."

Tess nodded. "Yes, please."

"It'll be ready in ten minutes," Grace added, directing the comment to me. "I'll dish up if you want to get changed. Since it can be a messy meal, I thought we'd eat at the table instead of on the sofa."

"Sounds great." I was just grateful not to have to come up with anything for dinner myself. My creativity was limited and my recipe repertoire small. "Thanks so much for cooking. It smells delicious."

She smiled, and her eyes softened in a way they never used to. It felt intimate, as if she was sending a special message just for me. "Let's hope you enjoy it."

I went to my bedroom and changed from work clothes into a pair of worn jeans and a T-shirt. When I returned to the living area, Tess was already seated at the dinner table, still reading, and Grace was serving portions of kofta and rice onto plates.

"What can I do to help?" I asked.

She gestured along the kitchen counter. "Can you dish up the flatbreads and move them to the table, please?"

"Absolutely." I did as she asked, pausing to appreciate the scent of freshly baked bread. Was there anything better? Once I'd done that, I poured a glass of water for Tess, a wine for Grace, and cracked the top off a beer for myself. Grace carried the plates to the table, and we all sat. I looked meaningfully at Tess and cleared my throat. Without taking her eyes from the page until the last possible second, she inserted a bookmark and closed it.

"Tell me about your weekend," I said to Tess. "Steve mentioned that you went shopping with your mum."

"We did." Tess's face scrunched with concentration, and she began cutting into a kofta. "We went to Queenstown and got new leggings and shirts and a new pair of shoes for school, then we went to a bookstore, and Mum let me choose three books." Her tone was reverent. I grinned. It was cute how much she loved bookstores. She could never come out without at least one purchase.

"What else did you do?" Grace asked.

"We went up the gondola and came down the luge." Tess stuffed her mouth full and swallowed before continuing. "I didn't want to do the luge at first. I thought it looked dangerous, and I was scared I might get hurt, but Mum showed me how to control the speed, and it ended up being fine."

"That's great, sweetheart. It's good to try new things sometimes, but also know that you don't have to if it ever makes you uncomfortable."

She nodded as though that was obvious.

While we ate, we chatted more about her trip to Queenstown, and then Grace updated Tess on where she was at with the story she was writing. I'd have to see if she'd consider making a kid-friendly version so Tess could read it when she'd finished. At one point, I noticed Tess slip Duke a piece of bread under the table and narrowed my eyes at her. She smiled angelically, clearly pretending the dog's loud eating noises couldn't be heard from only a few feet away.

After dinner, I cleaned up while Tess did her homework and Grace took Duke out the back to burn off the last of his energy before he turned in for the night. When we'd finished, we met in the living room and put on one of Tess's favorite shows about a group of teenage witches. I wrapped an arm around each of my girls, and a sense of contentment settled over me unlike anything I could ever recall. The three of us felt like a family. I basked in the perfection of the moment. This was how things were supposed to be. I'd never had this feeling with Maddy, and I realized now that it was because she hadn't been the right woman for me. I wouldn't change my past for anything because being with her had given me Tess, but I was destined for Grace, not Maddy.

When the second episode of the show finished, I took a sleepy Tess to bed and tucked her in, then returned to Grace. She hadn't moved from the couch, and Duke had jumped up to take my place beside her. I sat on the other side and drew her close, planting a soft kiss on her lips.

"You are incredible," I said. "Seeing you is one of the best parts of my day."

Her lips curved into an endearingly shy smile. "This feels really natural between us, doesn't it?"

"Yeah," I agreed, kissing her again.

She curled against me and rested her head on my shoulder. "I'm scared that it's all going to disappear."

My fists clenched instinctively. "It won't," I promised. "It might have taken me a long time to wake up to what was in front of me, but we're the real thing, and I'm going to do whatever it takes every day to prove it to you."

She tilted her face up for another kiss. I gave it to her. Then another and another. Eventually, I carried her to my room and made sweet, tender love with her until all the doubts had hopefully been erased from her mind.

44

———————

GRACE

"How's everything looking?" I asked Alice.

She raised her head and slipped her headphones off her ears, giving me a thumbs up. "It's good on the release front. The negative reviews aren't all gone, but they're outweighed by the positive ones." She grinned. "You're lucky your readers love you so much."

"I know." I let out a sigh of relief. "I really am. They're incredible."

Alice and I had done everything we could to salvage my book release, and now it was just a matter of letting the cards fall where they may. So far, sales had picked up, and while we hadn't undone the damage caused by the wrong file going out, the situation could be worse.

I glanced at my phone. "Want to get lunch at Taste of Destiny? My treat."

"Seriously? That would be great. Let me just do one last thing." She turned back to her computer.

I stood and stretched, my back protesting because I'd

been hunched over my laptop all day. I clucked my tongue, and Duke sprang to his feet and followed me out. I grabbed a treat from the pantry and put him in the backyard. Ryan and I had set up a doghouse for him, but he hadn't used it much, since he usually went wherever I did. Unfortunately, I didn't trust him alone in the house for an hour or two while we were at the cafe, so he'd have to make do.

By the time I got back to the office, Alice had her handbag over her shoulder and was ready to go.

"Walk or drive?" she asked.

"Let's walk," I suggested. "It isn't far, and I could use some fresh air."

"So, have you and Nate told Tess you're dating?" Alice asked as we walked.

"Not yet." Although come to think of it, we ought to discuss if and when that might happen. "I guess we'll probably wait until we're sure it's going somewhere."

Alice rolled her eyes. "You guys have been friends for half your lives. I doubt you'd have crossed a line unless you thought it would go somewhere."

"There's no point in rushing," I said. "We have plenty of time."

We arrived at Taste of Destiny, and the place was buzzing, with a line of customers out the door. A pair of elderly ladies were leaving a table in front of the window that looked onto Centennial Street, and Alice swooped in and claimed it as soon as they were gone.

"What would you like?" I asked Alice. "I'll order."

"One of their rosemary scones and a side salad, please. Coffee too."

"Got it." I went to the back of the line, taking a moment to study the other patrons while I waited my turn. Most were tourists, although I saw a few locals. London, who ran the animal shelter and riding school, was seated at a table opposite Cal, her boyfriend and Summer Braddock's business partner. Many people thought Cal and London were an unlikely couple, but their connection was obvious to anyone who cared to look. London practically glowed when they were together, and Cal's eyes softened every time they landed on her. My heart squeezed. I wanted that with Nate.

I gave Eden my order, took a number, and went back to our table, surprised to see that Summer had joined Alice. Summer, the only Braddock sister, had the same blonde hair as her brothers. Her eyes as she glanced up and smiled at me were a mossy shade of green that sparkled with intelligence.

"Hey, Summer." I placed the number in the center of our table and sat. "I'm surprised you're here. I'd have thought either you or Cal would need to be at the clinic."

She shrugged. "We decided to close for an hour over lunch. We both had chaotic mornings, so we need the time away."

Alice winked. "The perks of owning your own business, right?"

"It is pretty good," Summer agreed.

"Have you ordered?" I asked.

"Yeah. I asked for it to go but then saw Alice and thought I'd say hi." She leveled a mischievous look at me. "I heard through the grapevine that Nate finally got a clue. Rumor or fact?"

My heart skipped a beat. "Who told you that?"

As far as I knew, we hadn't shared our changed status widely—unless, of course, Alice had spilled the beans. She loved a juicy piece of gossip, but she usually knew when to be tight-lipped.

"Oh, don't glare at Alice." Summer laughed. "It was Maddy who told me. She brought their cat in for its yearly vaccinations this morning. She assumed I already knew."

I winced. "It's still early days, and we haven't talked about when we're going to tell people, so I'd appreciate it if you could keep it to yourself. Honestly, I didn't even know Nate had told Maddy." I couldn't hold it against him though. Transparency was important when it came to co-parenting.

"My lips are sealed," she promised. "But can I just say how happy I am for you?" She bounced in her seat, her smile stretching from ear to ear. "I've always considered you a sister, and it would make me so pleased for it to finally be official."

Her words made me warm and gooey inside. "I love you, Summer."

"Back at you, Gracie." She grabbed my hand and squeezed it. "Seriously, Nate is lucky to have you. I hope he realizes that."

"Thanks." I squeezed her hand back, then let it go. "But dating Nate or not, you'll always be my sister of the heart. That doesn't change."

"N'aww!" Alice clapped excitedly. "You guys are just too cute."

Summer rolled her eyes. She was about to reply when Eden called her name. She stood, intending to get her order, and nearly smacked into Asher, who was coming the other way.

He grunted and steadied her. "Be careful where you're going, Baby Braddock."

Summer scowled. "Maybe you should be careful not to get in my way."

Alice and I exchanged a glance. Every time Asher and Summer were near each other, sparks practically exploded between them. Based on the longing looks Summer directed at him when she thought no one was watching, I knew she yearned for him to see her as more than his best friend's little sister. She'd had a crush on Liam's broad-shouldered, dark-haired friend as a teenager, and it had never faded. I felt a pang of sympathy. I knew what that was like. Asher, on the other hand, was a dark horse. I'd never been able to tell what he really thought of her.

"Whatever." Asher stepped around her to address us. "Mind if I take that last seat while I wait for my order to be called?"

"Go for it," Alice said.

I watched Summer's back as she headed for the counter, wondering whether she'd return or take her food to go. With Asher around, I couldn't be sure either way. She seemed to take the opposite route to what I had with Nate and went out of her way to antagonize him—which wasn't hard, since he had a short fuse. In the end, she did come back, although perhaps only to spite him.

I was grateful when a waitress brought our lunch over and even more grateful when Asher left. I liked him well enough, but he made Summer tense, and I found it difficult to relax when my companions were on edge. The three of us chatted while we ate, and it occurred to me that we should do this more often.

Eventually, Alice and I headed home. But by the time we got there, I wasn't feeling so great. My stomach was cramped and bloated.

"Are you okay?" Alice asked, her brow furrowed with concern.

"Not really," I admitted. "Maybe I ate something that was off. I might lie down for a while. Do you have enough work to get on with?"

"Of course. I always do." She nibbled her lip. "Should I call Max to set up an appointment?"

"No. Hopefully I'll have a nap and be fine after."

But that wasn't what happened.

45

NATE

MY SHIFT WAS NEARLY over when my phone rang. I groaned. Hopefully there hadn't been an accident or anything that would mean I'd have to work overtime. I'd been looking forward to an evening with Grace and Tess. I withdrew my phone from my pocket and relaxed. It was just Tess.

"Hi, sweetheart," I answered.

"Hi, Dad. Something is wrong with Grace." Tess sounded distraught. "I went to her place after school like you said, since your shift hadn't finished yet, and she's in bed, throwing up. Alice is still here, and she's sick too. What should I do? Grace looks really bad."

Worry curled in my stomach. "Have you asked her if she knows what's wrong?"

"She says it might be food poisoning," Tess replied. "She and Alice both had lunch at the cafe today and started feeling sick not long after that."

At least if Grace had been able to communicate that much, she probably had enough presence of mind to know whether she needed a hospital or not. The fact that she'd chosen to go to bed instead of calling for help probably meant she didn't think it was anything major.

"Okay. You did the right thing by letting me know. I'm going to see if Max can come over and take a look at them. Did anyone else have lunch with them?"

"Um, hang on." I heard the sound of movement and then faint voices. When Tess returned, she said, "Summer was with them, but she ate something different. Alice said she and Grace both had salad."

"That's good to know. I'll be home as soon as I can, sweetheart. If either of them gets worse, call me back. Promise?"

"Yeah." Her voice was small. "Please come soon."

My heart squeezed at the plea in her voice. "I will. Love you."

I said goodbye and ended the call, then placed another to Max, who said he'd just finished at the Medical Center and would drop by immediately. Next, I called Summer.

"Sick?" she asked when I put the question to her. "No, I'm fine. Why?"

I explained what had happened with Grace and Alice.

"Do you think I should visit and bring them dinner?" She sounded concerned.

"I'm sure Alice would appreciate that, but Grace is staying with me, so Tess and I will make sure she's taken care of."

"Oh, I bet you will." Her tone was heavy with innuendo.

"What's that supposed to mean?" I demanded.

She laughed. "Nothing. Don't stress. Hopefully, this is just some kind of twenty-four-hour bug, and they'll both be fine tomorrow."

"Hopefully," I agreed.

We said our goodbyes, and I made one last phone call, to the cafe.

"Taste of Destiny. Eden speaking." The girl was out of breath. Perhaps there had been a last-minute rush before closing.

"Eden, it's Nate Braddock. I need to know if you've had any reported cases of food poisoning today."

"God no." She sounded shocked. "Why? The boss would have my head if something like that happened."

I hesitated, unsure whether to worry her when the illness could be completely unrelated to the cafe. "It might be nothing, but Grace and Alice ate lunch there, and now they're sick."

She gasped.

"Like I said, it might not be related," I hurried to add. "But if you get any other calls, please let me know."

"I will." She groaned. "Is it wrong for me to say I hope they've just caught a stomach bug?"

"I get it."

"I hope they're okay. Keep me updated?"

"You bet."

I hung up and checked the time again. I could officially clock out. I hunted down the officer who'd be in charge of the night shift and briefed him on the day's activities, then shut down my computer at record speed and rushed to Grace's place.

I had to park outside the neighbor's property since Alice's car was up the drive and Max's was parked along Grace's frontage. There was a light on in the cottage, but the house looked dark from here. Presumably, they were in the private quarters on the other side of the building. I unlocked the door and flicked on the hall light. Duke appeared from around a corner, his tail wagging. He barked once in greeting but didn't make a fuss.

"Where's your owner?" I asked, bending to scratch behind his ear. He leaned into the scratch, his tongue lolling out the side of his mouth.

I headed into the private living room. Alice lay on the couch, her head on a pillow, her complexion pale. Max knelt beside her, taking her temperature. He didn't look up until he'd finished.

"Hey," I said.

Max nodded at me, then turned back to Alice. "Your temperature is up but not enough to cause concern. Based on your symptoms and what you've told me, it's likely you've got a mild case of food poisoning. It's possible something in the salad wasn't washed properly. Whatever it is, you seem to be better off than Grace, which makes me think she ate more of the contaminated food than you did."

I frowned, his comment triggering a question in my mind. If Alice wasn't as unwell as Grace, was it possible that this might not be an accident? Could someone have tried to poison Grace, and Alice was just collateral damage?

"Where's Grace?" I asked.

"In her bedroom." Alice was clearly miserable. "Tess is there too."

"Thanks." I hesitated, uncertain what to say to her or whether to voice my suspicions. In the end, I decided I'd keep it to myself until I had the chance to speak to Max alone. "Is it likely to be contagious?"

"It's hard to know for sure," Max said. "If it's food poisoning, then no. But don't worry, I had Tess put on a surgical mask and told her to keep a little distance between herself and Grace, so she's unlikely to be exposed any more than she already has been."

"I appreciate it." I nodded to them and went to find my girls.

Grace lay on her back beneath the covers. Her hair was a

mess, and her skin was even waxier than Alice's. A cold compress rested on her forehead, and her eyes were open just wide enough to see me as I entered. Tess sat on the floor against the wall. Her expression crumpled with relief at the sight of me, and she scrambled up and threw her arms around me.

"It's okay." I soothed her. "Grace is going to be fine. She just looks a little worse for wear."

"Exactly what every woman wants to hear," Grace muttered from the bed.

"You're still beautiful," I replied automatically, then froze, realizing I shouldn't have said something like that in front of Tess, but my daughter didn't seem to pick up on it.

Max cleared his throat from the doorway. "Alice is fine to go home, although I'd prefer for someone to drive her there. I've told her to keep her fluids up, and the same goes for you, Grace. Plenty of water and take it easy. Neither of you should work tomorrow. Your bodies need time to recover."

"Okay," Grace agreed. The fact that she didn't argue spoke volumes about how poorly she must feel. She rarely took time off even if she was sick.

"If you start feeling worse, call me," Max said. "No matter what time it is."

"We will." I joined him and we walked to the exit together. "Thanks for coming."

"No problem." He grimaced. "I hate seeing them like that."

"Me too." I glanced around to make sure I hadn't been followed, then lowered my voice. "Is there any chance this might not have been an accident? Could someone have poisoned them intentionally?"

Max's eyebrows flew up. "Why would you ask that?"

I explained the situation with Grace, watching as his face grew graver.

"I didn't realize it had gotten so serious." He tapped his chin thoughtfully. "Yes, there are poisons that could have produced these symptoms, or if someone had access to their food or drinks, they could have knowingly introduced a contaminated food or liquid. It might not have happened at the cafe, although considering the security system in place here, that would be the most likely place."

My stomach clenched. "Are there any tests you could do to confirm whether or not it was poison?"

Max shrugged. "If it was a chemical poison, sure, but if it was just contaminated food, there's no way to be certain. I could draw blood for a test, but it will take time and money to get the results."

I nodded. "Do it."

46

—————

GRACE

After a restless night broken by intermittent rushed trips to the bathroom, I felt even worse than yesterday. Logically, I knew that my stomach had improved and it was just the throbbing in my head that made me so miserable, but that didn't stop me from wallowing in self-pity. Some days called for a little moping, and this was one of them.

I must have looked awful, because Tess was able to convince Nate to let her stay home from school to keep me company—on the condition that she wear a mask and keep a safe distance. Kennedy came by to see me too, but I slept through most of her visit.

When I woke again, my head was less fuzzy. I glanced at the clock and saw it was just after noon. Tess was curled up in an armchair Nate had dragged into the room, her feet tucked beneath her and a book on her lap. My mouth felt dry, so I gingerly sat up and looked for my water bottle. I sipped, grateful for the coolness in my mouth until my tummy started feeling queasy from the water sloshing around the empty space. I lay back against the cushion again.

"Are you hungry?" Tess asked.

"A little," I admitted. "I'll get up and make some lunch soon."

"No, you won't." Her tone was surprisingly stern. "Dad says you're not to get out of bed unless it's to use the bathroom."

Yes, that sounded like Nate. He somehow managed to be both caring and bossy, even from a distance.

"Is soup all right?" Tess put her book down and extended her legs. "We have some of that chicken noodle stuff where you just add hot water. I could bring you some bread too if you want."

Even though the thought of food made me feel nauseated, I forced myself to nod. Regardless of whether I wanted to eat, I needed to at least try. Without fuel, how was my body supposed to recover?

"That would be lovely."

I dozed off again, only waking when Tess murmured my name. I sat up, and she passed me a tray upon which were a small bowl of chicken soup and a hunk of wholegrain bread.

"Thank you, Tess," I said. "It's so sweet of you to look after me."

She went back to her spot on the armchair and picked up her book again. "I don't mind. I get the day off school, and I like spending time with you. You're the only person who doesn't think it's weird that I read all the time." She bit her lip and tilted her sweet face toward me. "Mum and Dad buy me books and take me to the library, which is really cool, but they don't get it like you do."

Tess's confession warmed my heart.

"Reading is wonderful," I agreed. "It's one of my favorite

things. My parents didn't understand either. They both had more important things to do with their time."

Tess scowled. "More important than reading?"

If I didn't feel so awful, I might have laughed. "So they said." I tried not to harbor resentment against them, but sometimes I couldn't help it. They hadn't exactly been nurturing and supportive. "You're lucky to have your mum and dad."

"I know." Her nose crinkled. "Some of the kids at school whose parents are divorced seem sad all of the time, and their parents are always angry. Mum and Dad have never been like that, although Dad gets angry sometimes."

"He feels things strongly," I said diplomatically.

I scooped a spoonful of soup and tentatively sipped it. It wasn't bad, although my stomach wanted to revolt. Hopefully if I took it slow, the soup would stay down.

"Mum was angry the other day too," Tess said. "She's not normally like that. Maybe she was having strong feelings."

I frowned, unsure whether I should ask more. Maddy wasn't my business. But if Tess wanted to confide in me, I'd listen. "I'm sorry."

She shrugged. "She said that Dad is being selfish and that he's stupid when it comes to anything to do with his perfect, beloved Gracie. Do you know what she meant?"

Ouch. "I'm not sure."

Although I could hazard a guess. Maddy probably didn't approve of Tess being near me given my potentially dangerous situation. Honestly, if that was the case, I didn't blame her. Although I supposed it was also possible she was upset because Nate and I had gotten together.

"Oh." Tess looked disappointed. As I raised the spoon to my mouth, she asked, "Can I tell you a secret?"

"Sure. If you like." I hoped it wasn't anything else about her mother. That would be awkward.

She glanced around as though expecting an eavesdropper to appear from nowhere. "Sometimes, I come up with my own stories."

I smiled. "You're a writer?"

She toyed with the pages of her book. "Not like you are. Nobody will want to read my stories."

My heart ached for her. "Oh, sweetie. I'd like to read one someday, but only when you're comfortable with it."

She squirmed in her chair, obviously feeling awkward about what she'd shared. "I want to get it perfect first."

I sighed. "I feel that. But being perfect isn't everything, because you're going to get better every day. So what's perfect for you today might not be perfect for you tomorrow. You've just got to do the best you can and be proud of it."

She smiled shyly at me. "I can do that."

She opened her book and started reading. It was only after I'd finished my meal and closed my eyes that she spoke again.

"When I'm ready, I want you to be the first person to read one of my stories."

Emotion swelled within me. God, I adored this beautiful girl. Tears prickled at the backs of my eyes, and I blinked them away. I loved Tess just as much as I did her father. I'd never stood a chance of resisting her. She and her dad had my whole heart.

47

___

NATE

WHEN I ARRIVED home in the evening, I went straight to the bedroom to check on Grace and was surprised to find her sitting upright, a book on her lap. In the neighboring armchair, Tess looked like her mini-me. My heart warmed. Could anything be more perfect than coming home to these two?

I kissed Grace's cheek, then Tess's.

"You look better," I told Grace.

"Thanks." She smiled. "I was feeling pretty terrible until a few hours ago, but I'm much better now. Tess has been taking great care of me. She made soup and wouldn't let me out of bed."

"Good job." I patted Tess's shoulder. "I knew I could count on you."

Tess beamed. "I even made sure she drank a glass of water every hour because Uncle Max said she needed water."

I grinned. My daughter was incredible. I had no idea

how I'd created her. I'd been a little shit at her age, more interested in playing outdoors and getting as muddy as possible than in helping others.

"That's great, sweetheart." I touched the backs of my fingers to Grace's forehead. It was warmer than usual but only barely. "Do you think you're up for dinner at the table?"

She smirked. "If I'm allowed to leave the bed."

"Yeah, yeah." I rolled my eyes. "Get up. I'm going to change and dig around in the freezer. I think Mum put a casserole in there a while ago."

"I can help," she said.

"Nope, not going to happen. You just sit down at the table and take it easy."

There was a knock at the door.

I frowned. "Expecting anyone?"

"Desdemona said she might drop by after closing," Grace replied. "It could be her. I'll check."

"No, I'll do it." I turned to Tess. "Make sure Grace goes directly to the living room and sits down, will you?"

"Yes, Dad."

I winked. "You're my number one."

I left the room, noticing as I exited that Duke was curled on a bed in the corner, dozing. Hopefully he hadn't been too hyperactive today.

At the front door, I opened it a crack and peered through, then opened it all the way as Desdemona's face framed with purple dreadlocks came into view.

"Hello, Nathan." She patted my cheek like I was a child, and the scent of patchouli and something else—*was that weed?*—wafted toward me. "I woke up this morning and knew that something was wrong with Grace. I need to do a reading for her." She held up the small wooden box I knew she kept her tarot cards in. "How is she?"

"Much better now than she was." I stepped aside to let

her in, my nose crinkling as I got another hint of that darker scent. "They should be in the living room. I'm cooking dinner. Would you like to stay?"

"That would be lovely." She glided down the hall, her gauzy coat billowing behind her, making her look almost supernatural. I shook my head. Now I was being fanciful. Desdemona had her quirks, that was all.

I went to the kitchen and found the casserole in the freezer. I started defrosting it and peeled carrots and potatoes to accompany the meal. While I was working, I listened carefully to Desdemona and Grace, who'd moved to the dining table so Desdemona could do her tarot reading. She made a few comments as she turned cards over, none of which made much sense, but as she drew the reading to a close, she said something that chilled me.

"Someone is deceiving you."

A shiver rippled along my spine.

Someone is deceiving you.

I didn't put much stock in the woo-woo practices Desdemona structured her life around, but I had noticed that she was an unusually perceptive woman, and her words had a ring of truth about them.

Grace laughed halfheartedly. "That sounds sinister."

"In this case, it may well be," Desdemona replied. "Tread carefully, dearest."

Grace choked out an acknowledgment, sounding as disturbed as I felt, then she changed the topic, asking Desdemona how her shop was doing. They talked for a while, and then we all ate together.

Not long after dinner, Desdemona announced that she had to go home and feed her cat. I offered to walk her out.

As we reached the door, she put her hand on my arm and stopped. "So, Nathan, what do you need to ask me?"

I was only slightly surprised she knew I had an ulterior motive for wanting to get her alone.

"You said that someone is deceiving Grace. Do you know who?"

She sighed. "I wish I did, but no." Her gaze turned speculative. "You'll keep watch over her for me, won't you? You love her as much as I do, even if the shape of that love has recently changed."

My mouth dropped open and I gaped. "You know?"

She waggled her eyebrows. "Not much slips past me, even if my eyesight isn't as good as it used to be."

I chuckled. "So it would seem. Don't worry, I'll keep her safe."

"Good." She patted my cheek the same way she'd done when she arrived and breezed out the door into the darkness of the night.

I returned to the living room. Tess was reading in the armchair, and Grace was napping on the couch.

"Psst," I hissed.

Tess glanced up and cocked an eyebrow. I gestured at the door. She got up and followed me out. A snuffling sound and rapid footsteps indicated Duke had come too. I went to Tess's bedroom and sat on her bed, which was neatly made, in stark contrast to mine.

"I have an important question for you, Tessie," I told her. I was nervous, but having Desdemona guess that Grace and I were now together had reinforced the fact I needed to discuss it with my daughter before someone else let the cat out of the bag.

"What is it?" She looked worried. "Something about Mum? I know she was angry at you."

"No, nothing like that." I gave her a quick hug. "It's not bad—or at least, I don't think so."

"Okay."

I sucked in a breath, let it go, and told myself to get it over with. "How would you feel if I dated Grace?"

Tess's forehead furrowed in confusion. "You mean, if she was your girlfriend, like when Mum and Steve got together?"

"That's right."

She seemed to think for a moment. "What would change? You guys spend all your time together anyway."

I considered my words carefully. "Well, for starters, it would mean we might live together one day, and if that went well, maybe we'd marry."

I'd never thought I'd marry again. Maddy did a number on my self-confidence when it came to being a good partner, but I was starting to see that had more to do with how wrong we were for each other and less to do with me personally. Now, I was open to the idea. Especially if Grace was the woman who'd become my wife.

To my surprise, Tess launched herself into my arms. I embraced her, unsure whether she was excited or upset. I waited, trying to gage her mood. When she backed away, I realized she was smiling.

"If Grace lived here, then I'd get to see her even more." She sounded thrilled. "Grace is already family in my heart. If you got married, then she'd be my family properly—like a stepmum, except not an evil one. I'd like that."

My heart full, I scooped her into another hug. "I'm so glad you feel that way."

She looped her arms around my neck. "I love weddings."

I huffed a laugh. "The wedding is a while away yet. I've got to ask her first, and who knows? Maybe living with me will drive her crazy first."

"It won't," she said with the complete confidence of a child.

I really hope not.

I wanted this thing with Grace to go all the way. House, wedding, pets, family. But before that, we needed to find out who meant her harm.

48

———

GRACE

It was a subdued author and assistant who showed up at the office on Thursday. Despite sleeping well and being healthy enough to get out of bed, I still didn't feel completely better, and Alice looked worse for wear as well. She'd only applied mascara and lip gloss and hadn't bothered to style her hair. For her, that was the equivalent of moping around in unwashed clothes.

"I'm so sorry," I said to her when we were each seated behind our respective computers.

"What for? Food poisoning? It's not as if it was your fault."

I pursed my lips, debating whether to share Nate's theory that the poisoning may have been deliberate, but if Alice had been caught in the crossfire, she deserved to know. "It might not have been an accident."

"What?" That had her attention.

I ran my hand through my hair. "Nate thinks there's a

possibility someone intentionally contaminated our food because they wanted to hurt me."

"No!" Alice's eyes widened, and she covered her mouth with her hand. "Who would do something like that?"

"I don't know." I wished I did. "But if you want to work from home until we figure it out, I'll understand. I don't want you to be at risk."

"Hell no." Her shock was beginning to fade, and she looked outraged. "I'm not letting some creep dictate our lives. Screw them."

"Are you sure?" I prompted. "You can take some time to think about it. Your safety might be on the line."

"No." She shook her head, expression determined. "I'm not leaving you."

"But what if—"

A ringing phone interrupted. I grabbed it from the desktop and checked the screen, then frowned. It was Ryan. I hadn't expected to hear from him, and it was unusual for him to call during the day.

"Hold on, I'd better take this." I stood and excused myself from the room, closing the door behind me with both Alice and Duke on the other side. I clicked the Answer symbol. "Hi, Ryan."

"Are you okay?" Panic filled my ex's voice.

I halted abruptly, nearly tripping over my own feet. "Yes, why?"

"Thank god." A shuddering breath came over the line. "I was so worried."

"Why?" I demanded. "What's going on?"

He released another long breath, then seemed to gather himself. "Darrel Weich was just here."

I turned cold inside. "Where? At your place?"

"No, at the tattoo parlor." His tone was strained. "He

barreled into the shop and started yelling about how you were in danger and he needed to save you."

My knees felt weak. I put my hand on the wall to steady myself. This was a nightmare. I'd gotten Darrel Weich out of my life and hadn't heard from him since, but with one act, it was as if I was back where I'd been five years ago.

"Do you think he'll try to kidnap me again?" I asked tremulously.

"I don't know." He sounded exasperated. "I tried to ask what he wanted, but he wouldn't talk sense. I got close enough to touch his shoulder and tell him to calm down so I could understand what he was saying, but then he grabbed me and slammed me against the wall. After that, he freaked out and ran before anyone could stop him."

I clutched the phone tighter. "Do you know where he was going?"

"No, but he was seriously worked up about something. If there's even a chance he could have figured out where you live, you need to get out of there."

"I will." I bit my lip hard to ground myself in the present. I couldn't let the trauma of the past dig its claws into me or I wouldn't stay calm enough to do what needed to be done. "Thanks for calling. I'm sorry he barged in there. I hope it didn't cause you too much trouble."

Ryan scoffed. "Don't be ridiculous. It's not your fault the guy lost it. I'm just sorry we didn't stop him from leaving." He hesitated, then added, "Seriously, Grace. Go somewhere safe. Lie low. And please let me know you're okay. If I don't hear from you, I'll worry."

"I'll keep in touch," I promised. "I doubt he found me or he wouldn't have come to the parlor, but even if he has and he's coming here, you gave me a good head start."

"I hope it's enough."

"It will be."

We said goodbye, and I pushed off from the wall, swaying slightly as I tried to straighten. I made it to the living room and flopped onto the sofa, then I opened the contacts on my phone and found Nate's number. He answered on the second ring.

"Hey, Gracie. Do you feel sick again? I knew you should have stayed home."

"Nate," I said more firmly than I thought I was capable of in my current mindset.

He stopped rambling. "Yeah?"

"Ryan called." As calmly as I could, I explained what had happened. Nate's responses grew terser with each detail. I could tell he was pissed. He viewed Weich's actions as a personal affront because Weich was disturbing my life and Nate had assigned himself as my protector.

"I'm glad you called me immediately," he said. "I'm going to issue an alert for people to be on the lookout for Weich. In the meantime, can you and Alice pack everything you need and go to either my place or hers?"

"We'll go to yours," I agreed, knowing Alice liked to keep her work out of her home as much as possible.

"Good. Make sure you aren't alone. We don't know where Weich is, but it sounds as if he's had some kind of mental break, and he might be dangerous."

"I'll stay with Alice," I promised. If he turned up, Alice would probably fight him herself. She was fierce like that.

"Thanks, Gracie." His voice softened. "If we find anything, you'll be the first to know."

49

GRACE

"THAT MUST BE MADDY," I said, hearing a knock on the door. "Tess, are you all packed?"

Tess nodded, her eyes downcast. Nate had called Maddy and asked her to take care of Tess until he could locate Darrel Weich. On the off chance my former stalker was able to find us, he didn't want to risk Tess getting involved. I knew it was hard for him to ask Maddy to step in. He worried that she might see it as either his new relationship or his job interfering with his ability to be a good parent. While he hadn't outright said it, I suspected his dedication to his job had caused problems in their marriage.

"Grab your pack, then," I urged. "We better not keep your mum waiting."

Tess stood and slung her backpack over her shoulder. "Grace," she said hesitantly.

"Yes, sweetie?"

"Dad isn't sending me away because I did something to upset him, is he?"

"Oh, honey, of course not." I hugged her with every fiber of my being. "I promise, it has nothing to do with you. There's something going on at work that means you're best to stay with your mum for a little while, but he isn't upset with you, and we'll see you again really soon."

She gnawed on her lip. "You promise?"

"I do." I kissed her forehead. "Come on."

Tess looked brighter as we opened the door to greet Maddy.

Maddy pulled Tess close and wrapped an arm around her. "Hi, baby girl. I'm so excited I get to spend some extra time with you."

Tess perked up further.

"Thanks for taking her," I murmured to Maddy.

"No problem." She ruffled Tess's hair. "Can you go sit in the car? Mummy just needs to talk to Grace for a few minutes."

Tess glanced from one of us to the other, suspicious, but she agreed.

"Don't forget to lock the doors," Maddy reminded her. She adjusted her stance so she could keep one eye on the car and Tess inside it. "Grace, I just wanted to say that I'm sorry about the problems you're having. I know you and I haven't always gotten along, and it upsets me that Tess might have been exposed to danger because of whatever is going on, but I do hope everything turns out all right for you."

I blinked at her, no idea how to respond. Although we'd known each other for years, this was the first time she'd been warm toward me. I'd never expected it.

"Um, thanks." I gave a weak smile. "Hopefully it won't be for long. If it stretches on, I'll go and stay with Kennedy and Liam instead. It's not fair to interfere with Nate's ability to see Tess."

Maddy rolled her eyes. "As if he'd let you out of his sight."

My lips parted, and I forced myself not to stare. What did she mean by that? If it came down to spending time with me or his daughter, I wouldn't let him choose me. His relationship with Tess was more important. But my fingers were crossed that the situation would be short-lived.

"I can out stubborn him," I muttered.

She arched a brow. "Maybe, but I'm not sure you'll choose to. We both know how long you've wanted him."

I winced, but she didn't sound angry. She was just stating facts.

"Stay safe," she said, and with a nod, she left.

I turned to go back inside. As I was locking the door behind me, my phone rang in the other room. I hurried to find it. Alice met me in the hall and handed the phone to me.

"It's Max," she mouthed.

I answered and raised it to my ear. "Hi, Max."

"Evening, Grace." He sounded relaxed, and tension leached from my shoulders. Nothing was wrong, then. "I'm just calling to check on my favorite patient."

I smiled and gestured for Alice to precede me to the living room. "I'm on the road to recovery. Alice is too. She's here at the moment."

"I'm glad to hear it. Have you been taking it easy as I suggested?"

"Yes, doctor." I laughed. "We worked a little this morning, and we've been watching a movie for the last couple of hours."

"Good." I could hear the smile in his voice. "Are Tess and Nate home?"

"No. Nate hasn't finished work yet, and Tess just left with her mother."

"She did? Why?"

I explained the day's excitement.

"It was a good decision to send Tess away," Max said. "We can't let anything happen to her."

"I know, and Maddy was good about it." I hesitated, then added, "Actually, it was a bit strange, considering Tess made it sound as though she was quite upset about things."

He hummed in thought. "Good for her. I think she's matured a lot since meeting Steve. Either that or...." He trailed off.

"Or what?" I asked when he didn't finish the sentence.

"No, it's nothing." He sounded distracted. "Forget I said anything."

I frowned. "Or what, Max? I need to know what you meant."

He sighed, and I could picture him rubbing his temples in frustration. "Look, it was a stupid thought. I just, for a few seconds, wondered if Maddy could be the one behind your recent problems. I know she used to be jealous of you. Maybe she blames you for her failed marriage."

I laughed in disbelief. "Maddy, jealous of me? Why would she be? She was the one Nate married."

"Maybe so, but you didn't see him after you left. He wasn't the same. He lost his spark. I think she saw that and resented it."

"Really?" Oddly, I felt sorry for her. I'd always envied her for having what I wanted, but seeing it from her perspective of being with a man who depended emotionally on another woman must have been a challenge. I wouldn't have handled it well myself, and Maddy had always been more volatile than I was. More like Nate.

I shook my head. "No, I don't believe it's Maddy. She's happy with Steve. Why would she come after me now?"

"I don't know. Psychology isn't my forte. Just think on it, okay?"

"I will, but I really think she's got nothing to do with it." Maddy might be manipulative and snarky at times, but she wasn't the type to take such a cold-blooded approach to revenge, was she?

50

NATE

As I was leaving work, frustrated by our lack of success in locating Darrel Weich, my phone rang. I checked the screen and saw it was Max, so I answered.

"Hey, any news?"

"Not exactly." There was something off in Max's tone, but I couldn't quite pick what. "Just a thought I had."

When he didn't elaborate, I prompted, "Well? Go on."

"I talked to Grace—"

"Is she okay?" I interrupted, suddenly worried this call might be more serious than I'd thought.

"Yes, Nate, she's fine." He was placating me. "Or at least, as fine as she can be. But she told me about an interesting conversation she had with Maddy when she came to pick up Tess."

I frowned, unsure of what he was getting at. "Did Maddy upset her?"

"No, the opposite, actually. Well, for the most part."

A little of the tension in my shoulders eased. "That's

good." After her comments the other day, I hadn't been sure how Maddy would react when I called her earlier.

"Yeah," Max agreed. "But it got me thinking. Maddy is someone who doesn't tend to let things go, and I think she blames Grace for the breakup of your marriage—at least in part."

"So?" I shrugged, heading for my car. "She's engaged to Steve. Why would she care about Grace and me now, even if she used to hold a grudge?"

"I don't know." He sounded frustrated. "Perhaps it's an ego thing, or maybe she feels like she wasted years of her life on you when she could have been with Steve. My point is that if she feels that way, she might enjoy causing problems for Grace in order to get even."

I snorted and shook my head. "Nah, Maddy isn't that kind of person. I'm not blind to her flaws, but she's happy with Steve, and it's not as if I was much of a prize while we were together."

"You'd know better than me. I just thought I'd mention the possibility."

"I'm glad you did," I said. "But I can't believe it."

He hummed in thought. "Grace said the same thing, and honestly, I didn't want to think it either, but if there was any chance it could be her, I knew I had to bring it up."

"Thanks. I appreciate you looking out for Grace." Once again, I wondered if maybe Max had feelings for Grace, even if he'd never admit to them. "Are you sure you're not—"

"In love with Grace?" Max huffed. "No, I'm not. Like I said before, it crossed my mind that she and I could be comfortable together, but I'm not in love with her and I never have been. That said, if you hurt her, I'll make sure you regret it."

I unlocked my car and got in. "I thought you were the nice brother."

"Only to an extent. Everyone has their limits."

Interesting. I wondered what else would cause my level-headed brother to throw caution to the wayside.

"Has it ever occurred to you that maybe you shouldn't be looking for a comfortable partner?" I asked. "Perhaps you need to find someone who pushes you out of your comfort zone."

"I don't want someone I can't be comfortable with." He sounded unimpressed. "I need to sort out my paperwork so I can go home. Call me if anything changes with Grace's case."

"I will." We said goodbye and hung up.

I started the car and began driving home, but then turned the corner onto the road Maddy lived on instead. Max had planted a seed of doubt in my mind, and if there was even the slightest chance that Maddy might have something to do with Grace's thefts and that threatening note, I needed to investigate it. Even if just to hear from her own lips that she wasn't involved.

I parked outside her house and sent her a message to ask her to join me. I didn't want to knock at the door because if Tess was to answer, I'd have to explain why I was there, and I didn't have an excuse at the ready. A few minutes passed, and I considered calling her, but then the door opened and she emerged, wrapped in a puffy coat with a beanie pulled down over her ears. She glanced over at the car and hurried toward it before opening the passenger door and climbing in.

"What's going on?" she asked with a scowl. "I had to leave a nice toasty house. Is there a reason you couldn't come in?"

My stomach churned. I knew what I had to ask would upset her, but I couldn't help that. "I didn't want Tess to overhear our conversation."

Her scowl morphed into concern. "What's wrong?"

I met her gaze, needing to look into her eyes so I could see whether she was being truthful. "You don't have anything to do with the problems Grace is experiencing, do you?"

Maddy's eyes widened. Her nostrils flared. All signs she was mad as hell. "You can fuck right off with questions like that. If you so much as suggest I'm capable of that kind of assholery again, I'm going to punch you in the balls."

I winced. "I'm sorry, I had to ask."

"No, you fucking didn't." She gripped the door handle as if she might tear out of the car at any second. "You should know me better than that."

"I do," I assured her. "But I have to ask anyone who might have reason to hold a grudge against Grace. It's my job."

Maddy released the handle, but she was still fuming. "Despite what you apparently think, I have no reason to hurt Grace. If anything, I owe her an apology."

I frowned in confusion. "Why?"

Her eyes searched mine. "You don't know?"

"Know what?" I grumbled.

"Huh. She never told you." She looked surprised. "The night you and I first hooked up, Grace turned up while you were in the shower. She had some of those lemon drops you love and a couple of tickets to the dance. I assume she was going to ask you to go with her."

My heart skipped a beat. "What?"

Maddy rolled her eyes. "She had the biggest crush on you. It was obvious to everyone else, but I figured you weren't interested in her or else you would have noticed, so I went ahead and made a move."

"She did?" Grace had said she'd had feelings for me for a while, but why would she keep something that big from me?

Then the rest of Maddy's story sank in, and I clenched my fists. "What did you say to her?"

She shrugged. "I didn't need to say much. I was in your room, naked apart from your shirt. I just told her to go before she embarrassed herself, and I took the lemon drops. I figured they weren't going to do her any good, so I may as well take advantage of them."

My teeth gritted. "I remember," I ground out. "When I came back from the shower, you offered me one." I'd thought it was sweet that she'd paid attention to what I liked.

I turned away from her and stared through the windshield, emotions roiling inside me. Anger heated my gut, but I didn't know who I was angry with. I felt as if I'd been robbed of years I could have spent with Grace, but I'd been the one who decided not to pursue her. The night she'd come over, Maddy and I had just had sex for the first time. We'd both been virgins. Of course Maddy wouldn't have thought I'd wanted Grace to ask me out. I'd been with her. It would've been pretty damned insulting and unfair if I'd slept with Maddy and then moved on before the sweat had even dried on our skin. But it would have been nice to know that this had happened. Perhaps then I would have understood Maddy's dislike of my best friend.

And Grace....

Poor Grace. I couldn't imagine how she must have felt. She'd wanted to ask me out and finally worked up the courage to do so only to discover I was seeing someone else in a way that must have shocked and hurt her. My stomach cramped. How many times had I unwittingly hurt Grace over the years? And Maddy. I'd inflicted emotional wounds on both women. I didn't deserve either of them.

"I'm sorry," I said.

She cocked her head. "I thought you'd be angry."

I buried my face in my hands and growled, then dropped them onto my lap. "I don't know what I am. I just know that I hurt you, and I hurt Grace, and I didn't mean for any of it to happen. But at the same time, I can't regret anything. We may not have been the best fit for each other, but we had Tess, and she's the most important thing in my life. I'd never wish her away. But I wasn't the husband you needed, and I regret that. I wasn't there for Grace when she needed me, and I regret that too."

Hesitantly, Maddy laid her hand on my shoulder. "You and I were a mess together, but I've made peace with it, and I'm happy with how things turned out. I'm sorry I said cruel things to you during the divorce. You weren't a bad husband, just not the right one for me. I don't want you to beat yourself up over the past, and I'm sure Grace doesn't either. Just do the best you can for the future."

I forced a smile. "You're right. Thanks, Mads." I patted her hand. "Sorry about tonight. I'd better go home before Grace wonders where I am."

51

GRACE

When Nate arrived home, Kennedy—who'd been keeping me company so I wasn't alone—gave me a bone-crushing hug and left. It had been nice to spend more time with her, knowing that she would be able to understand better than anyone else what it felt like to have Darrel Weich come out of the woodwork once again. I'd confessed my fears to her, and she'd listened and sympathized, then made me promise both to do whatever the police suggested and to call her whenever I needed to talk again. Even though being with her hadn't improved my current situation, I felt lighter as I waved her goodbye.

After Nate had changed out of his work clothes, I offered him a curry I'd made for dinner, and he joined me to eat, but his mind seemed to be a million miles away. He was distant, and I caught him frowning into space more times than I could count. Eventually, I couldn't handle the brooding silence any longer.

"What's wrong?" I asked gently. "Is it about the call from Ryan?"

He shook his head, then waved his hand back and forth. "A little, but not really."

"Then what? I can tell something's on your mind. Talk to me."

He set his cutlery down and pushed his plate away. "I don't know why you want to be with me."

My eyebrows drew together. "You're a good person. You're loyal, and when you care for someone, you care fiercely. You've stood by me any time I needed you."

"But I haven't." He grimaced. "The times you've needed me most, I wasn't there. Even if I was physically present, I didn't pay enough attention to you."

My frown deepened. "Where is this coming from?"

He pressed his lips together. "I've been thinking it over for a while. Each time I learn something new about you— something I overlooked or that you felt you had to hide—it reminds me that I let you down. Tonight, I talked to Maddy, and she made me aware of something else I didn't know.'

My arms felt shaky, and when I glanced down, my fingers were trembling around my knife and fork. I set them aside before Nate could notice. "About?"

From the way he'd said it, I was afraid I knew the answer. She'd told him about what happened our senior year. My chest ached and my breaths seemed to come in shallow gasps. Would he be upset? Angry?

He looked at me. "You know what, Grace."

Just Grace. Not Gracie. Did it mean anything?

I intertwined my fingers on my lap. "What do you want me to say?"

"I don't know," he growled. "Why didn't you tell me?"

I inhaled as slowly as I could, determined not to freak out. I still hadn't figured out what was going on in his head.

"It was embarrassing," I admitted. "I felt like an idiot. At the time, you were with Maddy, so there was no point saying anything about it because I didn't want to be responsible for breaking up your relationship if you felt the same, and if you didn't, well, I preferred not to know."

"But didn't I deserve to have that information?" he asked. "So I could make an informed decision?"

I leaned forward slightly, needing him to see my perspective. "What good would that have done? It could have irrevocably damaged our friendship, which was the most important thing in the world to me. You were with Maddy. It would have been wrong of me to do anything to interfere with that."

His eyes softened, and he reached across the table and laid his hand on the surface, palm up. Hesitantly, I took my hand out from under the table and rested it on his. Palm to palm, our fingers laced together, the contact felt more intimate than sex.

"You're right." He drew circles on the back of my hand with his thumb. "I know you are. I also know how much pain I must have caused you over the years." His blue-green eyes burned with intensity. "I wish I could take it back. I can't do that, but I'd like to spend the rest of my life making it up to you."

My breath caught. "You would?"

He nodded. "More than anything."

A slow smile curved my lips. "You have nothing to make up for, but I'm not going to stop you trying."

"Good." He allowed himself a small smile but then turned serious again. "Do you know what else Maddy told me recently?"

"Something else?" God, how could there be anything else?

He gave my hand a reassuring squeeze. "She said that

during a lot of our relationship, she felt like she came second to you. I hate that I made her feel that way when she was supposed to be my priority, but I think it's a sign that my heart was always yours. I just didn't know it yet."

I felt a pang of sympathy for Maddy. We'd both been in a tough situation and done the best we could, but at times she must have hurt as much as I did, if not more. I couldn't bring myself to regret how everything had worked out, though, because I finally had the man I'd always loved.

I stood and rounded the table. He pushed back his chair and swept me into his arms. Our lips met eagerly. I softened against him as he took the lead with tender but passionate kisses that grew more and more heated until we were both breathless. He led me to the sofa and sat. I straddled his lap and took his face between my hands. I brushed my mouth softly over his, then more firmly. His tongue touched mine and—

Bang. Bang. Bang.

Hammering at the door interrupted us.

I pulled back, shocked by the urgency of the knocking. "Are you expecting anyone?"

"No." Nate grabbed my hips and guided me off his lap. "But it sounds like it's important."

I started to follow him, but he stopped me with a hand on my shoulder.

"Wait here. I'll be back in a minute."

52

NATE

I YANKED THE DOOR OPEN, ready to lay into whoever was on the other side for interrupting my time with Grace, but I drew up short as a stocky, balding man tried to barrel past me. I grabbed his shoulder with one hand to stop his momentum and reached for my gun with the other, only to realize I didn't have it on me.

"Grace!" the man gasped. "Grace!" he yelled more loudly. "I need to warn you! You're not safe!"

He made another attempt to dart past me, but I blocked his way and twisted him around, maneuvering his arm into a position I knew he wouldn't be able to get out of without injuring himself.

"Let me go," he spat. "I'm not going to hurt her. I'm here to help. She's in danger."

I partially turned him until I could see the side of his face. Flushed cheeks, watery brown eyes, and thin lips set in a fleshy face.

Darrel Weich.

"If she's in danger, it's because of you." My voice was low and furious. "You're the one hunting her halfway across the country."

"Hunting?" He paled. "No. I would never."

"Oh, really?"

"You don't understand. Someone else is trying to get to her," he insisted. "I need to talk to her in private so I can explain."

"Like hell are you getting near her." Thankfully, Grace hadn't appeared behind me. She must have heard the commotion and was wisely staying away. She was probably terrified. I wished I could go to her, but without a weapon, I had no way to control Weich, so I couldn't release him. "I'm not letting you touch one hair on her head. If you want her, you'll have to go through me."

He bucked against me, but not violently, just as if testing the strength of my grip. When I didn't budge, he stilled. "It's not like that." His voice was strained. "I have important news she needs to hear."

At that, I paused. He was probably making it up or living some kind of delusion, but on the off chance he did know something, I needed to hear it.

"You can explain everything to me at the police station," I said, silently trying to determine the best way to get him there without backup to restrain him.

He moaned in distress. "The police never believe me."

I snorted. "I wonder why."

"Come on. I'm not a threat."

"You charged at me," I pointed out.

"Only so I could get to her." He growled in frustration. "You're not going to believe me, are you? No one ever does."

Deciding on a course of action, I angled my face away from him and toward the living area. "Gracie," I called. "I need you to bring me some cuffs and my keys, then lock the door behind us. Don't open it to anyone other than my family or Desdemona. Got it?"

She didn't answer, but a few seconds later, she appeared silently behind me and handed me the cuffs. Her scared eyes lingered on Weich, and then she hurried away again. Sensing her presence, Weich tried to look over his shoulder, but I manhandled him into the cuffs before he could. I pressed the button on my keys to unlock the car and guided him down the stairs, pausing until the door shut behind us and I heard the lock click into place. Weich mumbled something incoherent.

I opened the back door of the vehicle. "Get in."

I half-expected him to run for the house again, but he got into the car, only his glare telling me how unhappy he was. I locked him inside and made a brief phone call, then got into the driver's seat and headed for the police station.

"She's not safe by herself," Weich said as we began driving. He seemed to have calmed down.

"She won't be alone for long." I had already asked Liam and Kennedy to go to her. I'd considered sending in the whole Braddock clan, but Grace was already overwhelmed. She was close with Kennedy, and the other woman understood what she was going through, so Liam and Kennedy were the obvious choice to keep her company.

At the station, I called Mehrtens and Patton, who'd been most involved with the investigation, and asked them to come back in. Mehrtens arrived first and joined me in the interview room. I informed Weich of his rights and started the audio recording.

"It's about time," he said as soon as I was done. "This is taking too long. Grace is in danger, and we're all here sitting on our asses."

"Why don't you tell me more about why Grace is in trouble?" Mehrtens suggested. We'd agreed she'd take the lead on questioning him, since I might blow my top and do or say something to jeopardize the case.

"Someone emailed me yesterday," Weich said. "They told me where she lived and sent me photographs of her." He glanced from Mehrtens to me. "I've been going to therapy every month for years, and I understand now that I made a mistake when I broke into Grace's house. I was sick, and the only defense I have is that I genuinely believed she loved me and needed to be rescued. But this is different. I'm on my meds and I'm doing okay. That's how I know that whoever sent me those photos wanted me to hurt or scare Grace. I can't think of any other reason why they'd send them. I'm not dangerous to her anymore, but whoever it is doesn't know that." He looked at me pleadingly. "You don't have any reason to believe me, but you can ask my therapist."

"Who's your therapist?" Mehrtens asked.

Weich gave her the details.

"Do you have any proof that you're telling the truth?" I asked, unable to help myself.

His expression was blank for a moment, but then he nodded, visibly relieved. "The email is on my phone."

"Which is where?"

"My pocket."

Mehrtens approached him, taking a plastic glove from inside her uniform and putting it on her right hand. "Please stand. Do I have your permission to take it out of your pocket?"

"Yes."

Mehrtens extracted the phone and swiped the screen.

"The pin is four-two-seven-zero," Weich said.

She entered the pin and navigated into his email app. A moment later, she showed me the screen and raised her eyebrows meaningfully. I frowned. The email was exactly as he'd said, but it was the sender's email address that turned me cold. Ezra.Mendel@gmail.com.

I caught Mertens's gaze. "I want Mendel brought in immediately. Get Patton to do it. I need you to track the IP address the email was sent from."

"Yes, sir." She left the room, and I followed close behind.

"So you believe me?" Weich called after us.

I nodded once before locking the interview room door. I dialed Weich's therapist's phone number and listened to it ring. At this time of evening, he'd probably left work, but hopefully he'd still have his phone on. The call rang out once and I tried again. This time, he answered.

"Dr. Wong speaking."

"Dr. Wong, this is Police Sergeant Nathan Braddock. I'm calling about a client of yours. Darrel Weich."

"What's going on?" His tone had become guarded.

"Mr. Weich is assisting us with a case. We need to know his state of mind with regard to Grace Smith, the author who took a restraining order out against him."

"Do you have a warrant?" the doctor asked.

"No, but your client suggested we speak with you."

"I'll need to hear that from him."

I exhaled slowly, clinging to the frayed ends of my temper. Of course Dr. Wong would need to hear it from Weich himself. "Just a minute. I'll put him on."

Half an hour later, we had Ezra Mendel in the interview room adjoining Darrel Weich's, and Dr. Wong had confirmed that he thought Weich was likely telling the truth and that he didn't pose a threat to anyone. Just as I prepared to enter Mendel's room, this time with Patton in support, Mehrtens raced down the hall toward us.

"Sarge," she exclaimed. "I thought you'd want to know before you start the interview. The email Darrel Weich received originated from an IP address in Destiny Falls." She paused, then added, "Somewhere in the block of houses where Grace lives."

"So it might have come from her own property," I clarified.

Mehrtens nodded. "Yes."

"Excellent work." If the email had originated from Grace's property, that must mean it had been Ezra behind everything all along. Thank god we already had him in custody, where he couldn't cause Grace any more distress. Only two questions remained. Why had he done it, and was he working alone?

53

GRACE

WHEN I FINALLY GAVE UP ON sleep and went in search of coffee, Nate still hadn't returned. Kennedy was dozing on the sofa with Daisy and Duke curled around each other on the floor beside her. She must have moved from the spare bed when Liam left for his shift at the fire station. I padded barefoot to the kitchen and made two mugs of coffee, then searched the cupboards and the fridge for ingredients to make scrambled eggs. I whipped up a batch and was plating them when Kennedy joined me, wiping her bleary eyes.

"Sorry if I woke you," I said. "I couldn't sleep, and I was going crazy in bed. I needed to get up and do something."

"Trust me, I get it." She scanned the counter. "Coffee?"

"Here." I handed her a mug.

She inhaled the steam. "Mm. I need this."

"Didn't sleep very well either?"

She pulled a face. "This situation brings back a lot of memories. I'm just glad they got Ezra locked up before he did any serious damage."

"Me too." I was lucky. Kennedy's stalker hadn't been captured until after he'd drugged, kidnapped, and shot her. While I was shaken, I'd been relieved when Nate had called to say the email to Darrel Weich looked to have come from Ezra. It was hard to believe the guy I'd thought of as strange but harmless was to blame, but I was grateful to know I'd soon be able to put this whole mess behind me.

"I'm sorry if it's stirred up too much for you." I'd been selfish, wanting her near me because she'd understand how I felt. I hadn't fully considered how it might impact on her.

"Hey, none of that." She put her mug down and pulled me into a fierce hug. "I'm exactly where and with whom I want to be."

My eyes teared up. I loved this woman like a sister. "You're incredible."

"We're both pretty wonderful," she replied. "Come on. Serve those eggs, and let's eat before they go cold. Hopefully they'll call soon with an update."

I passed her a plate of scrambled eggs and finished dishing the rest for myself, then we shared our breakfast at the worn dining table. We didn't talk much, but we didn't need to. The comfortable silence between us said more than words. But despite the easy company and the relief of knowing Ezra had been found out, my mind whirred, jumping from one thing to another in its sleep-deprived state. I knew I couldn't sit around all day. I needed to channel my restlessness into something productive.

"Do you think it would be all right for me to go back to my place to do some work?" I asked Kennedy as we cleaned up after breakfast.

She hesitated. "Given the circumstances, I don't see why it would be a problem. The guy is locked away, and you said Nate thought everything was pretty much wrapped up."

"True. Besides, Nate has Darrel Weich at the station too,

so either way, there shouldn't be an issue." It was strange to think I was finally safe again.

"I'll come with you," Kennedy said. "That way you won't be alone."

"Thank you, that would be great."

"No problem." She laid her hand on my arm. "I'm happy to be there for moral support. I'm sure you were scared after that guy turned up on the doorstep last night."

"I was, and you're right, I don't want to be alone yet." Seeing Darrel Weich had made me realize just how easily someone could get to me if they wanted to.

I showered and dressed while Kennedy got ready to go. We drove to my place in Kennedy's car. Hopefully she or Nate would drop me back at Nate's house at the end of the day—presuming I still needed to stay there. If Ezra was charged, perhaps I wouldn't need to spend all of my time with Nate. Would he want me to go back to sleeping in my own bed? We hadn't discussed it yet, and that felt like an oversight. What came next could signal exactly where—and how fast—our relationship was going.

When Kennedy pulled up outside my property, Alice's car was already there. Of course, it was a normal working day for her. I hadn't thought to message to let her know what had happened last night, so she'd turned up at her usual time. She was probably confused as to why I wasn't in the office.

"I forgot Alice would be here," I said. "She'll keep me company. There's no need for you to hang around while I'm working."

Kennedy frowned. "Are you sure? I'm happy to curl up on the couch and watch a movie or read something."

"Don't be silly. There's no reason for you to be bored out of your mind when Alice is already here." I grinned. "Do you really think she'd let me get away with brooding over anything?"

She brightened. "Good point. She'll make sure you're all right."

"She will," I agreed. "But thank you so much for staying with me overnight and for being willing to be with me today. It means a lot."

"No problem, and I'm on the other end of the phone if you change your mind and want to call me back. I'll drop everything and come right over, I promise."

"Thanks, Kenz." I reached across the seat to give her a one-armed hug, then got out of the car and opened the back door of the vehicle so Duke could leap out too. Daisy tried to follow, and I had to usher her back in.

"Sorry, girl, not this time."

I waved Kennedy off and wandered up the drive. The front door was locked, so I used the key to let myself in and went in search of Alice. I found her in the office.

She took one look at me and asked, "What happened?"

I explained the drama of the night before, and her eyes grew wider and wider. When I finished, she tossed questions at me one after the other. I tried not to get frustrated with her, but I was functioning on less than a couple hours of sleep and wasn't as patient as I might otherwise have been. Eventually, she seemed to realize I was struggling and smiled sheepishly.

"Sorry," she said. "Why don't I make us both a coffee?"

"Yes, please." I could use more caffeine.

While she did that, I got to work. She returned soon after and settled in next to me. Our routine was much the same as usual for the next hour. At one point, I heard my phone ring, but Alice answered and checked the screen.

"Looks like one of those international scams," she said, and rejected the call.

"Thanks."

I tried to return my focus to writing, but no new words would come, so I gave up and went in search of more caffeine. I headed to the kitchen and started another brew. I was engrossed in my task when the sound of a footstep sent goosebumps prickling up my arms. That wasn't the click-clack of Alice's high heels. It was the soft tread of a sneaker.

I spun around. Ezra stood at the entrance to the kitchen, breathing heavily. His hair was a mess, and his expression was unreadable. I stumbled backward, shocked. Shouldn't he be locked up? I grabbed blindly for something to defend myself with. From down the hall, I heard a muffled bark. I risked glancing away from Ezra for long enough to spot the knife block, which was only just out of reach. I edged closer to it, and his eyes followed the movement.

"What are you doing here?" I demanded, my voice shakier than I'd have liked. Why would Nate have let him go? Unless they didn't have enough for an arrest to stick, and his lawyer had made a fuss about them holding him. But if that was the case, Nate would have called and made sure I knew about it.

"It's not what you think," he said, his eyes wild. "Just let me explain."

"Everyone seems to be saying that lately." Someone had to be lying.

He took a step forward. "I didn't lie to you about who I am, but I didn't tell the whole truth either."

He took another step forward. I edged closer to the knife block.

All of a sudden, he jolted, his face contorting. I lunged for the knives and yanked one out of the block, only to stare in disbelief as he toppled to the floor with a thud. Alice stood behind him, holding a taser.

"Oh my god." I nearly crumpled with relief. "You saved my life."

She smiled with grim satisfaction. "Just doing my job."

"Ha!" The laugh that burst from me surprised me as much as it did her.

Duke trotted into the room and stopped to sniff at Ezra's prone body, then growled.

"You're okay." Alice dropped the taser and moved toward me slowly, as if wary of my mental state. "Why don't you give me the knife?"

I glanced down at my hand, stunned to realize I was still gripping the weapon so tightly, my knuckles were white. I passed it to her, handle first.

She used her free arm to hug me, and I closed the distance between us, coming to an abrupt stop when something punched me in the chest, robbing me of my ability to breathe. I looked down, barely able to believe what I was seeing. The knife I'd handed Alice was buried in my lower chest, the blade puncturing the skin beneath my breast and angling upward.

Pain ripped through me, blazing hot. I raised my eyes to Alice's, my mouth hanging open. The taste of blood filled my mouth.

"I... I d-don't...." I dropped to my knees.

"No, you don't," Alice whispered, her voice harsh. She leaned close until only a couple of inches separated her face from mine. "You don't deserve everything you have. You owe it all to a pair of incompetent judges. If the universe were fair, your life would have been mine."

I tried to shove her away, but my strength was leaching out along with the blood that soaked the front of my blouse. Alice twisted the knife handle and slowly drew it out. I screamed in agony and scrambled backward, trying to escape as she raised the knife for another strike, but there was only so far I could go while I was on the floor. As the knife arced toward me, I threw my hands to block it and screamed as the blade sliced into my palm.

A blur of dark fur passed my face, and then Duke launched himself at Alice, sinking his teeth into her arm. She shrieked and shook him off, but he latched onto her calf, easily tearing through the thin fabric of her pantyhose and piercing the flesh. She tried to dislodge him, but he growled furiously and refused to let go. I reached for her other leg to pull it out from under her, but she swung the foot and booted Duke in the face. He yelped and released her. She lashed out at him again, this time with her pointed heel. He grunted and fell back. Alice yanked her other shoe off and sprinted out of the kitchen.

I tried to get to Duke, but I couldn't seem to make my body move. My limbs were heavy. My vision flickered at the edges. Duke dragged himself toward me and licked the side of my face.

"It's okay, boy," I whispered.

But nothing was okay.

I summoned all of the energy I could muster, but instead of getting up off the ground, the ceiling seemed to grow further away. My head had hit the floor. Darkness crept across my vision. Before I let it overtake me, I had time for two thoughts.

Please let Duke be okay.

I should have told Nate I loved him.

54

———

NATE

IT WAS with gritty eyes and a weary heart that I tried calling Grace again. I'd been surprised the first call had been rejected, but I figured she must have been sleeping and had turned it off reflexively. I had to get in touch with her soon so I could share the news that would turn her world upside down before Ezra got to her and spilled the beans himself. I would have accompanied him back to her place, but Mehrtens had pulled me aside to discuss a possible lead and by the time I'd heard her out, Patton had already released Ezra. As we'd discovered, Ezra had a legitimate reason for wanting to spend so much time around Grace, and given the circumstances—and how distraught he'd been—there was no reason to think he was behind anything. That meant Grace may still be in danger.

When she didn't answer, I tried again. The call went to voicemail. I told my staff I was taking a break and drove home, but she wasn't there. Kennedy's car was missing too. Figuring she'd probably taken Grace back home, I returned to the car and raced to Grace's place. When I got there, Ezra's car was the only one in the drive. My heart sped up. Was I too late? Had he already confronted her?

I went to the door and knocked, but there was no response. I tried the handle and found it unlocked. I frowned. She should know better. I pushed it open cautiously and strained to hear the slightest noise, but it was eerily silent. With dread clawing at my gut, I withdrew my gun from its holster and cleared each room as I made my way through the house. Perhaps it was overkill, but my instincts were screaming that something was wrong, and when I got to the office, which looked like Grace had only stepped away from it for a few minutes, my suspicions were reinforced. I checked Alice's computer and saw that it was shut down. My jaw tightened. Even if she'd thought she was safe, what would have possessed Grace to be reckless enough to come here alone?

I continued up the hall. The living area was empty, but when I entered the kitchen, my heart nearly stopped.

Blood everywhere.

Smeared on the floor and pooled around the woman I loved.

Kneeling over Grace, one hand pressed to her throat and the other to her chest, was Ezra Mendel. Duke lay curled against her side, panting and barely conscious.

My gut turned over. I'd assumed that what we'd discovered about Ezra, combined with the fact he'd provided evidence he wasn't in town during Grace's first problems, meant he'd been set up, but it would seem I'd made a fatal mistake.

"Get away from her," I snarled. "Put your hands on the back of your head and move away."

He glanced over his shoulder. "She's still alive."

Relief rushed through me. I'd gotten to her in time.

"Her pulse is weak," he continued. "She might not have long."

"Back off," I ordered, wondering if he was playing some kind of mind game. I didn't understand whether he was helping her or hurting her. Damn, I never should have let him leave the station alone. I should have ignored Mehrtens or instructed Patton not to let him go without one of us accompanying him.

"I can't," he bit out. "If I stop putting pressure on her wound, she might lose too much blood."

I kept my gun leveled at him with one hand while I reached for my radio with the other. "If you try anything—"

"I won't." He gave me a look. "You know I won't."

"I'm not sure I know anything when it comes to you." He may be trying to help, as he'd said, but the situation was very incriminating, and it was better to be safe than to let Grace's attacker get away.

I used the radio to get a hold of Officer Mehrtens. "I need backup and an ambulance at Grace's house," I told her. "Immediately. She's sustained trauma to the chest and is bleeding heavily."

"It's a stab wound," Ezra said.

"Possible stabbing," I informed Mehrtens. "Person of interest on the scene."

Ezra paled. "You think I did this?"

"It doesn't look good, does it?" I glanced at Duke and spoke into the radio. "Call Summer too. We need a vet."

"Yes, sir." Mehrtens disconnected.

I removed my shirt and folded it. "I'm going to take your place." I didn't trust him to be the one to care for Grace, no matter what he'd revealed to us earlier. After all, if he wasn't responsible for this, then who was?

I shouldered him aside and pressed the folded shirt against the seeping hole in Grace's chest. I had to agree with his assessment. It looked like a knife wound, but not a clean one. Whoever had done this had either stabbed her at a strange angle or twisted the blade to inflict maximum damage.

Grace's eyelashes fluttered.

"Come on, Gracie," I urged. "You've got to live." I glanced up at Ezra, who hadn't tried to run. "Handcuff yourself."

He blanched. "Excuse me?"

I narrowed my eyes. "If you want me to believe you didn't do this, then handcuff yourself. I can't care for Grace properly while I'm worried whether you'll attack me."

He stared at me for a long moment, and I half-expected him to turn and leave. It wasn't as if I could stop him. But then he came closer, unhitched the cuffs from my belt, and slowly put them on.

I turned back to Grace, grateful to be able to give her my full attention. Her eyelashes fluttered again, and I caught a glimpse of her hazel eyes before they closed.

"You've got this, baby. Keep breathing." I checked her pulse. It was rhythmic but weak, as Ezra had said. Feeling that faint throb, it struck me how close I'd come to losing her. Emotion burned at the back of my throat. Grace meant everything to me. I didn't know how I'd go on without her.

"I love you, Gracie," I choked out. "I know I'm an idiot, and it took me too long to realize it, but I love you with my whole heart. Please be okay. I need you to be okay."

Sirens sounded outside, and I was vaguely aware of people entering the house. They surrounded us. Ezra was guided away, and someone knelt beside me and tried to move my hands.

"I can't let her go," I snapped. "She needs the pressure."

"I've got her," Asher promised. "Let me do my job. She needs to be taken to hospital."

He pulled at my arms gently, and I shifted away from her, tremors wracking my body.

"Will she survive?" I asked as Asher replaced me at Grace's side and began assessing her.

"You know I can't make promises." His tone was all business, but I understood. When dealing with something this personal, people needed to disconnect from their emotions in order to get through it. "She has a good chance though. It's a good thing you got here so soon."

Not soon enough. I should have gone to her the instant Mendel was released.

Asher and the other paramedic lifted Grace onto a stretcher and carried her out. I started to follow, but Patton intercepted me.

"Sarge, should we begin questioning Mendel?" he asked.

I watched Grace disappear around the corner, wanting to be with her more than anything. I struggled to get my thoughts in order. I couldn't help Grace right now, but I could figure out who'd done this to her.

"You and Mehrtens can question him. I'll observe." I couldn't be part of the interrogation. Not when I was emotionally compromised and had such a strong conflict of interest.

A few seconds after Grace went out of sight, Summer appeared in the doorway. She was panting, and if I had to guess, I'd say she'd run from the car.

"What happened?" she demanded.

"Grace was stabbed." I tried to sound as detached as Asher had, but my voice was rough. I gestured toward Duke. "He's been injured too."

She followed my motion and gasped. "Who would hurt a puppy?" She rushed to him and knelt, then carefully palpated his body. He raised his head weakly. "I think he'll be okay." She released a sigh of relief. "I'll take him to the clinic, but Nate, I want to hear whether Grace is all right the second you get any news."

"I'll let you know," I said.

"Great." She scooped the puppy into her arms, and I was surprised to see no sign of strain on her face. Duke was hardly a lightweight.

I faced Patton again. "Head to the station now. Get Mehrtens to call a crime scene team. There's too much for her to process on her own, and we need her at the interview."

He nodded. "On it."

I waited until he'd left, then made a quick call to my parents to ask them to go to the hospital so Grace wouldn't be alone if she woke. Mum was hysterical, but she promised she and Dad would collect Desdemona and leave immediately. It was a weight off my mind to know they'd be there for her. Her own parents may have abandoned her, but mine never would.

I made my way to the police station in a haze, but all of my senses sharpened as I entered the interview room and claimed a chair in the corner.

Patton stated the time, date, and who was present for the recording. "Do you understand your rights?" he asked Mendel.

"Yes." Mendel sounded as exhausted as I felt.

"You are choosing not to have your lawyer present?"

"Against his advice, yes."

I cocked my head. Perhaps he really hadn't had anything to do with the stabbing, but considering I'd found him standing over her, questions had to be raised.

Patton asked Mendel to describe the events leading up to when I'd found him in Grace's kitchen.

"I went there to talk to her," Mendel said. "I knew Nate

would tell her the truth about who I was, and I wanted her to hear it from me first."

"Where was she when you arrived?" Patton asked.

"In the kitchen."

"You let yourself into the house?"

"It wasn't locked."

Patton and Mehrtens exchanged a glance.

"When you saw her, what did she say?"

Mendel squirmed in his seat. "She was scared. She wanted me to leave. I asked her to hear me out."

"Then what happened?" Patton leaned forward, his tone becoming firmer. "Did she refuse, and when you got angry, you stabbed her?"

"No!"

"Then what?" Mehrtens asked, more softly.

He sighed and rubbed the back of his neck. "It was like all of my muscles went rigid at once and everything hurt." He dropped his hand onto the table. "I think I might have been tased."

I cocked an eyebrow. Tased? It was just strange enough to be the truth.

"What happened next?" Patton prompted.

"I heard voices, but I wasn't able to move. It felt like I was just on the edge of blacking out. When it stopped hurting and I got up, Grace was already on the floor, bleeding."

Mehrtens made a thoughtful sound in the back of her throat. "Would you mind me looking at your back?"

"Um, sure." He stood and held his chin high as she circled the table and lifted the back of his shirt.

"Turn around, please," she said.

He did.

Mehrtens pointed to a pair of small red marks on his back. "These could have been left by a taser, although we'll need an expert to examine them to be sure."

I got up and went over to study them, then cursed. She was right. We'd all had to practice with tasers at police college, and this looked a lot like the mark I'd had after one of my fellow trainees had tased me.

I scanned Mendel and something else struck me. "There's not enough blood."

"What?" Patton asked, but Mehrtens seemed to know what I was thinking.

"If he'd been the one to stab her, he'd have been covered in blood," she said. "This is more like what you'd expect to see on a first aider or a first responder."

I gritted my teeth. It seemed Mendel was being honest, which meant we were back to square one.

55

NATE

AFTER WE'D GOT ALL the information we could squeeze from Ezra's hazy memory, Patton arranged to have his clothing collected for evidence and for him to be checked over by Max in case he had any underlying injuries as a result of being tased. Meanwhile, Mehrtens and I returned to Grace's house to see if there were any clues that could help us identify Grace's assailant. Mehrtens was driving, which I was grateful for when my phone began to ring.

"Sergeant Braddock," I said into the receiver.

"Nate, it's Summer."

I dropped the formality. "How's Duke doing?"

"He's going to recover just fine." I could hear the smile in her voice. "But I have news that might interest you. Duke had traces of blood on his teeth. It's possible it's from Grace, but based on where I found it, I think he might have bitten the person responsible for this."

For the first time since I'd seen Grace lying prone on the ground, my spirits lifted. "What a good dog."

"Such a brave boy," she agreed. "Don't worry, I'm giving him plenty of treats. I've collected as much of the blood as I can. Should I drop it off at the station?"

"No." I thought quickly. "We'll come by now. Hang tight."

I hung up and explained the discovery to Mehrtens.

Her eyes lit up. "If it is his blood, then we'll be able to confirm the assailant's blood type, and we'll have a comparison for DNA analysis. This could be exactly what we need."

I nodded. I understood the importance of the find.

We stopped outside the veterinary clinic, and Summer came to meet us. She passed me a small vial, and I sealed it inside a Ziplock bag.

"Get the bastard" was all she said.

I ruffled her hair, ignoring her scowl. "We will."

I'd just gotten into the car when my phone rang again. It was Kennedy.

"What's up?" I asked, positioning the phone between my shoulder and ear while I did up my seatbelt.

"I just heard about Grace." Her voice was thick with tears. "I'm so sorry, I knew I shouldn't leave, but Alice was there too, so it seemed safe enough."

Mehrtens started driving.

"Wait, Alice was there?"

"Yeah." She hesitated. "Her car was parked out front, anyway. Wasn't she there? Obviously not or you wouldn't ask. Oh my god. Do you think she's okay, or could she have been hurt too?"

I tried to summon an image of the kitchen into my mind. There had been plenty of blood, but it had been pooled around Grace, and there was no sign anyone had been dragged through it. I couldn't recall seeing blood anywhere else, although there must have been at least some because the attacker would have been covered in it as they left.

"I don't think she was involved in the attack at the house, but I'll send an officer to look for her." I ended the call and was about to radio in the information when we arrived outside Grace's house, and I spotted Alice near the gate, looking paler than usual and carrying two takeout cups. She was eyeballing the row of police vehicles and the crime scene tech's van warily.

"I'll talk to her," I told Mehrtens. "You get the vial to the tech guys."

I gave her the vial, knowing she'd be aware of the proper protocol for logging it and passing it on. As soon as we exited the vehicle, she was pulled into conversation with another officer, and I strode toward Alice. As I got closer, I noticed how ruffled Alice's composure seemed to be compared to normal. Something else looked different too. I studied her for a moment before I realized she wasn't wearing makeup, and instead of her usual dress or skirt and shirt, she was wearing tailored slacks and a blazer. The dark colors only served to emphasize her pale complexion.

"W-what happened?" she asked, her voice wobbling.

"Where have you been?" My tone was harsh, and she backed away a step. "Kennedy said you were with Grace."

"I was."

My eyes narrowed. "Then why was someone able to stab her without you knowing about it?"

Her mouth fell open. "She was *stabbed*?" She shifted her weight from one foot to the other. "Oh my god. This is all my fault. Is she okay?" Her expression was miserable.

"She was alive when emergency services arrived. That's all I know."

Her face pinched. "Thank god."

"So," I prompted. "Where were you?"

She shrugged. "Grace was a bit emotional, so I went to get coffee and scones from Taste of Destiny to perk her up, but then my stupid car broke down. I had to wait for Warren to tow it before I could come back."

I watched her carefully. My instincts were telling me something was off, and I was going to listen to them. She was too agitated and antsy. I didn't like it.

"We'll need to take your statement at the station. You might have seen or heard something before you left that will help us find the person responsible." Hopefully phrasing it that way would get her into an interview room without any fuss. "Wait a moment." I radioed Mehrtens, afraid that Alice might leave if I took my eyes off her, and explained where we were going. When I was done, Alice followed me meekly to the car and got into the passenger seat, placing the cups in the holder between us.

"So, you don't know who did that to Grace?" she asked eventually. "They were already gone when you got there?"

I forced myself not to look at her, knowing my thoughts would show on my face. "Did you think they'd stay and wait to be caught?"

"No, I guess not." She gave a small laugh. "I sound crazy, don't I?"

I didn't answer because she didn't sound crazy, she sounded *guilty*. As if she'd expected the police to find someone with Grace. Someone like the man who'd been immobilized by a taser for a few crucial minutes. Mendel had already said he wasn't certain whether the voice he'd heard had been male or female, which meant it could have been Alice.

In the station, I escorted her to the room Darrel Weich had recently vacated. Since he'd been under police supervision at the time of the stabbing, we knew beyond a shadow of a doubt that he wasn't responsible. I locked her inside, found Patton, and asked him to join me. We sat opposite Alice at the table, and Patton ran through the routine preliminaries. By the time he'd finished, Alice was whiter than a ghost.

"Why all the pomp and circumstance?" she asked.

"It's protocol." Patton's tone was flat. I'd briefly explained my concerns to him on the way to the room.

"When did you first see Grace this morning?" Patton asked.

"When Kennedy dropped her off." She sat on her hands, and in this position, I was reminded of how small she was. Not the five-foot-eight to six-foot height of the person previously recorded withdrawing money from the ATM with Grace's card. But then, she liked to wear heels, and a platform wedge or a pair of pumps might put her into the right ballpark.

"What time did you leave to get coffee?" Patton asked.

"A bit before nine, I think." She chewed on her lip, and her lack of makeup and out-of-character fashion choices nagged at me again. She wouldn't let herself be seen like this unless she thought she had to. After she'd been sick, she'd still gone to the effort of applying mascara and lip gloss. Perhaps she'd prioritized getting the coffee to make her story seem authentic over redoing her makeup after she'd showered off Grace's blood.

I chewed the inside of my lip. Why would she want to hurt Grace? Grace was her boss. Her friend.

Patton tapped his pen to his notebook. "What type of coffee?"

Alice frowned. "Why does it matter?"

He gave her a look.

She rolled her eyes. "A vanilla latte for Grace and a mocha for me."

"Any chance you still have that coffee and are willing to share with a sleep-deprived police officer?" he asked.

She snorted. "Ask your boss. It's in his car."

I hid a grin, clearly able to see that Patton's tactic to relax her had worked.

An instant later, his expression grew serious. "Why the pants? Aren't you usually a dress or skirt kind of girl?"

"It's cold today."

"Are you sure it's not because you're hiding a dog bite?"

She rocketed to her feet, stumbling slightly, as if her leg was sore.

Bingo.

"Of course not!" she exclaimed, her voice too high-pitched to be believable.

Patton stood. "You won't mind if we check, then."

She stepped backward. "Don't you dare." She placed her hand on her hip. "I don't consent, which means that's assault."

Patton held up his hands in a gesture of peace. "Then I won't touch you now, but we will get a warrant."

Her eyes narrowed, and in my mind, her next words confirmed her guilt. "I want my lawyer."

"But—" Patton began to interject.

"Lawyer," she snapped. "Or I'm not saying another word."

56

———

GRACE

MY MIND WAS a haze of pain and confusion.

I could hear muffled sounds around me. Beeping. Voices. A door clicking shut.

I tried to open my eyes, but the lids were heavy. I succumbed to the fog and let it claim me.

Sometime later, I became aware of voices again. A male and a female, both familiar. I strained to make them out. Was the man Nate?

"Nate," I murmured, butchering the name because my tongue felt thick and my mouth like it was full of cotton wool.

"Gracie?"

Definitely Nate.

A gentle touch smoothed over my forehead.

"Are you awake?"

My eyelashes fluttered, and I fought to hold them open. Light burned into my retinas, and I flinched.

"Shh, it's okay."

The light dimmed, and I blinked a few times as the world slowly came into focus. I tried to move my hand, and it throbbed painfully. When I struggled to sit up, someone urged me back down.

"Take it easy," Nate's gentle, reassuring voice said. "You're safe."

I turned my head to the side and finally laid eyes on his gorgeous face. His eyes were bloodshot with dark circles underneath, and he looked as if he hadn't slept in a month.

"Wha' hap'n'd?" I rasped.

"Here." Something touched my lower lip. A water bottle. I sipped, the water relieving the dryness of my mouth.

"Grace?" a hesitant voice asked. Female. Tess? The little girl came into view as she leaned over me. "Are you awake?"

"Yes." The water had helped. I sounded stronger already.

"Good. I was so worried, but Dad said I shouldn't be because you're the strongest person he knows."

My heart squeezed, but then something lower in my chest began to burn. I frowned, finally recalling what had happened.

Alice had stabbed me.

Alice, my friend.

I didn't understand. Had she been the person behind everything that had gone wrong recently? I tried to think it through, but my mind was too muddled.

"Alice?" I asked.

Relief flooded Nate's face. "She was the one who did this to you?"

I started to nod, but pain burst through my temples, and I stilled. "Yes."

He leaned over and kissed my cheek. "I'm glad you remember. We've already arrested her on suspicion of attempted murder, but your testimony will be the nail in her coffin."

I glanced at Tess, wondering how much we could discuss in her presence, but my need to know the truth outweighed my hesitancy. "How did you find out it was her?"

"She wasn't present at the scene when, according to Kennedy, she should have been. She had an excuse for that, but even after we spoke to Warren, who was supposedly her alibi, the timing didn't quite work out, and she was behaving strangely. When we questioned her, she demanded a lawyer. She hasn't spoken to anyone other than her lawyer since then, but we got a search warrant for her house and found traces of blood that match your type. There were no bloody clothes, but we're scouring the neighborhood's dumpsters and trash cans. She's smart enough to dispose of them somewhere they won't be directly linked to her. We've also confirmed that her blood type matches traces of blood recovered from Duke's teeth, and she has puncture wounds that are consistent with a dog bite. We're going to take a cast of his teeth to prove they match."

My brain hurt. His words made sense, but the reason behind Alice's actions didn't. "Duke?"

"He's staying with Liam," Tess chimed in. "Summer says he'll be fine in a few days."

Nate nodded. "He had some bruising and a puncture from a sharp implement—not a knife—but she stitched him up and he's recovering nicely."

"Alice's shoe," I told him. "She kicked him with her high heel."

He shuddered. "Poor dog."

"And Ezra?" I asked, recalling the way he'd fallen to the floor. "Why was he released, and is he okay?"

"He's fine," Nate said. "He explained a few things to us that changed our perspective of him, but I'll let him share the details with you himself."

"Okay." I closed my eyes, tempted to disappear back into the mindlessness of sleep, but I forced myself to stay conscious. "Do you know why she did it?"

"Not the whole story, but we've pieced together parts of it." He pursed his lips. "Are you sure you're ready to hear it? You only just woke up."

I reached for him with my uninjured hand, and he clasped it between both of his own. "I need to know."

"Okay." He glanced at Tess. "Keep this to yourself, okay, honey?"

"Yes, Dad." We both knew Tess wouldn't breathe a word. She was a vault when she needed to be.

"On Alice's computer, we found evidence that she was a finalist in a writing contest you won several years ago. The prize was mentoring from a successful author. She got second place. An email she sent to a friend of hers made it sound like she thinks that mentoring was what launched your career and that if the judges had scored differently, then she'd be the one with all your success."

"Wow." I struggled to comprehend that. "I had no idea. If I knew she was a writer, I'd have helped her. She never mentioned it."

He grimaced. "I doubt she wanted your help. We found a number of manuscripts on her laptop with your pen name on them, but they aren't among the titles you've published. This is pure guess work, but it's possible she intended to publish them under your name after you were gone. Posthumous works can bring in a lot of money, and she could have claimed she'd found them on your computer and was making them public to honor your memory. I think she was obsessed with you. We were looking for someone who wanted you to be theirs when we should have been looking for someone who wanted to *be* you. It was right there in her note."

Your life is mine.

I recalled wondering what it meant and whether someone thought I owed them my life or intended to take it away. In a way, the truth was more sinister. Alice believed she deserved to have my life.

I felt sick.

"How did I not see the ugliness inside her?" I asked.

He kissed the back of my hand. "You weren't the only one. I should have noticed something was off with her. In less than a year, she became completely enmeshed in your life."

"She was my assistant. She was supposed to be."

He sighed. "I'm still sorry I wasn't there when you needed me. When I saw you on the floor, it took years off my life."

"You saved me," I reminded him. I couldn't remember what had happened, but if he'd found me and I was still here, then it made sense he was responsible for that. "You did exactly what I needed."

He released a shuddering breath.

"Can I have more water?" I asked.

He let go of my hand and guided the water bottle back to my mouth.

I drank enough to wet my lips and allow me to keep talking. "When I thought I was..." My chest tightened, but I forced myself to go on. "...dying, I wished I'd told you how much I loved you." Despite the pain radiating throughout my body, I managed to smile. "I love you so much. I always have. I love you too, Tess. You're my family."

"We love you back," Tess replied immediately, her face appearing over mine again.

Nate smiled tenderly. "We do." He took my hand again. "I love you with my whole soul. I couldn't stand not knowing whether you'd be okay. I need you around for another few decades yet."

The whoosh of a door indicated someone else had entered the room.

It was Desdemona. "Oh, thank the stars!"

I smiled as my aunt rushed to my side and embraced me as though I were breakable. I breathed in her familiar scent of patchouli, and tears prickled in the backs of my eyes. I was surrounded by my family, and I'd never felt more loved.

57

NATE

ON SATURDAY, after Alice had been formally charged and remanded in custody, I delegated my duties to Patton and returned to Queenstown with Tess in tow. We ran an errand and then went to the hospital. Desdemona and Max were already in Grace's room. Desdemona sat at her bedside, talking to her, while Max observed from his position against a wall near the door.

As we entered, my gaze lingered on Grace. Her skin was still pale, especially in contrast to her dark hair, but she was beautiful nonetheless. She met my gaze and smiled. I felt the force of that smile in my heart.

Max grabbed my hand as I passed him. "Are you sure you want to do this now?" he asked softly. "It's understandable that you're having a strong emotional response to the trauma, but—"

"I'm sure," I interrupted just as quietly. "What happened gave me a metaphorical kick up the ass, but this is absolutely what I want to do."

"Okay, then." He let me go.

As we drew near to Grace, Desdemona stood and offered me her seat. I took it, and Tess perched on the edge of my lap—something she hadn't done since she was younger.

"Hey, Gracie." I leaned over to kiss her forehead. "How are you doing?"

"Better." She sounded weary but more awake than yesterday.

"I'm glad to hear it." I swallowed, trying to choose the words that would express everything I wanted to say. I was better at action than words, damn it. "I love you so much. I know our relationship is new, but in a way, I've loved you for years. You're my best friend. Other than Tess, there's no one I trust and care for more. We've let time slip away from us, and I don't want that to happen again."

I nodded to Tess, who reached into her pocket and withdrew a small black box. She opened it to reveal a white-gold engagement ring. The design was simple but elegant. I thought it matched Grace perfectly.

Grace's eyes widened and her breathing hitched. She looked from the ring to Tess and me, a question in her eyes.

"This diamond represents our past," I told her, indicating the smaller gem to the left of the central one. "All our years of friendship and the foundation we've built together."

She raised a trembling hand to her mouth.

"This is for our present." I pointed to the large stone in the center. "And this third one is for our future. I hope it's long and bright, because you make me happier than I ever thought I could be." I paused for a moment, then took the plunge. "Will you marry me?"

Tears sparkled in those warm hazel eyes I'd stared into so many times before.

"Yes," she said. "I would love to marry you."

Thank god.

I let out a breath. I'd hoped she'd say yes, but our relationship had changed so recently that I couldn't be sure.

"Tess, honey, why don't you help her put the ring on?" I suggested.

With a wide grin, my daughter carefully took the ring from the satin cushion and held it out to Grace, who slipped it onto the third finger of her uninjured left hand.

"I'm glad you said yes," Tess confided in Grace. "Dad would be a mess without you."

"Hey!" I protested, but Grace and Tess just laughed. I glanced at Max, who arched an eyebrow as if he agreed with Tess.

"I told you change was on the horizon," Desdemona said, beaming at Grace. "I'm so happy for you, dearest."

Grace looked at her affectionately. "You could have let me know it was something good."

Desdemona shrugged. "All good things come with bad. Where there are new beginnings, there are also endings."

Grace's lips quirked. "I love you, Auntie."

I loved them all. My wonderful family. Perhaps it had taken a while for us to get this right, but we'd finally done it, and I was happier than I ever could have imagined.

58

———

GRACE

Shortly after my visitors left, I heard a noise at the door and looked up, assuming they must have returned. It wasn't the Braddocks or Desdemona though. It was Ezra.

I stiffened, and the movement tugged at the stitches in my chest. I glanced at the button to summon medical help for emergencies and wondered whether I should push it. Even though I knew Ezra hadn't been the one to stab me, and Nate had said he had a good explanation, I was still wary of him.

"Hi, Grace." He stopped in the doorway and held his hands out in a gesture of peace. "Can I come in?"

I hesitated. "That depends on what you want."

"Just to talk." He looked anxious, and that was what helped me decide how to react to his presence.

"Okay, but sit over there." I motioned to the seat furthest from the bed.

He did as I said, scanning me as I lay on the bed. I felt self-conscious and confused.

"I'm sorry for scaring you," he said. "I didn't know how or when to approach you after... well, you know."

My pulse beat rapidly at the base of my throat. "Nate said you have something to tell me."

"I do." He looked down at his hands for a few seconds, seeming to gather his thoughts before raising his eyes. "When my dad died recently, he left me a letter."

"Okay." I didn't understand what that had to do with anything.

"In it, he told me that I'm adopted."

I frowned. Again, interesting, but how was it relevant? "You didn't know?"

He shook his head. "I asked Mum about it. She was upset at first because she hadn't realized Dad was planning to tell me, but when she calmed down, we talked it through, and she told me my birth parents' names. I looked them up and found out that they had another child. A daughter." He clasped his hands on his lap. "You."

My lips parted. "What?"

"Yeah." He nodded in confirmation. "Three years before you were born, your mum gave birth to me, and then put me up for adoption."

"That can't be right." I searched my memory, but as far as I could recall, Mum and Dad had never mentioned having a son. Surely that was the kind of thing I'd have had an inkling of. But then, my parents weren't exactly big sharers. I could imagine them doing what Ezra had said if they'd had an unplanned pregnancy.

"I assure you, it is. I did my homework."

"So, what? You came here to meet me?"

"I was curious about you." He sounded guilty, as though admitting to his curiosity was a sin. "I wanted to know what you're like and why our parents kept you when they gave me up."

My stomach bottomed out. If he was telling the truth, I couldn't imagine how much it must have hurt for him to learn his parents hadn't wanted him but had wanted me. That sort of thing haunted a person.

"You didn't miss out on much." Perhaps knowing more about our parents would help him see that he might have been the lucky one to have been given to another family. "Mum and Dad are all about the big picture. They're only happy when they're fighting for a cause. They gave me the necessities growing up—a home, food, and material things—but they never seemed to care about what I wanted. I always felt like I was getting in the way of the things they'd rather be doing. As soon as they could, they left me with my aunt and joined a crew of volunteers in Africa." I grimaced. "I know it's awful to complain when they're working hard for an important cause, but I was never the priority. Maybe they did you a favor."

He hummed thoughtfully. "I hadn't thought of it that way. I saw that they'd left the country, but I wasn't sure why."

I studied his face, this time noting that his eyes were a similar shade to mine and that his hair was dark too. The slopes of our noses were similar. We'd want to get a DNA test, but it wasn't outside the realm of possibility that he was telling the truth. We could be related. I might have a brother.

A brother.

I turned over the word in my mind. I'd always envied the Braddocks for their large, boisterous family. Would it be nice to have a sibling?

"Why didn't you tell me who you were from the beginning?" I asked.

"I didn't know how. I wasn't sure how you'd take the news. It seemed easier to stay there and get a sense for who you are first, and then after your problems started, I could never get you alone to talk in private."

That, I could understand. We'd done as much as we could to make sure I was always with someone. I hadn't anticipated that he might want to see me privately for a legitimate reason.

"Will you try to find my parents to meet them?" I asked, then corrected myself. "*Our* parents, assuming you're right."

"Maybe one day, but not now." He shrugged. "For whatever reason—perhaps they weren't ready, or maybe it was something else—they chose not to have me in their life. You never got that choice, so I'm more interested in you." He gave me a shy smile. "I know I haven't made the best first impression, but I'd like to get to know you better if you're interested."

"I'd like that too." A thought occurred to me. "Oh, we'll have to tell Desdemona as well. She'd be thrilled to welcome you to the family."

His smile relaxed. "She seems like a character."

"She is." I maneuvered myself into a better position and faced him. "I'd love to hear more about your adoptive parents. Hopefully, they were more nurturing than our birth parents."

59

———

NATE

GRACE DOZED as we drove back to Destiny Falls. She'd been discharged from hospital this morning, but she needed plenty of rest and more time to heal. Ever since I'd picked her up, I'd been trying to figure out how to ask her to move in with me. I wanted to be able to look after her properly, which would be easier if she shared my home. Besides, we were engaged now, so it would make sense to live together.

Still, I knew she was proud of her own home and rental cottages. She'd bought the property while she'd been in college, with a little help from Desdemona, who she'd long since paid back. She'd put a lot of care into them and might not want to leave. If that was the case, I'd gladly move in with her, but I didn't want to just invite myself to do so.

As we passed the turnoff road to Destiny Peak Ski Field, Grace's eyelashes fluttered open. She made a sleepy sound and stretched, then winced.

"I keep forgetting," she said. "Ouch."

"It won't be forever," I assured her. "You'll feel better

before you know it."

Especially if she allowed me to coddle her.

She gazed out the window, admiring the view of the snowy mountain. "You're taking me to your place, right?"

I glanced at her, surprised. I'd assumed we were going to her place. I'd even hired a cleanup crew after the crime scene team had finished there to make sure it was presentable.

"Uh, why?"

She turned to face me, wearing a breathtaking smile. "I finally have you. Why would I want to be without you?"

I tilted my head in acknowledgment. The lady had a point. "My place it is, then."

"I'd like that." Her smile grew sad. "With everything that's happened at mine, I think I need some distance from it until the memories fade. Between everything Alice did and what happened to Kennedy, it feels like there's a lot of bad energy there. I know I sound like Desdemona, but maybe there's some truth to what she says."

I reached across the space between us and clasped her hand. "You're welcome to stay with Tess and me for as long as you like. If you eventually want to return home, we'll come with you, if you're open to that."

"I am." Her eyes twinkled, the green flecks brightening with excitement. "We're moving in together."

I laughed. "Damn right, we are. And not a moment too soon."

She bit her lip. "By the way, I might have called Summer and asked her to gather the family at your place. I want to see everyone, and I figured it could be an impromptu house-warming if you said yes."

I laughed again, my heart lighter than it had been in ages. "That's absolutely perfect. I love you, Grace Smith."

"I love you too, Nate Braddock. Every day of my life."

60

GRACE

I WAS tired and achy but had no regrets as we pulled up opposite Nate's house and saw several other vehicles already there. My heart was whole. A little bruised by Alice's betrayal, but full of love for the kind, caring people who'd shown up for me. My family, both those by blood and by choice. As I got out of the car, the front door opened, and Heather raced toward us.

She stopped a yard away from me and opened her arms wide. "Can I hug you? Is that allowed?"

"Yes," I said at the same time that Nate grumbled, "Be gentle."

Her eyes flicked from him to me, and she grinned and gathered me into a soft embrace. "Welcome to the family, officially. You've always been part of it as far as I'm concerned, but it's about time that son of mine saw what was right in front of him."

My heart swelled, almost bursting with joy. "Thank you, Heather. That means the world to me."

She kissed my cheek and smoothed my hair away from my face. I leaned into the contact, enjoying the affectionate touch my own mother had never given me. "If anything had happened to you...."

"It didn't." I gave her another hug. "I'm okay."

"Thank the lord for that."

She wrapped her arm around my back, and we walked inside together. I was ushered to an armchair and seated while each of the Braddock siblings took turns to fuss over me. Bailey and Asher were also there to wish me well. I spotted Desdemona behind them, patiently waiting her turn, and blew her a kiss. Then I noticed another figure hovering in the entrance.

"Ezra," I called.

Several curious faces turned to the newcomer. He didn't shrink away. Instead, he smiled nervously and stepped inside, a bouquet of roses clutched in one hand.

"These are for you," he said, clearly unsure of his reception. We'd exchanged numbers yesterday, and I'd told him he was welcome to come over, but he obviously wasn't certain what the Braddocks would think of him. By now, I was sure word of who he was to me would have circulated.

"They're beautiful, thank you."

"Such a gentleman." Summer took the flowers from him. "I'll put them in a vase." She gave him a flirtatious smile, and I barely concealed a laugh as Asher scowled at them both. Perhaps Summer's feelings weren't so one-sided after all.

"Come in," I said. "Have you been properly introduced to Desdemona?"

He offered my aunt his hand. "We talked briefly at your shop. I'm Ezra, but I suppose you know that."

Desdemona brushed his hand aside and hugged him tightly. "None of that formality. We're family, dearest." She took his hand and tugged him away. "Come and talk with me. I want to know everything there is to know about you. I knew my sister had given a baby up for adoption, but she swore me to secrecy and I never dreamed I'd get the chance to meet you."

I smiled, glad the introduction had gone well. I'd expected Desdemona to be welcoming. That was her way. I could already see that they would get along.

"Grace?"

I glanced up at the sound of my name and jerked in surprise, gritting my teeth as the now familiar pain seared through my lower chest. Maddy stood beside me. I hadn't seen her arrive. When I looked around, I noticed Tess was with her dad. Maddy must have brought her over. Nate eyed us warily, and I sent him a reassuring smile. Maddy and I were grown women, both in happy relationships, who shared a love of the same little girl. We'd be fine.

"Hi. It's good to see you."

"You're looking better than I expected." She knelt as though she was uncomfortable standing over me. "I hope it doesn't hurt too much."

"Only when I move," I joked, then added, "It's not too bad."

She smiled tentatively. "I'm glad to hear it." She hesitated for a moment, then met my eyes. "I owe you an apology for the way I've behaved over the years."

"There's nothing to forgive." I held her gaze so she'd know I meant it. "If I'd been with Nate and someone else had wanted to make a move on him, I'd have defended our relationship too."

Maddy's smile widened. "Perhaps we could get a coffee sometime, just the two of us. It would be nice to talk more. I feel like we've known each other for years but don't really *know* each other, if you get what I mean."

"I do." Her words warmed me. "We can get together whenever you're free." I gestured at my chest. "It's not like I'm able to do much else at the moment."

"I'll call you." She stood again. "I'd better go. Steve is waiting in the car."

"Thanks, Maddy. Take care."

I rested against the back of the chair and closed my eyes for a few moments, the day beginning to take an emotional toll on me. When I opened my eyes again, Bailey was crouched in front of Tess, saying something that made the girl smile, but her focus wasn't on Tess. It was on a man behind her. Max. I had to look away because the yearning written across her face was too private for me to witness. I'd never realized Bailey was interested in Nate's quieter twin brother. She flirted with everyone, and nobody took it to heart. I wondered if she'd ever tell him how she felt. Perhaps I should give her a little encouragement. Max was a good guy. He deserved to be happy. I'd do that later, though, when I had more energy.

Nate appeared in front of me. "Hello, beautiful."

"Hi, handsome."

"What's got you so smiley?"

"Everything." I gestured around. "This is all I've ever wanted."

His expression grew tender. "You'll always have it." He held out his hand and I took it, allowing him to help me to my feet. "The dogs are outside. They want to see you."

I followed him.

In truth, I'd follow him anywhere.

EPILOGUE – 5 MONTHS LATER

*"A successful marriage requires falling in love many times,
always with the same person."*
~ Mignon McLaughlin

GRACE

"Stunning," Kennedy proclaimed.

"Absolutely beautiful," Summer agreed.

"You look like Cinderella," Tess added.

I smiled, studying myself in the floor-length mirror. They were right. I practically glowed. I supposed that was a side-effect of being wonderfully happy. Well, happy and pregnant. None of them knew about the pregnancy yet though. It was a secret between Nate and me until the beginning of the new year. We were being cautious since I wasn't far along.

"What do you think?" Bailey asked. She'd been the one to do my hair and makeup. I could have hired specialists from Queenstown, but this was a low-key wedding, and I liked it that way. Everyone involved was a friend or family member except for the dress designer. I'd seen the dress at an expo and fallen in love with it. The designer, an Auckland-based woman named Clarissa Mitchell, had won awards, but I didn't care about that. I just knew the dress was made for me.

The fabric was more champagne than white, which was fortunate because white didn't suit me. The bodice was simple with a high neckline and only a few beads on the shoulders for adornment, but the skirt was gorgeous. A confection of tulle and lace that was, as Tess had implied, fit for a princess.

I stopped admiring the dress and looked at my face instead. Bailey had done exactly as I asked, using natural colors that enhanced my features. My hair was twisted into a sleek knot at the back of my head.

"I love it," I said honestly. "You did a wonderful job."

Bailey's face creased into a smile, and she pretended to wipe sweat off her brow. "Thank god. You had me worried for a moment."

"Seriously, thank you, Bailey. You've gone above and beyond." I gave her a hug and turned to the others—my bridesmaids and flower girl. "Are we ready to go?"

Kennedy grinned. "Nate is going to go crazy when he sees you."

"He'd better," Bailey said. "We put enough effort into it. But no sneaking away and messing up your hair and makeup until after lunch, okay?"

"I promise," I said solemnly. "We'll behave."

"Good. That's what I like to hear."

Summer took her phone out of a pocket sewn into the seam of her cobalt blue bridesmaid dress. "Let's wait another few minutes. The bride is supposed to be fashionably late, and Nate needs to know not to take you for granted."

I laughed and swatted her hand. "Put it away. There's no sense in making anyone worry. Let's go."

NATE

I STOOD beneath the arch that had been erected out the back of my parent's property, tugging the collar of my shirt. Damn, it was hot as hell today. It figured our wedding would fall on the warmest day of summer. The sky was a vivid blue, not a cloud to be seen for miles, and a slight breeze was the only thing keeping me sane. I felt a hand on my shoulder and turned.

"This is it," Dad said, squeezing affectionately. "The start of a new chapter for you."

In more ways than you know.

But I kept that tidbit to myself. We'd tell Mum and Dad they were going to have another grandchild once we were ready. For now, it was our joyous secret.

"I can't believe I'm getting married again." I said it more to myself than anyone else. If asked a year ago whether I'd marry again, I'd have answered with a resounding no, but fate had other plans, and I would be eternally grateful for that.

"You and Grace will make a lovely family," Max said. Along with Dad, he was my groomsman. I hadn't wanted to choose between my four brothers, but Max was my twin and we'd always been close. The others understood that. They also got why I didn't want our wedding to be a massive event like my first one was. Back then, I'd included them all in the bridal party, and we'd dropped a crazy amount of cash to get married at the ski resort, but it hadn't been what I'd wanted. Maddy had made all the decisions, and in hindsight, my disinterest should have been a red flag. She'd planned a beautiful wedding, but just like she and I hadn't been the right fit, nor had the wedding.

This time, it was perfect. Just close friends, family, and a delicious homemade lunch.

A song started playing, and everyone fell silent.

Tess emerged from the house first. My heart felt like it doubled in size at the sight of her. She was smiling, her hair loose around her narrow shoulders as she made her way down the stairs and across the lawn, scattering white petals in her path I could imagine her grown, at her own wedding, and tears filled my eyes. I blinked them back. Nope, this was not the moment to start bawling.

Summer came next. My sister looked fresh and pretty in a blue dress that made her golden hair shine with vibrancy. She grinned at me and waggled her eyebrows. "Wait 'til you see her," she mouthed.

Kennedy followed behind Summer, and in the front row, Liam's chest puffed with pride. I fought the urge to roll my eyes, but I understood how he felt. Every time I saw Grace, I wondered how I'd managed to get so lucky.

I waited with bated breath until, finally, Grace stepped through the doorway. My heart skipped a beat. She was exquisite. As elegant as ever, and an essence of goodness seemed to radiate from her pores. She was smiling, the slight tremble of her lips giving away her nerves. I caught her eyes, and a shock rolled through me.

Holy shit, this gorgeous woman was about to become my wife.

I couldn't look away.

As she neared, she reached for me, and I took her hand and pressed a kiss to her palm.

"I love you," I told her, ignoring Ezra, who'd been about to begin speaking. He'd become a certified officiant so he could conduct our wedding.

"Love you," she whispered. "Let's get married."

I couldn't think of anything I wanted more.

THE END

WISH YOU WERE MINE EXCERPT

SUMMER

"Are you sure you want to do this?" Bailey asked as we wove between people, making our way to the makeshift dance floor at Drunken Destiny. Bodies writhed as our graduating class let loose, celebrating the end of our school career and the beginning of whatever came next.

"I'm certain." Despite the nerves that rioted in my gut. "I've waited long enough. It's time."

I was officially no longer a high school student. I was old enough to vote, drink, and have sex. I was a woman now, not a girl, and it was about time Asher Heaton realized it.

Bailey sipped her juice. "How are you going to ask him?"

"I'm going to get straight to the point. I've been practicing in the mirror."

She rolled her eyes, her mouth curling in a smile. "Of course you have."

I drank a few mouthfuls of raspberry vodka, my eyes finding Asher in the semi-dark. After years of seeing him at nearly every family gathering, recognizing his profile was easy. He stood beside my older brother, Liam.

His best friend.

I couldn't see Asher's face, but I knew it was gorgeous. Square, but with a pointed chin. Dark eyes and rich chocolatey colored hair. Then there were those broad shoulders. I'd spent so much time staring at his back that I could practically draw them blindfolded.

"So...are you going to do it?" Bailey asked, perhaps concerned by the fact I hadn't moved an inch. "If you don't want to, that's fine. There's no rush."

I brushed my hair away from my face. I'd left it loose because Bailey said it made me look older.

"I'm just preparing myself," I said.

After all, it wasn't easy to tell a man you'd loved him since the dawn of time. Or for the past few years, at least. Although I'd decided not to use the word "love", in case that scared him off. But that didn't make the prospect of spilling my guts to him any less intimidating.

"You've got this." Bailey hugged me. "You're stunning. You're smart. You're kind. He'd be lucky to have you."

Aww.

"I love you," I told her.

"Love you too, beautiful. Go and get him."

I straightened my back and clasped the bottle more tightly. I took one step, and then another. Out of the corner of my eye, I saw Sam from school ask Bailey to dance. She set her glass aside and took his arms as they began to move.

Another step.

I made my way slowly around the people watching the action. Neither Liam nor Asher were on the dance floor. In fact, they were hardly paying the dancers any attention at all.

A guy tripped in front of me, and I darted out of the way as he caught himself in a drunken stumble and managed not to fall. I waited for him to get out of the way before continuing. Finally, I stood before Liam and Asher, my heart beating a mile a minute.

"Um, hey." I cleared my throat, and they both turned to me.

A smile creased Liam's face. He was my third oldest brother, after the twins—Max and Nate—and he fell solidly in the midzone as far as brotherly protectiveness went. Nate and Connor were the most protective, while Max and Toby tended to think I could take care of myself. Liam sat somewhere in between.

"Hey, Summer," he said. "You're officially done with school. How's it feel?"

"Pretty good," I admitted. "Although I'm still going to be a student."

He shrugged. "It's a bit different though, isn't it?"

"Yeah." I glanced at Asher, and he sent me his charming, toothy smile. "Liam, can I talk to Ash alone for a minute?"

"Sure." Liam looked surprised but didn't argue.

"Thanks." Before Asher could protest or Liam could change his mind, I took his hand and pulled him toward the corner. Actually, this would probably be best done outside. There would be less risk of being interrupted or overheard.

"Do you mind going outside with me?" I asked.

"That's fine."

He disentangled his fingers from mine but followed close behind. A shiver of awareness rippled up my spine. He was so much bigger than me. Wider through the shoulders, with strong arms I'd dreamed of having wrap around me. He always smelled of the woods, and I longed to bury my face in his chest and breathe him in.

We left through the main entrance, and I slipped around the side of the pub, into an alley between Drunken Destiny and the neighboring building. I shivered again, this time with anticipation.

Asher shrugged off his jacket and offered it to me. "You're cold."

I bit my lip. Of all the times I'd imagined myself wearing his clothes, it had never been out of practicality. More of a silly fantasy where he instructed me to walk around naked except for his T-shirt.

Still, this was romantic because it was real. Even if I wasn't actually cold. I took the jacket and slipped my arms into the sleeves, inhaling his scent.

"What's up?" he asked, putting his hands in his pockets.

"I...' I gathered all my courage and took a breath. "I like you."

His mouth quirked. "I'm glad to hear it."

I rolled my eyes. Men are so dense. "No, I mean I like you. I think you're really handsome, and maybe we could date."

The last words ran together in a nearly incomprehensible stream.

His eyebrows knitted together. "Summer—"

"I'm eighteen now," I blurted out, cutting him off. I couldn't read his expression, and since he hadn't swept me into his arms, I was scared of what he might say. "I'm not at school anymore. I'm an adult."

He winced and tugged his hand through his hair. "You know I care about you."

My stomach sank. Somehow, that didn't sound good. "I do."

"I know you used to have a crush on me," he said.

I fought the urge to bury my face in my hands as humiliation swamped me. He knew?

"I thought you'd gotten over it," he continued. "I'm sorry, Summer, but I don't see you that way."

I looked down. There was absolutely no way I could gaze into his eyes as he crushed my heart. To my mortification, tears welled in my eyes. I blinked rapidly, and tried to swallow but there was an enormous lump in my throat.

"Have you tried?" I asked quietly. "Maybe you've just never tried to look at me that way, but if you do, you'll see how good we can be together."

He put his hand on my shoulder, and I immediately shook it off. "I'm really sorry, but it's not going to happen. To me, you're Liam's little sister. That's just the way it is."

Then, I couldn't stop the tears. They streaked down my face, and I felt every inch a girl and not at all a woman.

He reached for me. "Don't cry, Summer."

"Don't touch me," I sniffed, pulling away from him.

For five years, I'd had a crush on him.

I always pictured us sharing a happily ever after in Destiny Falls once I was old enough.

What a joke.

ALSO BY ALEXA RIVERS

Destiny Falls

Stay With You

Come Back to You

Always Been Yours

Haven Bay

Then There Was You

Two of a Kind

Safe in His Arms

If Only You Knew

Pretend to Be Yours

Begin Again With You

Let Me Love You

Little Sky Romance

Accidentally Yours

From Now Until Forever

It Was Always You

Dreaming of You

Little Sky Romance Novellas

Midnight Kisses

Second Chance Christmas

Blue Collar Romance

A Place to Belong

ACKNOWLEDGMENTS

Thank you to the wonderful team who made this possible. Kate, for providing early feedback and suggestions, and then for polishing the final story. McKinley, for smoothing out the rugged edges, and for your enthusiasm.

To Shannon and Lindee for the stunning cover design and photography, and to the models for lending your gorgeous faces.

Thank you to my husband for your ongoing and unwavering support, and to my family, and in particular Mum, for your support and feedback.

Lastly, thank you to my readers and reviewers, and to everyone who helps spread the word and share this book. Thank you, thank you, thank you.

ABOUT THE AUTHOR

Alexa Rivers writes about genuine characters living messy, imperfect lives and earning hard-won happily ever afters. Most of her books are set in small towns, and she lives in one of these herself. She shares a house with a neurotic dog and a husband who thinks he's hilarious. When she's not writing, Alexa enjoys travelling, baking cakes, eating said cakes, cuddling fluffy animals, drinking copious amounts of tea, and absorbing herself in fictional worlds.